Something inside him was surf. to. Some basic mistake of her own or something she'd overlooked—which would mean she'd failed as a mother to a stunning degree—or maybe that some resonance of their problems with the marriage was rising up inside him to take a terrible toll . . .

. . . she knew she wasn't responding well at all. She was afraid of this behavior! And being afraid led her straight to a kind of irrational anger. He was scaring her . . .

"Kids do lots of weird stuff," Arthur said. "It'll pass. You'll see. It's just some stage he's going through."

He was trying to be reassuring but what he was actually being was infuriating.

It was not some stage.

Her son was in trouble. Trouble right across the board. And this compulsion of his. This meant something . . .

Gordian Knot Books is an imprint of Crossroad Press Publishing

Copyright © 1995 Dallas Mayr
Cover by David Dodd
Design by Aaron Rosenberg
ISBN 978-1-941408-76-6
For information address Crossroad Press at 141 Brayden Dr., Hertford, NC 27944
www.crossroadpress.com

First Crossroad Press Edition

STRANGLEHOLD

JACK KETCHUM

GORDIAN
KNOT
BOOKS

PROLOGUE

LEGACY

Ellsworth, New Hampshire
Easter 1953

Enough, she thought.

Goddamn it, that's enough.

The baby cried.

The baby wanted the nipple. Or the baby wanted to be held. Or else the baby had shit or pissed itself or maybe it wanted to piss or shit on *her*, maybe it was holding it, storing it up inside, waiting for her to come check its diaper so it could blow its filth out into her face. It had done that before.

She got out of bed and walked to the crib. The man slept on.

She picked the baby up and felt its diaper. The diaper was dry. She bounced the baby up and down. It cried some more.

Well, it wasn't getting the nipple.

Her nipples were already sore.

She was still a good-looking woman. She was going to stay that way.

Tomorrow you go on the bottle, she thought. I don't care what the doctors say.

I can do whatever I want with you, she thought.

You know that? *You're mine.*

She was still a little woozy from all the port wine after dinner. Her head hurt. She wasn't much of a drinker. Except lately. Right now she wanted nothing more than to get back into bed and sleep it off, but no, she had to deal with the baby again. Every night the same damn thing. Every night the baby. Her husband *never* woke. Once or twice maybe but then all he did was roll over and tell her that the baby was crying, as if she didn't know that already, as if she wasn't lying there waiting the baby out.

Well, if the baby didn't have to pee, she did.

She took the baby with her, thinking that maybe just carrying it back and forth would put it back to sleep. You never knew.

She padded down the hall to the bathroom and pulled up her nightgown and squatted, the baby in her arms, its face splotched angry red, its mouth open wide and the noise coming at her filling the tiny room, nonstop, unrelenting. She smelled her own strong urine and the baby's warm peculiar fleshy smell and the smell of its crying.

Some people liked a baby's smell.

She didn't.

To her the baby didn't even smell human.

When she stood up and flushed, the baby screamed.

Really screamed.

She shook it. "Jesus Christ," she said. "Will you for god's sake *shut up*?" The baby cried. She felt a hot wind blow inside her. *I'll shut you up*, she thought.

No more.

She lifted the toilet seat and took hold of the baby's feet, turned it upside down and thought, am I really going to do this? *Am* I? And the answer was damn right I am, I'm up to here with screaming whining sucking drooling pissing shitting I'm up to goddamn here with all of it.

She lowered its head into the water.

And held it there.

Bubbles.

Squirming.

Pathetic, puny.

Coughing.

Weakening.

The baby dying.

Her baby.

Oh jesus oh jesus god oh jesus.

She pulled it out dripping wet, its tiny eyes wide, astonished, its mouth open wide streaming water from the bowl and there was silence, for a horrible moment it simply wouldn't breathe, its mouth was open but nothing was happening and then she started patting it, slapping its back and it started coughing and then screaming like she'd never heard it or *anything* scream before, staring at her wide-eyed all the while like he was seeing her there in front of him for the first time, staring straight into the sick wild soul of her so that she had to hug him close if for no other reason than to get away from his eyes, from that astonished accusation, holding him tight to her, thinking what did I *do*? what in god's name did I do? and saying to him *baby, baby baby.*

ONE

CHILDREN

Wolfeboro, New Hampshire
June 1962

The little girl had quit pounding at the door. It wasn't doing any good.

She couldn't even hear them outside anymore.

The cabin smelled of earth and old decaying wood heavy in the damp still air. It was nearing dark. The light through the cracks in the windowless walls grew dimmer and dimmer.

They'd wedged something into the door frame, a piece of wood or something, and she couldn't budge it. She sat huddled against the sweating, slimy wall, smelling wet clay soil and the rich musky smell of her own tears and thought, *nobody will find me.*

She imagined them out there in the swamp water somewhere, maybe half a mile away by now—it was possible—slogging through shallow black water and mud that could suck your galoshes off, stabbing at frogs with their two-pronged metal spears. Jimmy would have a few by now dead or dying in his bucket. Billy was not as quick as Jimmy and might have come up empty.

You gotta see this, they'd said. This's cool.

The old log hunter's cabin lay out there in the middle of nowhere, what her daddy called a *misbegotten construction* that for years had been slowly sinking into the bog. Nobody used it for hunting now.

Liddy was only seven.

She hadn't wanted to go inside.

The boys, Jimmy and Billy, were nine and ten. So why should *she* have to go in first?

Why was it always *her*?

She was thinking that but stepping through the open door anyway because they were boys and she couldn't let them know she was scared, when Jimmy pushed her in and hooted with laughter and one of them held the door closed while the other wedged something between the door and its frame and trapped her.

She pounded. Screamed. Cried.

She heard them out there laughing at her and then heard them sloshing through the water.

Then she heard nothing at all. Not for a long time.

She sat huddled by the door, staring down at the earthen floor and wondered if snakes came out at night and if they did would they want to get in here.

She bet it was supper time.

Daddy'd be mad again.

Her mom would worry.

"Come on. *Please*," she said to nobody at all, "let me *out*. Pleeeese!"

All that accomplished was to start her crying again.

The guys all talked about what happened up here after nightfall. They talked about it all the time. Everybody knew.

Murderers used this place. Escaped crazy people who liked to do things to kids.

Especially little kids.

Liddy hated Billy and Jimmy.

She wished they were dead. Then she wished she were dead.

Because she'd disobeyed again.

She should never have come along.

Her mom and her daddy both had warned her against the place. *You're not to go there under any circumstances* her mom had said.

But there were not many kids around and no girls at all to play with and you had to have *somebody*. And sometimes Billy and Jimmy were nice to her. Sometimes she'd get through an entire day without getting pushed or pinched or hit.

Like she was really somebody's sister.

So she'd told them okay even though she knew it was probably going to turn out wrong someway, even though she had to trust the boys completely, depending on them to even get her *up* here because it was way off the trail and she'd never even seen this part of the woods before.

She was actually kind of . . . lost.

Even if she got out of here.

She thought that if she had to stay here all night she'd go crazy.

There was a story Jimmy told about the swamp.

He said his older brother Mike had been up here alone a long time ago and he'd seen something in the water, that it had looked like a log at first but when Mike came closer he saw it was a man, a dead man with half his face chopped off—cut absolutely, completely clean from head to chin so that one open eye was staring at him, the other eye gone, half the nose split right down the middle and half the mouth open in a great big O so that Mike said the guy looked sort of surprised more than anything else and in the back of the head he could see this mess of brain and blood and bone. He ran for the police and brought them an hour later to the very same spot, but by then the guy was gone. The guy had disappeared. They looked everywhere.

Jimmy was a liar and so was his big brother Mike but Jimmy always said that now the guy haunted the place. That you could hear him at night moaning through half a mouth, breathing heavy through half a nose, dragging himself through the dirty snake-, frog-, and leech-infested water.

It was only a story.

But if she stayed here all night she'd go crazy. She was trembling all over.

It was getting dark.

"Mommy," she whispered.

She heard footsteps. Sloshing through the mud. Coming toward her.

"*Mommy*," she said.

Thinking about the dead man.

Not *help* but *mommy*.

Her long brown pigtail caught on rough weathered wood as she slid away from the door, her scalp burning as a clutch of hair pulled free. She got to her feet and ran to the wall farthest away. She felt tiny splinters of the old rotten wood nip the palm of her hand. She pressed back against it anyway, facing the door.

"*That's right*," said Jimmy. "Call your *mommy*."

He flung open the door. The hinges screamed.

"Sissy!"

He ran. Billy was right behind him.

"Wait!" she cried. She ran after them.

Bog muck sucked at her galoshes, splattered her bare legs and her shorts. She plunged through it. But she was never as fast as they were. Never. Not even close.

By the time she was out of the swamp they were up the hill and into the trees.

By the time she made it up the hill she couldn't see them at all.

She was alone again.

It was full dusk. Just minutes from darkness. The thick trees and brush almost made it seem as though it were already dark.

Which way?

She thought that maybe . . .

She walked the crest of one hill to another. Over that to another. She was scared and she was crying. Each hill looked the same as the one before it and none of them were familiar. Brush and evergreen and pale white birch and thick, nasty tangles of thorn. She moved as fast as she could. Against time and darkness.

She stumbled, fell, scraped her knee on a rock and felt her funny bone tingle and go all numb and then start to hurt bad, throbbing, and felt the splinters lodge deeper into the palm of her hand. She stumbled again seconds later on a log half-buried under leaves and fell to her side.

Onto the path.

Well-trod, hard-packed earth.

And now she knew and recognized that big rock over there, just ahead of her, peppered with fool's gold. Jimmy'd stood on it on the way here.

Yes!

She was not going to die out here after all, starved or killed by crazy people or bit by snakes, she was not even going to hear the sound of the breathing of the ghost of the split-skull man. She was going to make it home.

Tears streamed down her muddy cheeks. It was hard to believe a person could feel this good and this bad both at the same time. Her heart pounded with relief.

She made her way home.

Her father was waiting for her on the porch. He had a beer and he was still in his shirtsleeves from the bank and he was sitting in his rocking chair listening while she tried to explain.

She could see her mother in the doorway, watching from behind the screen, hands resting on her swollen belly. Her mom was eight months pregnant.

When she was finished telling her story her father set the beer down and then stood up and walked over to her, standing at the very edge of the porch.

"What is wrong with you?" he said. "Where is your intelligence? Where are your *brains*, Lydia? Don't you have any brains *at all*?"

She could think of nothing to say. She picked at her splinters. Her hand hurt. Her knee hurt. The knee was even bleeding. Didn't he care?

"Am I raising a *stupid* child, Lydia? I think I am." Her mother opened the screen door behind him.

"Russell . . ."

It was as though her mother weren't even there.

"Listen to me. You're not a *boy*, Liddy. Boys do things that are sometimes dangerous, sometimes foolish. You could say that's part of being a boy. Part of how boys grow up. But you are not supposed to be out doing the kinds of things that boys do. Do you understand that? Is this too *difficult* for you?"

"No."

She thought she was going to start to cry again. She wondered if the baby in mama's belly would be a boy.

"No *what*?"

"No, sir."

His pale blue eyes bore into her.

"All right. I don't know why I even have to tell you all this." He shook his head. "Honestly. Sometimes I don't know where the hell it is you came from." He turned and sat down in the rocker.

"Your supper's cold," he said. "And it'll damn well *stay* cold. Now get upstairs and clean yourself up. You'll wash those clothes yourself, young lady. Understand me?"

"Yes, sir."

She took off her muddy galoshes and placed them to one side beside the porch. Daddy sipped his beer and didn't say anything and didn't look at her. At least he wasn't going to hit her this time. Her mother opened the door for her, then stood aside as she climbed the stairs to her room.

She sat down on the bed and then remembered that she was dirty and that the bed was clean. She got up and brushed off the bed cover, limped down the hall to the bathroom and looked at herself in the mirror.

The face staring back at her was dirty and tear-streaked, sad-eyed and dopey-looking. Her pigtails were a mess and studded with burrs and twigs and hunks of leaves.

She felt as lonely as she had in the cabin.

Almost.

A little less scared, that's all.

Ellsworth, New Hampshire
August 1962

The boy lay listening in the dark steamy crawl space beneath the stairs. His mother was standing right above him, talking to Officer Duggan.

He could hear them perfectly.

"I'm not waiting any twenty-four hours, Ralph Duggan," his mother was saying. "No way I am. You're standin' right here, right now and I'm telling you."

"Ruth . . ."

"Don't 'Ruth' me. I knew you when you were Arthur's age, didn't I? That's right. You're damn well right I did. Now *you* tell *me*—would your mama have waited any twenty-four hours? Answer me that."

Arthur could hear Officer Duggan sigh. He knew what it was like to try to talk to his mother. He lay way back in the dark and didn't move an inch.

He stared through the wooden latticework and then through the overgrown bushes and hardscrabble grass. Even though it was getting on to dusk he could see almost all the way over the hill to the bridge and the beaver pond from here. He'd sneak down there sometimes while they were asleep.

The boy could see out but they couldn't see in. It was much too dark back here until your eyes adjusted and that took a while. His mother had already tried.

"The problem is, Ruth, we got no men to spare just now. Damn brushfire's pinning us all down. We got people come all the way over from Compton to help us out. Troopers, volunteers. But with this breeze and the land being this dry . . . hell, you can smell the smoke yourself from here. We'll be on this thing half the night as it is."

"I don't care about any brushfire. What I care about's my boy."

"You want your house to go up in flames, Ruth? It could, if we don't stop the damn thing."

"That fire's half a mile away."

"That's right. And the wind's blowing right in your direction. You got the Wingerter place and then you. Harry, talk to her, will you?"

It was the first the boy was even aware his father was there. His father could move as quiet as an Apache if he wanted to.

Unless he was drunk.

A brown wood spider was moving across the back of the boy's left hand. Crawling up toward his wrist.

He knew that the spider's bite could be nasty but he wasn't afraid of anything that small.

Certain people, yes.

Spiders, no.

Though spiders disgusted him.

He couldn't risk slapping it, though. They might hear. Instead he reached over slowly with his right hand and firmly crushed its body against his wrist. The spider went wet and sticky. He rubbed the spot until the wet was dry and only the sticky stuff remained.

He'd done okay. The spider hadn't bitten.

"It doesn't matter what my husband's got to say on the matter," his mother was saying. "That boy's never missed a single Sunday dinner in his life. Wouldn't *dare* to miss it. Nope. Something's wrong here. You and me, Ralph Duggan, we're going looking for that boy, and you'll walk right over to that car there and call in a proper missing persons report or else I'll step inside for a moment and you'll go looking with me at the point of a shotgun. How's that?"

"Ruth, do you know what you're doing? You're threatening an officer of the law."

"You want to arrest me, fine. You go right ahead. *After* we find Arthur."

"Boys forget. They get to doing things."

He could hear the policeman shift uneasily on the stairs.

"And I got a *fire* to fight!"

"So how do you know he's not in it?"

"What?"

"*In* your damn fire, Ralph. How do you know he's not lying out there hurt, right in the path of the damn thing? My Arthur had asthma when he was three. Had fainting spells. What if he's had a relapse or something?"

"Jesus, Ruth."

The boy smiled. His mother was going to win.

His mother always won.

Best of all she was using the same explanation he'd intended to use anyway—the fainting spells. And now he knew it was going to wash with them. It'd scare them. He didn't know why he wanted to scare them but he did. His mother would make a whole big thing out of it and he'd stay out of school tomorrow and maybe even the next day or the day after that. There might even be a doctor.

"All right, Ruth," Duggan said. "You win. You and Harry climb in back. I guess what we'll do is start behind the fire, close as we can, and then work back toward the house. Not a lot of light left, though."

"And you call it in."

"All *right*, Ruth. I'll call it in."

He heard them go down the stairs and heard car doors open and then slam shut and the police car starting up and pulling away and then there was just the familiar silence, crickets and frogs way down the road at the beaver pond across the hill.

He crawled out from under the stairs and sat down on the grass with his arms folded over his legs. Nobody was going to see him sitting there. He felt invisible, like he wasn't in the same world as everybody else, like he wasn't even there.

He sniffed his shirt.

The shirt still smelled of smoke. So did his jeans. Smoke and dirt.

He wondered if they would still smell like smoke when they got back later and if his mom would notice.

It was possible he'd get caught.

He felt a bright rush of fear at the thought. At the knowing that there was danger. It was very nearly the same thing he'd felt using matches on the pile of brush and then crouching there watching the fire crawl from brush to trees to more brush, smelling the smoke and listening to the crackling sounds.

Eventually the feeling had overpowered him and made him want to run and hide.

It felt very much like joy.

He was bad.

And now he was invisible.

And no one would ever know either of these things. He'd sit here until his senses told him to hide again and then he'd crawl back into the crawl space and listen to his mother's worry and his father's silence inside the house until he was good and ready to come out and no one would ever know.

TWO

TEENS

Wolfeboro, New Hampshire
May 1971

"Come on, Lyd. You know you want to."
    "I *don't* want to."
"Sure you do."
"I *don't*. Don't touch me."
"Look, you just wrap your hands around it. Hold it like this. Then you *squeeze* . . ."
The sound was deafening. The Budweiser can seemed to leap off the stump.
"*God*, Martin!"
"Is that something? Is that cool or what? As soon as my dad saw this movie he had to have one. Bet it could stop an elephant. Here. Try it."
"I don't *want* to stop an elephant."
"My dad wouldn't mind."
"Your dad *would* mind. And you know it."
"So? Who's gonna tell?"
"Couldn't we just go inside? I'm cold."
It wasn't true. The wind was blowing hard off the field but it wasn't a cold wind. In fact it was the first sunny day they'd had after a winter that seemed to go on and on, simply devouring the spring.
"Not till you try."
She didn't like the gun. *Dirty Harry* gun, he said. It was smooth and beautiful in the way that bright new polished silver was

beautiful but she didn't like the smell of it or the enormous sound it made or the way it had bucked in his hands like something alive over which you could have only a limited, conditional control.

She didn't trust the gun.

He fired again. Missed this time. There was an explosion of sawdust at the base of the stump and the impact of the bullet toppled two cans and rattled all the rest. Not even the protective gear could keep her ears from ringing.

"I'm telling you. You'll love it."

She doubted that.

He handed it over.

She held it and admitted its attractions. Balance, substance, smoothness, weight.

"Hold it like this. Both hands. You gotta spread your legs wide and balance your weight, okay?"

He was standing in back of her now, his arms around her, his hands cupped firmly over her hands.

That part at least felt nice.

"Okay, now line up the target to the sight and squeeze the trigger. Don't jerk it. And keep your elbows bent. She recoils like hell."

"She?"

He laughed. "Yeah. Kicks back at you. Like you do."

She did as she was told, aimed and squeezed. The gun was heavy for her and hard to hold steady. The trigger seemed to melt steadily, slowly toward her. Then the blast and the shock that traveled up her arms all the way to her shoulders.

On the stump nothing moved.

"High," he said. "You shot high."

How high? she wondered. She imagined the bullet traversing some infinite distance, going on forever across the field and the forest to the road and whatever was beyond it. She could not imagine so much power simply dropping from the sky out of sheer inertia.

Her bullet could kill someone the next town over.

She really didn't care for this at all. *He* wanted it. And here she was again, going along.

He stepped up behind her again, took both her hands in his and extended her arms.

"Take it farther out, Lyd," he said. "Just a slight bend to the elbows. You'll steady her better."

He pressed her tight. She could feel his penis against her buttocks.

It made her a little uncomfortable. So that she was sort of glad when he moved away. She knew he didn't particularly *want* to move away but it was part of the game, making her aware of him yet going no further. Not quite yet.

She knew *that* game.

And knowing it made her feel scared and suddenly a little angry.

She aimed the gun, squeezed and fired. A beer can danced and tumbled sparkling in the sunshine.

"Hey! I *knew* you could do it! Terrific!"

She turned and smiled for him.

"Can we quit now?"

He laughed. "Sure. Come on inside."

They walked up the hill and through the glassed-in porch, down the hall to the living room. She thought again how the house was not at all the kind of place you'd expect from the president of a bank. Its furnishings were Spartan and inexpensive. *Cheap*, to be truthful. They made her aware of her mother's quiet good taste in these things, which had continued even after her father's death—when many women, she guessed, would have just stopped caring. It was clear that Martin's mother, who *had* a husband, a live one, had no interest.

"You want a beer?"

He was across the room putting on a record—the Beatles' *Rubber Soul*. Music-wise it was as adventurous as Martin got.

"A *beer*?"

"Sure. They're not gonna miss a couple."

"Uh-uh. No thanks."

First we have guns and now we have beer.

As far as she was concerned, this wasn't going well at all. She wondered how well she really knew this boy.

She'd only been dating him for about three and a half months, though she'd known him for years through his family. Her father'd worked for his father. Martin's little brother was in the same class as Lydia's sister Barbara.

They had all come to her father's funeral.

In fact it was at Russell McCloud's funeral that Martin first seemed to notice her. At the reception afterwards they'd talked and talked. She did most of the talking and he seemed willing to let her. He seemed like a pretty good listener. She'd vented like crazy.

Though she hadn't told him everything.

"You sure you don't want one? Absolutely positively sure?"

"I hate beer. A Pepsi, though."

"Comin' atcha." He went to the kitchen.

Paul was singing "I've Just Seen a Face." The music is up too loud, she thought. Or else my ears are still sensitive from the gunfire.

She got up off the couch and walked over to turn the music down. They had a brand-new, state-of-the-art Magnavox amplifier/receiver and she couldn't find the volume at first amid all these other dials so Paul continued to blare sweetly at her. She found it just as the song ended and John started on "Norwegian Wood."

She turned and there was Martin right in front of her. Beer in one hand and Pepsi in the other. She came to a quick decision.

"I'll make you a deal," she said.

"What's that?"

She put her arms around his waist and hugged him. "You forget about the beer and we can . . . um, you know."

"Oh yeah? What's *you know*?" He was laughing.

She slapped his shoulder. "Don't be a smartass."

It was easy to make a deal like that. It was natural. There were girls her age who smoked dope and girls who drank and girls who had sex with their boyfriends. She had interest in only one of these.

She loved the feel of his body. And she hated beer. There had always been beer on her father's breath at night when he came to her.

When he came to her he had always been drinking.

And it was drinking—that and being dumb enough to be driving too fast on a dark country road that had killed him—and left her alone with her nasty little secret.

"You got it," he said. "Whatever you say. No beer."

He put the bottles down on the coffee table and kissed her.

Her father had never kissed her.

He hadn't done that at least.

But she'd thought she would never want a boy to touch her after what he'd done, that at sixteen she was through with sex forever. So she was surprised at how quickly and how much she'd wanted Martin.

She thought he was beautiful to look at and even more beautiful to touch. He was hard and warm and smooth everywhere. And if he got a little pushy sometimes like he had about the gun and was just a little too full of himself sometimes it didn't matter because men were like that. And the first time, in the backseat of his father's Cadillac, that he'd brought her to orgasm—she didn't really think it was possible for girls to have an orgasm despite what everybody was saying—she felt like she'd gotten her virginity back just to lose it all over again.

It was only afterwards that she felt like the same old damaged goods.

She always did. It was as though sex were some sort of drug that cured all the loneliness and guilt and unhappiness but was also, for her, a deadly poison.

She tried never to think about what it would be like afterwards. She wouldn't now.

He unbuttoned her blouse and pushed the bra up out of the way and cupped her breast. Her nipple rose beneath his palm and sluiced sudden magic through her body. He could make her have an orgasm sometimes just by stroking one of her nipples. He didn't know that.

He didn't know a lot of things about her. Nobody did. "Come upstairs," he said and took her hand.

She followed.

It was the first time he was ever rough with her.

She didn't know why. She wondered if it had anything to do with the gun. Some aggression thing.

Her nipples ached where he'd squeezed them. She ached inside too and there'd be bruises on her upper arms tomorrow.

She'd had no orgasm. Not this time.

When he dropped her off it was clear she was mad at him. She hadn't said a word but she knew he knew. The silence itself was enough to tell him.

What he didn't know was that she was probably just as mad at herself. For not stopping him.

She'd never even tried to stop him.

She'd just *let* him.

"I'll call you," he said. He sounded a little remorseful. Not remorseful enough.

She slammed the car door and didn't look back.

She wouldn't be taking any calls from Martin, she thought. Not for a good long while and maybe never. There were other boys.

You just don't do that to people, she thought.

You just don't hurt them for no reason. Just because you want to and somebody lets you.

She walked up the steps to the porch, opened the door and walked inside.

Her mother was sitting in the living room reading a day-old newspaper. Judging by the good, rich smell coming from the kitchen, dinner tonight was going to be ham and cabbage.

"Hello, Liddy," her mother said and looked at her over the top of the paper. She saw her expression darken. Then she put aside the paper.

"What is it?" she said.

And all she could do was cry a little while her mother got up and put her arms around her and hugged her and asked her what was wrong? what had happened? because she couldn't tell, she wasn't supposed to be making love to boys in the first place, not at her age, not coming from this family.

So Liddy had yet another guilty little secret.

Plymouth, New Hampshire
July 1971

They were sitting at a desk inside the small glassed-in cubicle when Harry Danse came shuffling through the stationhouse door. The glass was cloudy from years of cigarette smoke but Harry seemed to spot his son immediately. He walked over.

"Hiya, Ralph."

Duggan nodded. He saw Harry was putting on weight. His son wouldn't look at him.

"How's Ruth?"

"Same."

Ralph Duggan felt bad for the man. Harry'd married a pretty young woman who'd turned into one salty old ball-breaker of a wife and here was his boy Arthur in trouble again.

Only this time they'd caught the kid red-handed.

"Before we get into what, uh, happened here I'd like for you to see something," Harry said. He reached into his shirt pocket and pulled out a folded piece of paper.

"What's this?" said Duggan.

"High school report card. See what it says there? All *A*'s but for one *B* in algebra. See, the boy's doing pretty well, Ralph."

"This Ruth's idea?"

"I guess so, yeah. She'd of come down herself but she's not feelin' too well."

"Flu?"

"Uh-huh."

Duggan sighed and settled back into his chair. He looked the card over. Harry wasn't kidding. All A's. Duggan handed the report card back to him. Harry folded it and tucked it into his shirt as carefully as though it were a page from the family Bible.

"Let me ask you something, Harry. Sit down here. How's the store doin'?"

Harry sat.

"Not bad. Still the only place to buy beans and boots in the town of Ellsworth. Still a long way for folks to come into town here or on over to Compton."

"That new complex out on 93 hurt you any?"

"Some, maybe."

"How come the boy don't work for you, Harry?"

"We was planning on sending him to college next year."

"You can do that?"

"We think we can."

Duggan looked at the boy and then at the father. The boy was slumped in his chair, frowning, looking grim. He guessed the boy didn't much care for getting caught. The father leaned hunched toward Duggan across the desk. For whatever reason he reminded Duggan of a dog hoping for a treat—looking at him with sorrowful big eyes. Well, he wasn't getting any treats tonight.

He reached into his pocket and pulled out the fat red Swiss army knife.

"You stock these in the store, don't you?"

"Sure I do."

"They go for about how much?"

"That kind's twenty-five, twenty-six dollars maybe."

"So what's Arthur doing stealing this knife from Becker's?"

Harry looked disconsolate. He shook his head.

"Right. Damned if I know either," said Duggan.

He let the silence work awhile. He could do that much anyway.

"The fact is that Becker's not pressing charges. I got to tell you, that's against my better judgment. But Old Man Becker knows you and respects you, Harry, the two of you being in pretty much the same business all these years. If it were me, I'd see your boy in Juvenile Court. You know and I know this ain't the first time he's been in trouble, even if we couldn't make it stick to him."

He heard the boy mumble something.

"'Scuse me?"

"I just said . . . you never . . ."

"That's right. We *never*. But I'll tell you something, kid, all I had to do was take one look at you to know you were guilty as shit on that break-in last summer so don't you try to bullshit a bullshitter. You're right. *We never.* But someday, somebody's going to. You can bet your A-plus college-bound pants on that. Somebody's going to."

He looked at Harry. Harry reminded Duggan of that same old dog only now the dog'd been beaten.

Why was there always the fucking temptation to apologize to this man?

"You can take him home, Harry. Tell Ruth I said hello."

He opened the door for them. The boy went first, gangly and moving fast. His father followed more slowly a few paces back. They could have been a pair of strangers coincidentally walking down the same hall at the same time.

Duggan leaned out the cubicle.

"Hey, Harry?"

He stopped and turned. His son kept going out the door. "What college, Harry? Where's he going?"

"Boston University. Boston, Massachusetts."

He said it with what for Harry almost amounted to pride. Duggan nodded.

"Well, good luck, Harry."

He watched the man walk away. He lit himself a cigarette and sat back down at the desk.

He wondered if he'd seen the last of Arthur Danse. Probably. The boy was going to college in the fall. He couldn't say he'd be one bit sorry.

Boston University. The school had a fine reputation, even Duggan knew that. He was impressed by that much about Harry's kid, anyway:

A punk's a punk, he thought.

Probably Arthur was Boston's problem now.

THREE

CROSSED PATHS

Boston, Massachusetts
September 1974

"I thought you ought to hear this personally," the girl said to him.
"Go fuck yourself."

She turned to leave.

Oh, yeah, he thought. You're very tough. Sure. Play it that way.

But he'd made a hell of a mistake on this one. He had to admit it.

"I didn't know, Annie! I swear I didn't. Come on in, will you? Just listen to my side."

"*To hell* with your side, Arthur."

"Just give me a minute, will you? Hear me out."

He stepped to the side. He looked at her. She hesitated for a moment and then marched into his apartment. He could see she was seriously pissed. No act. He liked her mad. In fact he felt more turned on by her right now than he'd been when he was fucking her two nights ago.

"You realize how humiliating this is? I let you make love to me Friday, and then Saturday night you're screwing my *roommate*?"

He closed the door behind her.

"I didn't *know* that. Look, Annie. Why would I do a thing like that? Do I look stupid? Do I look like I have the urge to self-destruct here? You were just two attractive women, that's all—two *very* attractive women. Denise and I danced at the freshman party. You didn't go, you weren't there. Then later on, after the dance, I asked her out. That was last weekend, Annie. I didn't even *know* her. I *barely* knew you. You and I hadn't gone out yet, we'd only made the *date* to go out. So who could tell how you and I were going to . . . get along? I sure didn't know we'd be making love the night before last, now did I?"

"But you knew it *last* night, didn't you, you bastard. And you fucked her anyway! What are you, the goddamn junior class Romeo or something? God's gift to the little freshman girls? Well *FUCK YOU*, Art! *FUCK YOU!*"

"I've got neighbors, Annie."

"Yes and I've got a dormitory full of women who think I'm a goddamned *joke*! Well, probably Denise can handle that—Denise's a fucking doormat—but don't you think you can pull that shit on me!"

"I'm sorry, Annie. Honest I am."

Her face was tight with scorn. She was beginning to piss him off.

"And *don't* you call me Annie, you son of a bitch! My *friends* call me Annie. NOT YOU!"

"Look, take off your coat. Sit down, relax a minute. Let me get you a drink or something."

He turned away from her toward the narrow cluttered counter that separated the tiny kitchen space from the living room. There was a bottle of cheap red wine in the corner. For her it would do.

"No thanks."

"Just one."

"I don't want a thing from you."

"Look, do you think this is pleasant for me? Do you think I like this? Believe me, honest, it's . . . I feel terrible . . ."

"No, I do not think this is pleasant for you, you selfish little *shit*, and you know why? *Because you just screwed yourself out of a damn good lay and a damn good woman!* Oh, and you also fucked yourself out of Denise too, by the way. You might care to know that, Mr. Class Secretary Big Shot. Because even doormats get humiliated. You know? And if you think she's going to . . ."

"Fuck you," he said. He'd done his best but enough was enough. "Fucking whore. You come here, to my home . . ."

"What? What did you say to me?"

"I called you a fucking whore."

"WHAT?"

He whirled and punched her.

In the stomach. Where it wouldn't show.

She doubled over and gasped for breath and he had no trouble just pushing her over. She fell to the side by his ratty old couch still clutching her stomach and rolling. He got down on his knees and let her have it again. Lower this time. Harder.

She attempted a sort of half scream but he could see she could barely breathe. He straddled her. Saw her face go red with pain. Pain was what she'd asked for, pain was what she got. He put both hands to her throat.

"Whores get fucked," he said. "They get fucked *quietly*. If you say another word to me or you fight me in any way I'm going to kill you, you dumb bitch. Because you have said *enough* to me! Got that?"

He tightened his grip, making sure she understood. And oh yes, it definitely got her attention.

He released her throat and grabbed the zipper of her jacket and ripped it open. She was coughing now and crying. He unbuttoned her blouse carefully and saw that she wore nothing underneath it and shifted further down on her legs so that he could unzip her jeans and then pulled them down over her hips so that the panties came off with them. She started to try to get up then but he gave her a straight-arm to the chest and her head slammed back against the floorboards.

Down you go, bitch.

He got off her and grabbed her legs and flipped her over, moved around and took her arms and dragged her to the couch and flung the top half of her over the couch and she was really sobbing now and she was kneeling on the floor with her face pressed down into the backrest muffling the sounds while he unzipped his own jeans and got it out—hard, *real* hard—and knelt and grabbed her around the belly and lifted and parted the cheeks of her ass with his other hand and stuck it in up her ass so that she emitted a single stunned shriek but he shut that up fast, smacking her head with his fist, another place it wasn't going to show, thinking she's never gonna tell after getting fucked this way, not up the butt, no way, she's gonna take it and shut the fuck up and go the hell on home.

His bonus was her roommate Denise would never know.

Despite what she'd said he still had hopes for Denise.

She might forgive him after all.

She did sort of strike him as the doormat type.

She might. If not, there were plenty of others.

Ann had cleaned up in total silence in the bathroom of his apartment but walking back to the dormitory she found that she could not stop crying. He'd handed her tissues at the doorway.

Knowing she'd need them.

And she did.

Her father was the Reverend Richard Fletcher of the Ames, Iowa, First Methodist Church. He would never have understood this in a million years. Why she would even go to his apartment. Let alone allow him to do . . . *this* to her.

Without dying first.

Her father had no idea that she even knew what the word "fuck" meant. He hadn't a clue. He would have fully expected her to resist him with all her might.

But her father hadn't seen the look in Arthur Danse's eyes the moment he turned and hit her.

She thought she was going to die in there.

She peered at her reflection in the glass double doors to the dormitory and saw how bad she looked. She'd have to make up some story. Though probably half the dorm already knew about her sordid little triangle with him and Denise and probably that would do to cover any questions.

The girl on desk duty noticed right away.

The girl was a freshman like Ann and her name was Lydia McCloud, from Maine or New Hampshire or something. She got out of her chair and asked if she could help, if there was anything she could do. Asked what happened. The girl seemed sincere, considerate, very nice really—but Ann was going to go to the grave with this one.

She could do that.

Her family had always had grit.

She might not have been tough enough to fight him back but she was tough enough to do this.

No regrets, Annie, she thought. You did what you thought was right going to his apartment and it turns out you messed up bad. So you lie in your tub for a while and hope he didn't hurt you too badly inside. And then go on with your life.

Like he never fucking existed.

You warn people that he's bad news if you can but you don't go into particulars. You warn Denise.

If you see him, he's invisible.

She went up the stairs to her empty room and sat on the bed and permitted herself to cry.

Boston, Massachusetts
March 1978

Lydia smoothed the skin tight across the old man's withered arm and neatly found the vein on the first try. She released the ligature and drew the blood and then withdrew the needle.

Beside her, Gloria Leonard, RN, nodded approval. The clinicals called Leonard "Pressure Cuff" behind her back, which had less to do with mercury sphygmomanometers than with the way she made them sweat. A nod from her was heaven.

"Nothing to it, right?" Lydia smiled at the man.

"Nah." The old man smiled back. You could tell the man liked pretty girls even if all they were doing was poking him with needles and stuffing thermometers under his tongue and waking him at five in the morning to hand him medication and change his sheets.

She patted his mottled hand. "I'll see you again tomorrow, Mr. Fischer, all right?"

"Oh yeah? You goin' off now?"

"Yep."

He glanced at Nurse Leonard, then at her. "You sure she's keepin' you busy enough?"

Lydia laughed. "Oh, I'm pretty sure. Yes."

In fact between her study load and the hours spent here at the hospital with her preceptor Lydia was running herself ragged. It was a happy sort of ragged though. She knew that her work was ranging from good to really excellent and that Leonard, her supervisor and teacher, appreciated that fact.

Finally. Something she was honestly good at.

She took the stethoscope and blood pressure gauge off the bed. She smoothed his sheets.

"You have a good night now," she said. "Is your wife coming back later?"

"Oh, sure. She'll be in."

"Well, say hi for me and tell her I'll bring her those clothes tomorrow."

"Will do."

They walked back to the nurse's station. She began the process of checking out, going through the paperwork. "Clothes?" Nurse Leonard said.

"Mrs. Fischer's temple has a used-clothes drive. I've got some old sweaters, blouses."

"Ah."

"That's all right, isn't it?"

"Sure. Got some myself. I'll bring them around."

She said good night and pulled on her sweater and headed for the elevator.

It hadn't been too bad today, actually. The ward she was working was mostly old people—heart, mostly—and during her shift the closest they'd had to a crisis was the remarkable efficacy of Mrs. Bragonier's stool softener, the result of which was a truly massive bowel movement and screams of outrage from her room.

It was time to go home. Grab some supper and then hit the books. *But first . . .*

There was a doctor she kind of liked working the emergency room. An intern. And she thought the attraction might be mutual. His name was Kelly. Jim Kelly. Blond and slim and, she thought, very bright.

She liked his hands.

The hands looked very gentle. Gentle was important to her.

She took the elevator down to one.

She walked the corridor past the treatment rooms and gazed into each of the rooms but he wasn't there. Marie Khurana was at the nurse's station.

"Seen Kelly?"

"You just missed him. He went off at five."

"Oh."

Marie grinned. "Is this a kind of a *thing* you've got here, Liddy?"

"You mean a *thing* like you and Daniels, Marie?"

"Hey. You're not supposed to know about that."

"Know about what?"

She laughed and walked away.

She passed Admitting and the row of patients waiting to see a doctor. She gave them a once-over.

Nothing really desperate for a change. No gunshot wounds. No stabbings. A young, good-looking guy holding a badly swollen hand. He looked vaguely familiar, but she couldn't place him. Probably broke a bone or two judging by the color and the swelling. She walked on past him out the door.

Arthur Danse watched her and thought she had a very good ass and that he had seen her somewhere. She was attractive. Too bad about the hand. It prevented him from following her, giving her some line, buying her a drink or something.

But the hand was priority.

He'd broken it against his own bedroom wall when he'd learned that they were not going to give him the scholarship for the Masters program. Now he'd have to find the money somewhere. Beg it. Borrow it. Steal it.

He'd figure something.

Meanwhile the hand hurt like a bitch.

He'd have to try to control that shit.

One of these days a guy's temper could get him into some real trouble.

FOUR

SEPARATE LIVES

Cambridge, Massachusetts April 1982

"It's just *work*, Jim. What in god's name is wrong with my wanting to work?"

"We've been through this."

"My little sister Barbara works and she's just a sophomore in college!"

"Barb needs the money. We don't."

"But it's not *about* money."

"My practice is fine, Lyd. You know that. Hell, I'm turning people away. We don't need it."

He wasn't hearing her. It was happening more and more these days—happening on many subjects but on two subjects in particular. Her getting back into nursing was one. The other was having children. And Lydia thought that Jim's patients weren't the only people he was turning away these days.

But she thought there was nothing to do but try again. She couldn't go on like this.

At least here in the restaurant he couldn't just walk away from her into the next room and turn on the TV or go to bed. They couldn't get into one of their shouting matches either.

"Jim, I'm bored to death here. Do you understand that? I'm twenty-seven years old. And you don't want children."

"Yet."

". . . *yet*, and you don't want me working. So what's left? We have an *apartment*, Jim. A big, beautiful apartment, but that's all it is—an *apartment*! I clean it. Fine. It doesn't take much. I pick up the groceries and do the laundry and then what? Do you know how much *time* there is between breakfast and dinner?"

"You have aerobics classes. You have the gym."

"Oh, for chrissakes, Jim. That's not a *life*."

"You have a life. You have friends."

"I have acquaintances. Casual friends. Mostly the wives of *your* friends. And even if I were close to them, that's no life either."

The waiter brought coffee and her slice of pecan pie. She was going to have to move this faster.

Jim looked disgusted with her. She'd seen the look before.

"Friends isn't a life," he said. "Having a good home and a husband isn't a life. What the hell is it you want, Lyd?"

"You *know* what I want!"

"I don't want you working."

"Because it's not going to fly over at the Club? That's no good reason."

"The Club has nothing to do with it."

"Of course it does. Be honest, for godsakes. *None* of their wives work. If I work, then you figure that you lose face. But you keep forgetting—*their* wives all have kids to raise."

"That again."

"Look, there's only one *other* reason I can think of. And that I like even less."

He looked at her. She took a deep breath.

"That you need to have total control over the purse strings. Control over me."

"That's bullshit."

"Is it? I hope so. I honestly do. But it's got to be one thing or the other. Or both. This business of 'we don't need to' just doesn't make the slightest bit of sense. I'm talking about me having a full life here, something in my life that's really mine. Not about what we need or don't need. I want kids or I want work."

"You're giving me some sort of ultimatum now, is that it?"

"Call it whatever you want. All I know is I just can't do this anymore."

She paused and then told him what, for her, was the simple but deepest truth of the matter.

"It isn't fair."

He looked at her for a moment over the coffee cup, then slammed it down. Lydia jumped. Coffee filled the dish.

"Damn you!"

He pushed up from the table and walked away. She turned and saw him hand his credit card to the waiter. The waiter moved fast to oblige him.

He was leaving her sitting there.

Just like that.

She guessed she was wrong. She guessed that there was always another room for him to hide in even if the room was Harvard Square.

That's that, she thought. For three long years she'd tried. At first to understand him. Then to cope with him. And then finally to survive him—to somehow exhume her own life from the empty crypt of her empty days.

They had a Picasso drawing, small but authentic.

They had nutske and a Steinway and two-hundred-year-old Japanese art.

Jim would succeed further. Jim was just getting started.

It didn't matter.

She found that, unsurprisingly, the women's group hadn't really helped her at all in one area. Despite what she knew to be true—that this was *his* fault, not hers—she felt she'd fucked up again.

That she'd asked too much, given back too little. For all the talk, when it came right down to it what she knew and what she felt were still two different things.

She finished the coffee and pecan pie at her own deliberate pace. It was a matter of pride. Then she walked past the waiter out the door and smiled at him and hailed a cab for home.

He wasn't there. That didn't surprise her either.

What there *was* was a note.

You want a divorce, get it.

She felt a tingling down her spine.

This was just too damn easy.

Wait a minute.

She knew him. Something else was going on.

She went to their bedroom. Searched through his bureau, through the closet. It wasn't long before she found it, a note off some other doctor's prescription pad, the doctor's name unfamiliar, written in a woman's hand and tucked into the side pocket of his navy blue jacket.

The note had a little round happy face at the bottom and said *2:30 Wednesday at the Copley Sheraton, Rm. 2208. Right after your meeting.* Today was Friday so that meant three days ago. Yes, he'd worn the navy blue that morning. She was sure of it. She wondered how often he'd been this careless or if lately it had been getting so that he wanted her to know.

You want a divorce, get it.

Okay, Jim.

She wanted.

Plymouth, New Hampshire
March 1983

It was nearly a half hour past closing time. The waitresses were long gone. They had the chairs up on the tables for the kid who swept out in the morning and most of the lights off and he was closing out the register but Jake, Arthur's night man, was still indulging this guy. The guy was seriously loaded and stooped low to the bar so Jake had put a cup of coffee in front of him gratis, but the guy preferred the watery dregs of his scotch to that. Sipping it slowly. The fucking idiot.

"Jake. You take off. I'll lock up."

"Sure, Art. Thanks a lot."

"Sir? You want to finish up your coffee now? I'd appreciate it."

Jake was right to feed the guy coffee because at least they could say they'd done that for him when the asshole wrapped his car around a tree a little while later.

Jake was a pretty good man. If he'd had a few more like him back in Boston he might have made a go of the place. Boston was a disaster.

Masters degree in Business, specialty in small-business management and here he was back in New Hampshire not fifty miles from where he grew up.

At least he was making a profit here.

"Night, Art. Take care now."

"Night, Jake."

He locked the door behind the barman and heard him fire up his Land Rover while he went behind the bar and finished closing out the register. They'd had another good night tonight. The Caves was popular with the older students and faculty at Plymouth State; his location out on 93 near the Polar Caves tourist trap was well chosen, and Arthur knew his business. He had probably the best bartenders around and definitely the best cook. Summertime and ski season he drew a bonanza.

The drunk lurched up from his barstool, muttered *'scuse me, gotta piss*, waved at Arthur, and started weaving his way through the tables toward the back of the restaurant.

Arthur slammed home the pseudo-antique silver-plated register drawer.

Asshole.

The guy looked to be maybe fifty, wearing a red-and-black checked hunting jacket.

A laborer.

Scruffy. *Not* a regular.

I've just about had it with you, buddy, he thought.

He tossed the rest of the man's coffee into the sink and rinsed and racked his cup. He poured a short Dewar's rocks for himself and lit a cigarette and then sat down at the bar, waiting.

How long could a piss take, anyway?

He sipped his scotch.

His mother and father had been in again tonight, dressed to what they thought was the nines. Of course they hadn't a clue. Usually whatever it was, was right off the rack at his father's store in Ellsworth. Arthur didn't mind. His staff all seemed to think they were sort of charming and old-fashioned. His parents always called him at home for reservations nights they wanted to come in as though *maître d's* didn't exist and he always made a point of being there when they arrived if that was possible. He didn't know why.

It wasn't as though he'd actually bother to sit down to eat with them or anything. He guessed he just sort of liked showing off the place.

He finished his smoke.

Jesus! How long *did* a piss take?

He got up and walked back to the men's room to face what he guessed was the inevitable and there the guy was, passed out snoring in the first stall.

"Hey. You. Up."

He slapped the man's face. The drunk just blinked.

God! this guy's shit stunk like he swallowed sulphur pills all day. He flushed the toilet.

Then slapped him again.

"Get up."

He grabbed the guy's arm and stood him up. "Mmmmm," the guy said.

"Pull up your pants." He had to repeat it twice. Then he had to tell him to button them and zip his fly.

"Come on."

He half-walked, half-dragged the man to the door. He unlocked it and stepped outside. The man seemed to revive a little when the cold air hit him. At least his eyes were open. Arthur looked around.

No car.

His Lincoln was the only one in the lot.

"Where's your car?"

"Hmmmm?"

"I said where's your car?"

Arthur still had to hold him up. The guy was heavy and he smelled like raw meat.

"No car. Took my license."

It wasn't hard to see why.

"So how'd you get here?" They were out on a highway for chrissake!

"Fella drove me. Friend a mine."

"Well, your friend's gone."

Arthur dropped him. The man crumbled to the pavement. "Hey," the man said.

He walked back inside and turned off the lights, switched on the security system, closed the door and double locked it. The man still sat there propped up on one arm.

Arthur had a notion.

"Listen," he said. "You want a lift? I'll give you a lift, come on."

The man crawled around to his hands and knees, concentrating, got his legs down under his weight and staggered to his feet.

"The car's over here."

He unlocked the driver's side and flicked the switch to open the passenger door. Then he got in and watched the man haul himself around the hood of the car to the passenger side. The man flopped heavily into his seat and sat there looking straight ahead, breathing hard and blinking.

"'Preciate it," he said.

"Where to?"

The man mumbled something.

"What?"

This time the guy *e-nun-ci-a-ted*.

"First road past Rumney Depot. Number two-two-three."

Arthur drove the dark quiet highway. He glanced over at the man now and then, saw the head bobbing and the eyes close. Soon the guy was snoring again.

He passed the Depot and turned off north into the mountains. It was a road he knew. He had taken women here from time to time, to see the sights he would tell them. There was never anybody around.

When the road finally went from macadam to hard-packed dirt he slowed the car so the bumps wouldn't jostle the guy awake. He didn't want him puking all over the Lincoln. He got to where he wanted to be and stopped and turned the car around so he was facing back toward civilization. He left the engine running and let himself out and walked to the passenger side.

The guy was leaning against the door. He opened it. The guy tumbled slowly into the dirt like a felled oak.

"Hey," the man said. His eyes couldn't seem to focus. This poor sad-ass drunk wasn't going to remember anything in the morning.

Except maybe this.

Arthur took him by both wrists and dragged him away from the car, dropped him down in the tall grass waving gray in the moonlight.

Then he kicked him.

Experimentally at first, not too hard, in the ribs and in the gut. The guy went *oomph* and *oomph* and tried to crawl away on rubbery legs. Art let him get a foot or two and then kicked him some more, harder this time so that he fell, then got in front of him and kicked him once in the face.

The guy rolled over lying in the grass, he was bleeding from the forehead, and Arthur moved again, kicked his legs apart so that he stood between them and then let him have one hard in the nuts.

The guy shrieked and doubled over puking all over himself. Then rolled to his side and lay there coughing, whining. Slime dribbling down off his chin.

Art walked back to the car, got in, and headed down the road.

It wasn't that he hated drunks particularly.

Drunks were just people.

People who were *easy*.

That was what he hated.

The careless, heedless, almost casual vulnerability of people. They'd put themselves in the damnedest, most pitiful situations with total strangers and then expect everything to go just fine. As though their innocence itself would protect them, as though innocence and virtue were a shield against the world *he knew* to be there.

He was put on the earth to do many things but partly he was put there to teach them.

Teach the truth.

That the world was a dark place.

Where you hid from what you caused to happen.

Everyone did, always. You forgot that at your peril.

And then you became a victim.

FIVE

DUET

Plymouth, New Hampshire
June 1985

It was something so lovely and painful to watch that Lydia could barely stand to see her sister, truly beautiful now out of the bridal veil and dancing, gliding—perfect—all in soft flowing white. Perhaps it was her own sense that it would never be this way for her sister again, this perfect, Barb's face bright with magic, the ancient ritual of bonding soul to soul resonant inside her, flushing her skin, reaching deep into something primal and good in human life lived together which, just for this moment, this day, radiated out to all who loved her. This, she thought, was the real virginity. Not the body's but the heart's. And once gone it was gone forever.

It would be that way for her sister too. If she was lucky enough and smart enough, what would follow would be the hard logic and gentle attentions of a good life together. Children maybe, enough money to live on, pleasurable sex and other pleasures, work she cared about, love, friendship. Yet she might also have none of these.

That made her beautiful too.

Their mother sat prominent to one side below the wedding party, her aunt and uncle flanking her. She could see in her mother's face a reflection of her own thoughts—a steely joy, the moment's fragile grace finding that narrow path through surrounds of pain and rough knowledge to her mother's heart.

It had not been easy for her, living with her father.

Certainly not easy for Lydia or Barbara but especially not easy for their mother.

She wondered what she was remembering.

There was a man standing at the double doors to the hall. Lydia didn't know him. She assumed he was with Alan's—the groom's—party, though she hadn't noticed him at the wedding. The man was looking at her with an open interest that was just shy of being rude because the eyes and smile were so friendly.

"Do you know that man?"

Cindy Fortunato, Barbara's ex-roommate from college, followed Lydia's glance. She sipped her champagne before answering. The champagne had kept coming all evening and Cindy was keeping up with it nicely.

"Sure. That's Arthur Danse. He owns the place."

"He's staring."

"Really?" Cindy laughed. "Hey, good for you. He's cute *and* he has money."

"He's the owner?"

"Uh-huh. You could do worse, Liddy."

She knew that her sister and her friends used to come here often to the bar and restaurant on the other side of those double doors while they were undergrads at Plymouth College. That was why Barb had chosen The Caves for her reception—that and the convenience for Alan's family, who lived right here in town. Supposedly the banquet hall had been a recent addition. Which meant that Cindy was probably right. Danse was doing quite well for himself.

Not that it mattered. What mattered right now, she thought—after her *own* three glasses of champagne—was more the cute part.

It had been a long time since Jim.

She decided that for once she didn't mind someone staring.

He finally had it—why he couldn't seem to take his eyes off her.

It wasn't that she was the most beautiful woman in the room—the bride, for one, was prettier—or the best dressed or most stylish or that she had the best body.

It occurred to him that there were women who seemed to have this weird sort of allure—who people seemed to want to talk to right away, to open up to right away. He'd never really understood the urge in others but he could tell she was like that. That she'd bring that out in people. Something about the eyes, their directness, the *interest* in the eyes, something about the way the younger girl who was sitting next to her leaned toward her as they spoke, as though she felt a kind of *pull*.

He knew instinctively that this was the sort of woman for whom the guy at the local service station would go the extra mile wiping down the windshield front and back and *wouldn't* cheat on the repair bills. The sort of woman other, maybe bolder women would always want to befriend and protect like some special little sister, even if they were actually younger than she was, and whom men would always desire.

Somebody you could *want*.

As he found that he did. If only to show a thing or two. That she wouldn't always be protected.

"Ask him over. Give him a nod. No, better yet, go to the ladies' room. You'll have to walk right by him."

"You're impossible."

"I'm sensible. Plus I'm smashed. Plus it's a wedding."

"What's that got to do with it?"

"It's a wedding. It's *romantic*, for god's sake."

"For my sister it's romantic."

"Bullshit. You're chicken."

"Cindy, I'm thirty years old. Married and divorced."

"So?"

"So I'm not about to go around picking up strange men."

"He's not exactly strange. I met the guy once."

"Sure. He nodded to you at the bar."

"Actually he *smiled* at me at the bar."

"See?"

"There's a difference."

"There is? Then *you* get up and go to the ladies' room. You go meet him."

"He's not staring at me. Besides, Eddie would shoot me. Come on! You're going to have to pee sooner or later anyhow, right?"

He really didn't believe he was doing this.

Walking right over.

Straight across the floor past the tables and the dancers to the bridal party.

It violated all his principles, business and otherwise.

First of all, it was their show. He was only there to make sure that things ran smoothly. He had no business fraternizing with the guests. Nor had he ever in his life made the acquaintance of a woman in quite such a public way. In such an exposed, unguarded way.

Yet here he was. Walking over.

"Everything all right here?"

"Everything's . . . just fine," she said. He could see the surprise in her face. "Dinner was excellent."

"Good. Plenty of champagne?"

She raised her glass and smiled. "Plenty."

"I wanted to introduce myself. I'm Arthur Danse. The Caves is mine. So if anything's not up to par you have me to blame."

"Really, everything's been perfect. And the room is lovely."

"Thanks. I got lucky on the decorator. You're . . . the sister of the bride?"

"Yes. Lydia McCloud."

"Pleased to meet you."

She reached for his hand.

Hers was warm and dry but not as smooth as he'd expected.

She works with her hands, he thought.

Yet she's educated.

Interesting.

She introduced him to the girl sitting next to her, one of the bridesmaids, Cindy something. Cindy Something was grinning at him like today was her birthday and he was her present.

Not likely.

Not with this one around.

"Listen," he said. "If there's anything you need, whatever, napkins, matches, or a B-52 from the bar, please just let me know."

"Excuse me? A *B-52*?"

"Gran Marnier, Kahlua, and Bailey's Irish Cream. Believe me, it's exactly what it says it is."

He turned and watched the dancers for a moment. "Looks like a good party," he said.

"Yes, it is."

"And your sister's a really pretty bride."

"Thank you."

He watched a moment longer.

"Well, I'd better get back to work," he said.

He smiled and turned to leave and then turned back to her again as he'd intended to do all along and gave it a beat, still smiling, looking puzzled now but knowing full well that this was a city girl. Hell, he could smell it on her.

"You're not from around here, are you?" he said.

"No. Boston. I'm just in for a few days, for this."

"Really? I went to school in Boston."

"Did you?"

"Had a restaurant there too—in Cambridge actually—but it went under. To tell you the truth it's been so long since I've talked to a city person I feel like there's hay sticking out of my hair. I don't suppose it would be possible to buy you a drink later on?"

"Well, I . . ."

"Or tomorrow night if that's easier for you."

"I . . ." She laughed. "Sure. I guess. Why not?"

"Tomorrow night, then. Great. Whenever it's convenient for you. I'll be here. It's good to meet you, Cindy." *Always be nice to the girlfriends*, he thought.

It was one of the rules.

He walked back across the room smiling, thinking, *now where is all* this *going*. He felt strongly attracted to this woman. Up close the eyes were a beautiful amber-green, the skin creamy and smooth and the scent of her a rich clean spicy smell, not sweet or flowery.

He liked the fact that she seemed a little shy, a little puzzled by him—off balance somehow. Maybe walking directly over had been the best thing after all. He hadn't really thought about it at the time. He'd just sensed for some reason that he could not afford to wait. That he had to grab this one fast or she'd be gone.

He wondered why he should care.

He wondered if he was good enough to get her to put off going back to Boston for a day or two.

It'd be interesting to see.

The band was playing a fairly respectable version of Springsteen's

"Hungry Heart." He didn't stick around to listen. He had things to do.

He was taking tomorrow night off.

Maybe, if he was lucky, the next couple of nights.

He wondered if Lydia McCloud knew that her life had already changed a bit.

Meeting him.

Lydia turned to Cindy and smiled. Feeling slightly foolish.

Here we go again, she thought. For better or worse, here I am again.

SIX

LONG DISTANCE

Plymouth, New Hampshire,
and Boston, Massachusetts
June 1985 to September 1986

He had a restaurant to run. She had a good-paying nurse's job at
Mass General.

They practically lived on the telephone.

She grew to know him this way, mostly through sleepy late-
night calls that would often last an hour or more, going over each
other's day. Her work and his. Her family and friends and his. None
of whom they knew in common.

Gradually she told him about her life with Jim—or her lack
of a life—and something, but not all, about her father. He was
sympathetic. He told her about the trouble he'd gotten into as a kid.
Truancy, stealing. It seemed to her that he still felt guilty about some
of it and she wondered why he should hold this against himself for
so long.

He seemed concerned about her interests, financial as well as
personal. She hadn't taken a penny from Jim so it was hard to get
along now living in Boston on a RN's salary. He advised her on a
few investments to increase her capital. They talked movies, books,
television. He seemed shy about expressing critical opinions, as
though afraid to offend, though when he did express them he was
smart and kind of funny. He made her laugh.

She thought it amazing and delightful to find that they had
actually gone to the same school together and at roughly the same

time, had probably passed one another at some point in the halls.

Sometimes he'd fly down to Boston for the weekend. Though it was hard for him because the restaurant was busiest on weekends, that was her only time off. Occasionally she'd drive to Plymouth.

In bed he was gentle, considerate, undemanding. She liked the feel of him, the smell of him.

She noted that while he had many acquaintances made through the business he seemed to have few friends. None of them close. She attributed this to his work schedule and a basic reserve in him. She had dinner a few times with his mother and father. The father seemed to warm to her immediately in his quiet way but his mother never did, nor Lydia to her. She thought the woman was probably a tough old bird—she was handling a severe case of rheumatoid arthritis with nothing more than the occasional dose of Tylenol and Lydia could admire that—but Ruth struck her as coarse, not the least endearing.

In July of 1986 they took a whole week off and flew to Jamaica to a resort where silly plastic shark's teeth substituted for money and the two of them lay basking in the sun drinking *piña* coladas and a lethal rum punch, dashing indoors to escape the drenching daily ten-minute rainstorms, dancing at night and eating the wonderful island food alfresco and making love, and at the end of that week, on a starless moonless night on the terrace of their hotel, he proposed to her.

She did not accept immediately. There was no question of his leaving the restaurant in New Hampshire. And it was hard for her to consider leaving behind her friends and job in Boston for a man she knew mostly from telephone calls and weekends. Hard to consider marrying any man again even though she had come to be very fond of this one. Almost, but not quite, in love with him.

She reminded herself that she had been in love with Jim.

And that was a disaster.

Love was not necessarily a requirement.

She consented in September over drinks at The Caves. Quite a number of drinks. Enough so that in the future she'd wonder sometimes how much they'd actually had to do with it. By then she'd seen certain sides to him that had not been apparent before and which would certainly have prevented her from marrying Arthur Danse had she known of them. No matter how many margaritas she'd had that night.

By then she knew all about the guns.

She knew about the father and mother.

She knew about the bouts of drinking.

She also knew that the expected had happened, that she had come to care for him despite all this. Sometimes she thought you could fall in love with anyone if you lived with them long enough and got to know them. She saw the remorse in the aftermath of his drinking. She saw the deep, almost childlike dependency upon his parents—especially upon his mother. She saw that to him firearms meant a kind of status and power and wondered why he needed them.

But for all this she doubted he was much different from any man.

That was how she felt at first.

It all changed when she had her baby. Their son Robert.

Their only child.

SEVEN

COMING OUT PARTY

Plymouth, New Hampshire
September 1987

He watched her read in bed.

The night was unseasonably mild so she had the bedroom windows open and the covers off the bed and she lay there on the sheets in the green silk chemise he'd bought her for her birthday. The chemise was scooped low in front and slim-strapped and plunging in back. Soft and smooth. His wife liked pretty things and he liked to give them to her. Her body had come back quickly after the baby. She hadn't worked at it. Some women had the genes, she said. They were lucky.

She was lucky.

Of course she was.

Her nipples were swollen from the baby's sucking and they had changed in color from a pale to a very much darker brown but that and a certain softening of the flesh, a certain overall voluptuousness, were the only major changes in her. She was still that woman whom all the men would want and all the women would want to know.

The softness only made her more attractive to him. He wanted to touch it, grasp it, almost all the time now.

He'd showered long and thoroughly, the water as hot as he could take it.

He was shaving for the second time that day and glancing at her over his shoulder in the clouded mirror.

Inside the boxer shorts his prick was hard already.

What he'd always taken elsewhere he was beginning to want more and more at home now.

It was funny.

Maybe he'd logged in too many miles on the car, traveled too many roads to too many places. On "business trips" to collect "supplies and equipment" for the restaurant or interviewing "potential business partners" who never quite came around to investing. Happily she didn't ask many questions.

But maybe he was getting tired of that.

Or maybe it was the baby. *His* baby. The thing he'd put inside her that had grown there and now claimed her attention utterly. The fact of that which excited him. The challenge to take her back.

Or maybe it was the softness of the flesh.

Whatever. It was time to show her.

Just a little.

He'd been patient. Amazingly so.

And she was ready. She wouldn't deny him.

The baby, Robert, made her happy. At least that was what she told him. And he couldn't see any reason to disbelieve her. Though it was hard to understand. It seemed to him that Robert was all demands. He cried. He wanted feeding or fresh diapers or to be held. What he wanted, he got.

He could understand that much at least.

But the point was that she was happy with the baby and consequently happy, he felt, with him. With life in general. Which meant it was time he showed her.

Just a little.

He splashed water on his face and toweled off and checked his upper torso in the mirror. Small pouches at his hips but not too bad, the rest of him still tight and young and strong.

He walked to the bed and stood over her.

"What's the book?"

"Novel." She showed him the cover. He pretended to be interested in the book. Something called *Hero Jesse* by Laurence Millman. He hated novels.

"It's about this retarded boy," she said, "or maybe he's insane, I don't really know yet, but he romanticizes the Vietnam War because his brother's over there and . . ."

"Any good?"

"Yes. Very."

He sat down next to her on the bed and rested his hand on her hip. He smiled.

"Okay. *How* good?"

She smiled back. She was flirting with him. She knew what he was after.

Or thought she did.

"I told you. Very good."

She went back to the book. And now she too was just pretending.

He moved his hand down over her hip beyond the silk to the soft-hard flesh of her thigh. He squeezed gently. She looked up at him still smiling and glanced across the room to the baby sleeping soundlessly in his crib and then she marked and closed the book.

"Okay, what?" she whispered.

"What?"

"Yes, what?"

"This."

His hand moved over and around her thigh and up to her ass and he cupped her cheek and pulled her toward him and kissed her, smelling her light perfume and his own fresh cologne. She put down the book and wrapped her arms around his neck so that he could feel her nipples hard already through the sheer jade silk. He slid the straps down over her shoulders and began to touch her, brushing the nipples side to side, up and down. She closed her eyes and moaned—and he thought of what he wanted to do.

He lay her down again across the cool white cotton sheets and pulled off the chemise and tossed it aside beside her and then spread her legs wide and moved his mouth down over her belly and down until his tongue was inside her, tasting how clean she always was there and smelling the cleanness too and then circling and crossing over the nub of her clitoris while his hands roved up over her thighs and belly to her breasts, his fingers mirroring on her erect swollen nipples the movements of his tongue.

He heard her moan and gasp and looked up over her pale body beginning to sheen with sweat while his tongue and fingers continued working on her, saw her toss her head again and again, back and forth, saw her clench her fists, her arms stretched wide.

"Come inside me," she whispered.

He shook his head. No.

He sucked and licked her and rolled the nipples, stroked lightly at their flat wide tips.

He felt her hips begin to buck and the body start to shudder and then she was bucking furiously, it was hard to stay with her when she got like this but he did until the fury of it was suddenly over and he knew that his fingers on her and his tongue were like slivers of glass which were punishing her, like fingernails on the blackboard of her body screeching throughout her nervous system, and he rolled away wiping at his slick chin. Relishing what was next.

"You now," she said.

Yes.

He entered her all at once and she gasped again. There was a sweet pain to this for her now, he knew. Each stroke would ignite pain and pleasure both.

He pulled out of her.

Her eyes flashed open. Almost a shock.

"Turn over," he said.

She looked at him, puzzled, but did as he asked.

He pulled her up to her hands and knees. He knew she was thinking that they had used this position only rarely because she didn't enjoy the angle of him inside her nearly as much as she did from the front. But the pleasure was his now. She wouldn't deny him.

"Press outward," he said.

"What?"

"You know. Like you're taking a shit. Press outward." It was dawning on her.

They had done this only once and she'd hated it. "Arthur . . .?"

She was worried now, looking at him over her shoulder. "Just now. Just this once."

"I don't . . ."

"Come on."

"Do you have to?"

Her reluctance, her tone of voice made him even harder, bigger.

"Yes. But I'm dry now. Move up a little."

She lifted her buttocks and he entered her vagina, stroked, stroked again, pulled out and shifted her down.

He went up her ass slowly, gradually opening her. She groaned. It hurt. She wasn't saying anything but he could tell. He reached around in front of her to the softness of her swaying breasts and squeezed them and pressed them back into her chest and squeezed at the nipples which were still so sensitive that he knew that would hurt her too and still she said nothing, only gasped and groaned again saying *ah, ah, ah,* as he moved faster, feeling like he was fucking some warm, soft, loyal thing he owned who'd do anything he asked and more.

He came and rammed it into her deep and held it there a moment, then collapsed on top of her onto the bed. And still she only lay there breathing hard beneath him.

He pulled out and went to the bathroom. He stood in front of the sink.

There was blood and shit on his penis.

Streaks of red.

Safe sex, he thought.

Sex with your wife. Who had had your kid.

It wasn't bad. Not bad at all.

He washed her off him.

He thought, hell, it's a beginning.

EIGHT

THE FAMILY OF ARTHUR DANSE

October 1987–December 1993

There were problems but she had determined to make it work, to go the whole distance. There was a child to raise.

And Robert clearly loved his father. No question.

From the age of three on he was always looking for his daddy. *When's daddy coming home? Can we go with daddy?* In the spring of '89 Arthur contracted with his chef and a bottling firm in Concord to launch a line of the more unusual sauces and salad dressings from The Caves to be sold at retail tourist shops throughout the White Mountains ski resorts and along Lake Winnipesaukee—even places as far afield as Stowe, Vermont—so he began traveling a lot. Sometimes for a week at a time they wouldn't see him.

When they did Robert was thrilled.

There were always presents for one thing. Plastic superheroes from the cartoon shows, dinosaurs, comic books, storybooks, and board games, and as he got older, games for Nintendo and Sega Genesis.

Arthur was a very attentive father.

They went out to movies, out for pizza—sometimes just the two of them, father and son—worked on his homework together, played baseball, and even though she hated it, football. He tried to be around for as many school and after-school activities as possible. She appreciated that. He took Robert fishing and taught him how to ride a bike.

The actual hard business of raising a little boy was left largely to her, naturally. Setting the rules and making sure the rules were kept. She often felt uncomfortably like the bad guy. But she guessed that just went with the territory. And compared to a lot of other kids Robert was an easy child.

Robert wasn't the problem.

The problem was Arthur.

Over time he seemed to withdraw. They talked less and talked *about* less. He seemed moody, distant. Except in the bedroom.

But that was a problem too.

More and more he wanted sex anally.

She hated the feeling. *Hated* it. Like having to go and not being able to go and having everything *pushed up* inside. It was easier for her to accommodate him now than it had been at first but that didn't make the act any less distasteful. It got so that she almost dreaded sex with him. Not knowing if he'd be wanting *that* again tonight.

Tension and sex were a bad mix.

She'd pretty much stopped having orgasms.

He didn't seem to mind. That hurt her too.

Once she'd simply refused him.

It was the kind of day where everything that could go wrong did go wrong, where the toilet broke down and getting a plumber in was hell and waiting for him to arrive had completely skewed her afternoon to the extent that she had to ask Cindy, whose daughter Gail was in Robert's class, to go pick him up after school and drop him off, and then Robert had one of his infrequent but *black* fits of pique because his Game Boy didn't work and they had no spare batteries around, like it was the end of the civilized world, and she practically shoved him out the door, ordering him to go out and play. Then she almost burned the lasagna. Rushing it.

So that night Arthur wanted to butt-fuck. *Jesus.*

"No," she said.

"Why not?"

She was exhausted. "No, Arthur. Please. Not tonight."

"Why?"

"Because I don't *want* to."

"*I* want to."

"Arthur, another time, okay?"

It wasn't okay. He slammed out of the room, awakening five-year-old Robert, and then she had to explain to him why daddy was sleeping in the guest room that night.

Something about a cold and germs.

Arthur'd sulked and glowered for over a week. He would say almost nothing to her and what little he did say was usually nasty. He ignored Robert as thoroughly as possible. The boy could see that something was wrong. He gave his father an unusually wide berth. Almost as though Robert was suspicious of him now. Yet she could tell that the boy was hurt and felt rejected. Her heart ached for him. And it disturbed her that Arthur would take their problems out on their son, as though Robert were just another hostage to him.

It was like living with a small cruel boy who had the power to make both hers and Robert's life miserable at whim. And was perfectly willing to do so.

Eventually he went off on business for a few days and when he came back the incident seemed forgotten.

But she never refused him again.

It wasn't worth it.

She had Robert's piece of mind to think of too.

She didn't even refuse him the night he came home from Concord with his little black bag of toys.

He was grinning as he dumped them beside her on the bed.

"It's fantasy," he said. "It's about fantasy and trust, y'know? Something different. It'll be fun."

Fun for who? she thought.

But it was different, all right.

Four black leather handcuffs with silver rings attached, two for the wrists and two heavier, thicker ones, for the ankles.

Four lengths of slender silver chain.

Eight two-sided spring-clips for attaching the chains together.

And a small black braided leather whip.

"You're kidding," she said.

"Don't worry. I'm not going to hurt you."

"Oh no? Then what's the whip for?"

He laughed. "Say . . . stimulation."

She pointed to the handcuffs. She could smell them. The new rich leather. The metallic smell of silver.

"You want me to put those on."

"Uh-huh. And this."

He reached into his pocket and withdrew a black silk scarf. A blindfold.

All she could do was look at him.

He shrugged, smiling. "Part of the game. But it's pretty, no? A present."

"Oh, thanks very much."

It was hard to take this seriously. *Bondage games.* They were out in New Hampshire, for god's sake, not someplace like New York, where she guessed they were used to this kind of thing. It struck her as pretty silly.

But there was also the other thing.

Some slight element of fear.

He could see her response. He could always read her.

"Come on," he said. "Just try it." Then he laughed. "Hey, I spent a lot of *money* on all this stuff, you know!"

Okay, she thought. What was the line? *Once a scientist, twice a pervert?* Might as well humor him. Just this once.

And who knew? Maybe he was right. Maybe it would be . . . sort of . . . exciting.

Excitement was in short supply these days.

"What do you expect me . . . what do you want me to wear?" she said.

"Nothing." He smiled. "Just this."

He held up the blindfold.

She took a deep breath.

"Okay," she said. "But none of . . . that other stuff."

He knew what she meant. She meant the anal nonsense. "No. I promise."

Robert had fallen asleep long ago, but Arthur closed and locked the door behind him.

She slipped the nightgown off her shoulders.

She felt suddenly very vulnerable.

"I don't know, Arthur."

"Don't worry."

If you're going to do it then get on with it, she thought.

"Okay. How do you . . . where do you want me?"

"For now just kneel there, right in the middle of the bed."

She did as he asked. He folded the scarf and draped it over her eyes and tied it behind her head. The world slipped into blackness and the scent and feel of soft, expensive silk.

He reached for her left hand and wrapped it with one of the handcuffs and buckled the cuff together.

"Too tight?"

"No." The leather felt soft actually.

"Can you slip your hand free?"

She tried it.

"No," she said.

And that was when she felt the first momentary thrill of honest-to-God fear—and it really *was* a little exciting, because once he had them all on there was no way she was going to get out of them again until he let her.

It was also kind of embarrassing.

She knelt and listened to the tinkling of chains after that as he attached them to the loops in the cuffs and then in back of her to the brass four-poster bed, telling her to spread her legs wide and then pulling the chains tight to the far low corners of the head post so that there was no way she could close her legs again, repeating the process higher up so that her arms were spread wide in back of her, chained to the top.

She felt suspended.

She couldn't fall forward to the soft protection of the bed and she couldn't fall to either side. She felt suddenly much too open to him. To whatever he had in mind. The thrill had become a kind of trembling. She felt weak and trapped and exposed. And for the first time, just a little afraid of him.

"Here's what we'll do," he said. "We'll play a game."

His voice seemed to come from everywhere at once.

"I've got eight guns here in the house, right?"

Guns? she thought.

"Pistols, rifles, shotguns. You've seen me polishing them, cleaning them, breaking them down a thousand times. Suppose we say the eight guns correspond to eight different parts of your body? Here . . ."

She felt the whip caress her inner right arm and she jumped at the touch.

"Here . . ."

Then her left arm, moving from shoulder to elbow. She jumped again.

"Here and here . . ."

Her inner thighs.

"Here, of course."

Her butt.

"And here . . ."

Belly.

"And finally here . . ."

Moving slowly, almost torturously over her breasts.

". . . and here."

The whip brushed her pubic hair.

My God, could he really be considering using a whip *there*?

No way. This was crazy.

"Arthur . . ."

"Let me finish. Here's the game. I touch you someplace like I did just now. Then I name one of the guns. You tell me the *caliber* of the gun. If you get it right, I don't use the whip there. Not at all. You get it partially right, I use it, but only lightly. You get it wrong, a little harder."

"Uh-uh, Arthur. No. Not possible."

"You can't refuse, Liddy."

"Arthur, it isn't funny."

"Liddy, you can't refuse."

"The hell I can't. Want to hear me scream?"

He laughed. "If you do that, you know what's gonna happen? You'll wake up Robert. Now how are you going to explain all this to Robert? You could have a problem there, right?"

"Arthur, you son of a bitch."

She was furious. How *dare* he?

And how did I let myself get into this?

"If you do this, Arthur, if you go through with this, I swear we're finished," she said. "I'm telling you. I'll divorce you. I'm not kidding."

"Lydia, it's a *game*. Just a game. Stop taking it all so *seriously*. Look, I know what's bothering you. We'll start with what you're obviously so damn worried about. Here . . ."

He let the whip move down over her pubic hair again. She flinched.

"Magnum," he said.

"What?"

"Magnum."

He brushed her again.

".357."

"There," he said. "See? There you go! You're playing. And you win, right? I don't do a thing."

Great, she thought.

I don't know your goddamned guns. I don't know half of them.

She felt the whip drift over the soft inner flesh of her right thigh. "Walther PPK."

She got the .3 in .380 right.

So that was an easy one.

Also, later, the Ladysmith .38 revolver because he'd made a point of telling her that this particular gun was hers, that he'd bought it for her protection. Though she'd never once fired it.

She also got the 12-gauge shotgun.

So that her right arm and her belly were spared.

But her buttocks weren't spared and he hit her hard there. She could feel the sting even as he moved on to the soft skin of her left thigh and her left inner arm.

Her breasts weren't spared.

And even though he used the whip more lightly there than anywhere else on her body in deference to their tenderness and sensitivity she wanted very much to scream then, only the thought of Robert holding her back, of Robert waking and wanting to know what was going on with mommy and daddy behind the locked door to their bedroom.

There were tears in her eyes when he was done.

When he released her she cursed him and showered and then she slept in the other room.

Another cold. More germs. Mommy this time.

"It was only a game," he said as she walked out the door. "Come on. You'll get over it."

The marks faded in an hour or so.

The memory never faded. She stored the memory like a chipmunk stores chestnuts for winter.

She never saw the handcuffs or the little black whip again. She assumed he'd thrown them away. Probably he was disgusted with her. Spoilsport.

She couldn't have cared less.

She threw the expensive black silk scarf in the garbage.

And for weeks there was nothing remotely like sex between them. Not so much as a peck on the cheek. She found that she didn't much mind that at all, either.

Arthur was withdrawing anyway. Spending more and more time away from the house. At The Caves. On the road. With his parents.

There were times she wondered if he had a girlfriend.

She wondered if she'd react the way she had with Jim.

She doubted it.

There were nights he'd come home with liquor on his breath and she always stayed clear of him then. His flash point, once seemingly nonexistent, was steadily growing lower and lower. He had never struck her in anger but that didn't mean she felt he was incapable of it. And his temper could be formidable. When he was angry and arguing he had a way of *stalking* her, moving toward her and then away and then forward again, each time getting closer to her, back and forth, until he was shouting right into her face.

There were times she considered leaving him.

She could do it. She hadn't much savings of her own but she could always dust off her nursing job again. They might be scraping a little but she could get by.

Then just before Christmas of '93 her mother died. The woman had been shoveling snow in the driveway, impatient with waiting for the overdue hired snowplow. The heart attack was swift, sudden and unexpected.

All three of them drove to Wolfeboro.

She was a basket case by the time they got there and her sister Barbara, who was living over in Hanover now, wasn't a whole lot better. They had never even *considered* their mother dying. Sixty-two wasn't old. And sixty-two-year-olds didn't come more vigorous than Kerry McCloud. After their father died she'd turned most of her backyard into a garden, grew her own vegetables and herbs and berries there, canned the vegetables and berries and gave them away. She worked on fundraisers for two charity groups, the public library, and the local Democratic Party. She held down a part-time job she didn't need in a bookstore just to be around the latest in hardcover fiction. She had bridge nights and a women's group for single widows. The only thing she didn't do was date.

And everyone knew the reason for that.

Just as everyone knew that Kerry McCloud had a drink or two every evening and slept, not in her marriage bed, but on the couch in the living room.

But Lydia and her sister were stunned at the loss. She found herself staring blankly at walls and remembering conversations and events as though they were being played out in front of her directly on those walls like a screen into her mother's history. A bookmark in an unfinished book, her mother's name on the daily junk mail which still arrived, a roaster left in the freezer—all were enough to undo her, to reach out to her unexpectedly and move her to sudden tears.

Robert, who was almost seven by then, had loved his grandma too, and despite the toys and books and games he'd brought with him could not seem to pry himself away from the adults and the spectacle of their grief. She doubted it was good for him. But it was harder to tell him to go out and play or banish him to another room while they were arranging for the funeral or on the phone with friends and relatives than it was to simply accept his presence, seeming always on the verge of tears himself—especially when she or Barb or both were going at it.

The real surprise was Arthur.

Not that he took charge—she almost would have expected him to take charge in some ways—but the surprise was the apparent grace, tact and dignity that he brought to the occasion. More often than not it was he who got the phone when it rang, fielding dozens of well-meaning but impossibly intrusive calls, telling the story over and over, how paramedics had rushed to the scene but failed to revive her, *at least it was fast, yes,* how there was no history of heart disease and no, none in the family history either.

To these calls and others of a more mundane nature—the sheer brain-numbing business of dealing with a death in the family— Arthur brought a kind of calm, a serious yet unsentimental style that relieved the burden on both sisters. There was to be no viewing. They both thought it barbaric. So that with Barbara divorced—she'd been more than right on that one, Barb's wedding *had* been the happiest day of her marriage—Arthur was the only man around most of the time all the way up until the funeral, and he was as gentle and generous with his hugs and time, his patience and consolation, with Barb as he was with Lydia.

The night before the funeral he and Lydia made love, the first time they'd done so in weeks. Arthur was never more tender and loving. Not even before they were married. And Lydia surprised herself with her ferocious hunger for him. She later remembered feeling for a moment that it was as though he was the earth, the land, and she was tying in a rushing wind, and she clung to him.

The day of the funeral she stood graveside amid thirty-five uncles, aunts, cousins and friends from all over New England, Robert to her left and Barb to her right, with Arthur standing behind them, one hand on each woman's shoulder. And she was grateful that he was including her sister this way because her sister was so alone.

At the reception it was his parents who were the last guests to leave. She thought that his mother Ruth looked like a scrawnier and tougher bird than ever but that Harry was becoming a shadow. Uncomfortable in his too-big suit now that he'd lost all that weight and even more uncomfortable being at the funeral of someone he barely knew. While his wife was all restless energy, taking over the kitchen from Lydia and Barb and somehow managing to make them feel like outsiders in the house they'd grown up in. She appreciated the help but was glad to see them go.

It had been unpleasant to discover that their mother had taken out a second mortgage on the house shortly after their father died. Apparently he hadn't left her as well provided for as she'd always pretended. Arthur arranged for its disposal with an agent. The agent said that Barbara and Lydia would each probably realize fifteen thousand dollars on the place. It wasn't much, but then Barbara was a single teacher with no children and wasn't strapped for money.

Returning to Plymouth two days later they were tuned to a Concord call-in talk show on the radio. The subject was a recent statewide rash of serial murders. Young girls, mostly, some not yet in their teens. People complaining about police inactivity, demanding that something be done. An expert in criminal psychology was discussing what type of person the killer might be, speculating on his motives, his personality, his childhood.

At first she barely listened. Not until the show's second guest, a state police lieutenant, began talking about the more personal side of it, about what parents and children should know in order to avoid becoming victims of this kind of thing.

"I hate that stuff," Arthur said.

"What do you mean? Why?"

"They try to make you feel as though if you do this or you do that, if you just take these precautions, you're safe. When you're not safe. You're never safe. Not from some people."

They listened a moment longer and then he changed the station.

It was only much later that she realized what he'd said to her and why.

NINE

ROBERT

Fall 1994

Robert dreamed that he was at the swimming pool and that the concrete was hot beneath his feet, burning hot, so that instead of sliding in or using the ladders, he jumped right in as fast as he could, even though jumping was against the rules.

For some reason there was no lifeguard that day to bother him anyhow.

He surfaced and saw that not only were there no lifeguards there were no other kids in the water either. And no adults. He had the pool all to himself. He wondered where everyone had got to, if there was maybe a parade or something and he was missing something, because there wasn't even anybody sitting *around* the pool like there usually was and here it was a nice sunny day. But then he just started swimming and was feeling pretty good in there.

He was best at swimming underwater so he did that, went almost the width of the pool crosswise before he had to come up for air so he decided to try it the long way and see how far he got. But he must have had his breathing wrong or something because he needed air way sooner than he thought he would and when his head cleared the water he saw that he wasn't in a pool anymore but in the middle of a lake with trees and bushes all around.

That was when he saw the snakes.

Three of them, black, right behind him, swimming right for him, he could see their heads sticking up pointed at him and the fast side-to-side motion of their bodies skimming the surface of the dirty black water under the suddenly darkening sky.

"Help!" he yelled but there wasn't anybody around and then he remembered that, sure, the lifeguard was off duty. He turned and started kicking his feet and pounding at the water swimming as fast as he could toward shore but the snakes were coming faster, he knew it, he could *feel* it, they were moving faster than he'd ever known any other living thing to move before like living torpedoes, and he knew he couldn't make it, thinking over and over *go away, go away, please go away* and praying that he'd been wrong, that the snakes weren't really coming for *him*, not for him, that maybe he'd been mistaken and they were going somewhere else and didn't like to bite kids his age and just *seemed* to be going in his direction so he turned to check that out, his one and only hope, and saw them inches from his feet and ready to bite, their snow-white mouths open wide and their needle-sharp fangs glinting, dripping thick venom in the sun, and he screamed and woke himself just in time. And he found he was still screaming into the wet writhing darkness of the room when his mom came in and grabbed him, held him—and he realized from the way the bed felt under him that he'd done that thing again.

Something was happening to Robert.

She could see it, his teacher Mrs. Youngjohn could see it, Arthur could see it. Even Ruth was commenting.

He'd begun stammering for one thing.

She'd stand by watching helplessly as he struggled to get some word out, his lips pursed tight together as though the word had somehow got trapped inside him fully formed, and then likely as not when he finally managed to pry it out of him it dropped out twice, uncontrolled, in rapid succession. His eyes would be blinking all the while, the muscles around them completely engaged in the effort.

She could count on nightmares awakening him two or three times a week.

And suddenly he was getting clumsy. Robert had more scraped elbows and knees these days than any kid she'd ever seen. He'd be running around and he'd trip over his own two feet. He'd topple off his bike. Drop things. Walk into banisters. The summer before she had been highly aware of the bruises on his legs, to the point that she hated to see him put on a pair of shorts for fear that somebody out there somewhere was going to take one look at him and accuse her and Arthur of child abuse. It happened.

He scalded himself one morning stepping into a too-hot shower. She was downstairs ironing. She heard him scream and ran upstairs and saw him standing sobbing on the bath mat, dripping wet, his right foot, leg, thigh, and the right side of his butt splotched lobster-red. She reached into the medicine cabinet for the antiseptic spray and covered him with the stuff.

"It's going to be all right," she kept saying, hugging his chest. Robert just kept crying.

Finally the spray had its effect and he calmed down. She took him by the hand and led him into his bedroom and laid him on his left side on top of the cool, fresh sheets.

"Just stay here awhile," she said. "Don't try to get dressed."

Then she went looking in his drawers for something big and loose for him to wear, pyjamas or something. Everything looked too tight so she went to her own bedroom and took a pair of Arthur's.

He looked at her and laughed when he saw what she was carrying.

"Those're *Daddy's*," he said.

"That's the point," she said. "They'll be nice and big on you."

"They'll fall down!"

"Let 'em."

He laughed again and then went suddenly serious on her.

"Daddy says pain's all in your head," he said.

"Does not."

"Does too. That's what he said to me, anyhow."

She thought about it. She guessed that Arthur'd been talking to him about Indian fakirs on beds of nails, fire-walkers, that kind of thing. But Robert wasn't talking about the mysteries of neurological functions now. He'd got it mixed up. It was clear he was worrying about *expressing* pain, ashamed of crying. He was talking about some ridiculous macho thing. Getting into the fakirs and fire-walkers now would probably only confuse him.

But she was going to scotch *this* one right away.

"Daddy's wrong," she said. "If you hurt, you hurt. Period. And it's all right to yell as hard as you want to or cry as hard as you want to. You don't have to try to tough it out just because you're a boy. Okay?"

He nodded. "Okay."

But then over time when he still kept falling and bumping into things she saw very little in the way of tears.

Not even after a nightmare. And he evidently had some doozies.

The worst thing, though, from both hers and Robert's point of view, was that at the age of almost eight he'd begun to soil the bed at night.

Not wetting it. Having bowel movements in his sleep.

It didn't happen every night but as many as three or four a week.

He hadn't done that since he was out of diapers. And now here he was back *in* them again, and damned humiliated by it. At an age when all the other kids wanted to go over to friends' houses on sleepover nights or have other kids to their house he could have none of it. He got asked and then he had to lie and say no, his mom was too strict and wouldn't let him.

Close friends like Cindy knew the truth. With most of the other mothers she simply backed his lie. Let them think what they wanted about her. She didn't trust them with his secret.

She didn't even tell his teacher, although she was working closely with Mrs. Youngjohn on some of his other problems. Lydia could see that just having it happen to him at all embarrassed the hell out of him. Other kids and parents knowing would be awful.

He started doing something very strange which she thought was somehow related.

The first time he did it she figured he was just being sort of perverse. Kids could be that way.

But later, as it continued, she wondered.

She walked into his room one night where he sat on the bed playing with his guys, bashing them into each other. Some superhero war game.

"Got to put this on," she said and held up the diaper. "Bedtime."

By then he knew the drill. But he didn't have to like it. "Just a minute, okay? Just one more minute," he said and continued bashing away.

"*Now,*" she said.

He sighed and made a face, making a big mock show of anger as he took off his clothes and got onto the bed.

And that was when he did what struck her as so completely odd.

He knelt on the bed stark naked and pressed his skinny chest directly to his knees.

His forehead rested on the mattress.

He dropped his arms behind him, fingertips touching his feet.

His pale white butt was sticking straight up at her. It was so unexpected that she laughed.

"Robert, what are you doing? How am I supposed to get a diaper on you in that position?"

She couldn't, obviously. It wasn't possible.

He didn't answer.

"Robert?"

He didn't move, either.

Protest, she thought. He doesn't feel like going to bed yet and he doesn't want the diaper on so he's found a brand-new wrinkle. *Kids.*

"Hey. Robert. This is not funny. Now roll over on your back so I can get this on, okay?"

He did as he was told.

She looked at him in silence as she worked. His expression was almost somber.

Poor little guy, she thought. Bromberg, the child psychologist he was seeing, wasn't doing him a damn bit of good. Bromberg said it would take time. Well, it was taking too damn *much* time. Every day she could see another grain of his happiness, his childhood, his personality being washed away like sand on a beach by these constant waves of exclusion and humiliation.

I'm different, he must think.

I stutter and I shit the bed so I'm bad.

And how to tell him that he wasn't bad without—just by discussing it—humiliating him further? Without admitting that any kid who did this all the time at his age had a pretty good *reason* to feel screwed up and different?

He was the only kid in his class who was seeing a psychologist.

He was aware of that too.

She was afraid to say anything to him at the moment, to call any more attention to his problems. Afraid to give them any more undue weight and substance.

Instead as she handed him his pyjamas she asked him about the other thing.

She smiled. "So what was that all about?"

"Huh?"

"Your cute little butt in the air. What was that stuff?" She thought he'd laugh but he didn't. He only shrugged. "Well, it's a whole lot easier on me when you're lying on your back, don't you think?"

He nodded.

She pulled the covers up over him and leaned over and kissed him on the forehead.

"Night, honey," she said. "You sleep well."

"Night, mom."

His voice sounded so small to her. Like the voice of a child half his age.

She turned off his light and went downstairs and hours later fell asleep on the couch wondering what to do for him or if there was anything she could do at all.

She thought that night that she'd seen the last of what she came to think of as the butt-in-the-air, knee-chest position. She hadn't.

It happened over and over. Irrationally and to no purpose. She'd walk into the bedroom with the diaper and there he'd be.

Like it was some sort of strange compulsion.

She tried to get him to explain what it was about. He would talk to her about plenty of other things but not about that.

All she got was an eerie silence.

And she was beginning to be afraid that her little boy was truly going crazy on her.

That something inside him was surfacing, something she'd been blind to. Some basic mistake of her own or something she'd overlooked—which would mean she'd failed as a mother to a stunning degree—or maybe that some resonance of their problems with the marriage was rising up inside him to take a terrible toll.

She told Bromberg and Bromberg tried to dig it out of him, the *reasons* for it, but Robert wouldn't speak to him either. Only shrugged like it was nothing.

When it was eating her up inside with worry.

It wasn't *normal*.

She knew she wasn't responding well at all. She was *afraid* of this behavior! And being afraid led her straight to a kind of irrational anger. He was *scaring* her.

A couple of nights she lost it, started yelling at him—*what's wrong with you? you know I can't put this on you when you do that! where's your* head, *Robert?*—and then hearing her own voice use the same words on him that her father had used on her so long ago, felt so guilty that she felt like crying.

Sometimes she thought that she was going crazy too. This was straining her sense of control, her feeling of being able to handle her life.

"Kids do lots of weird stuff," Arthur said. "It'll pass. You'll see. It's just some stage he's going through."

He was trying to be reassuring but what he was actually being was infuriating.

It was not some stage.

Her son was in trouble. Trouble right across the board. And this compulsion of his. This meant something.

TEN

PARTY TALK

November 10, 1994

"Okay," he said, once they'd taken off their coats and paid the sitter and she had gone outside into the cold night air. "What the hell did you think you were doing back there? I mean, *who do you think you are*, Lydia?"

It was the first he'd spoken to her since they'd left the party.

Since she'd told him what she'd done.

"Cindy's my friend," she said. "I think she has a right to know that that man is lying to her."

She wanted a cold drink of water. There was a taste of wine growing more and more sour in her mouth. She headed for the kitchen. He followed her.

"How do you know he's lying? What makes you so sure?"

"He tells you he's definitely decided he's staying with his wife? And then tells Cindy that he's madly in love with *her*? That's not lying?"

"Maybe he's undecided. Going two ways at once. *You* don't know. Plus it's none of your damn business."

She poured and drank the water. Arthur went to the refrigerator for another Miller Lite. She was tired. She didn't need the argument. It was late and she needed sleep.

"Listen, I'm not a gossip, Arthur. I thought about it a lot. I didn't just go off and do this thing. You think I wanted to say something? You think I enjoyed breaking the news to her or even getting involved in the first place? I didn't. I also know he's a friend of yours, even if not a very *good* friend . . ."

"Who says that? Who says he's not a good friend?"

She sighed. "Arthur, you see him two or three times a month. He comes into your restaurant. You talk to him. You buy him a drink. And that's that. Don't make out like he'd donate you a kidney or something, please."

"I happen to like the guy. Jesus Christ, Lyd, he's Chairman of the Board at *Groton Chemical*!"

"What's that got to do with it? Cindy's my best friend. Do you understand that? And she doesn't deserve to get jerked around by this guy! She got enough jerking around from Ed before the divorce."

She saw that the first beer had disappeared and he was already opening another. She turned on the water in the sink and started cleaning off some of the dishes. Even though she could have just as easily stuck them in the dishwasher or even left them for tomorrow. If she got busy maybe he'd go away.

"You *compromised* me, Lydia. You broke a confidence. I can't believe you'd do this to me! Do you know how much *business* this man throws my way?"

"I don't *care* how much business he throws your way. You don't need his business. You certainly don't need it as much as Cindy needs a decent life with a decent man who's not going to lie to her again the way her damned husband did."

"Maybe his intentions are good. Maybe he's just confused."

"That's ridiculous, Arthur."

"Look, everybody lies anyway. You lie to get what you want."

"I don't."

"No. *You* don't. You're fucking perfect."

"I didn't say I was perfect."

"You sure as hell seem to think you are."

She turned to him.

"I don't lie, Arthur. Do *you*?"

And she never saw it coming.

One moment his hand was at his side and the next moment he was slapping her.

She fell back against the sink, oddly aware that the water was still running and raised her arms to her face reflexively to fend him off because now that he'd put the beer down on the sideboard he was at her with both hands. The blows were getting through and they were hard, coming fast. He was using the heel of his hand and ball of his thumb, pounding at her, trying to hurt her, hitting at her head and cheeks and jaw, and she could smell the beer-stink on his breath and did not know whether she was more shocked or frightened at the attack.

She heard herself shrill his name once as she slid down the wall of cabinets to the floor and heard him growling at her, *bitch, you fuck with me?* grabbing at the collar of her blouse and pulling her up, ripping the fabric, so that she was kneeling in front of him held in place by one of his hands while he hit her with the other and she was crying, sobbing, she had her arms out in front of her but it wasn't any good, he was using his fist now, short tight jabs to the eye, to the nose. Punishing her. She could hear the pain roaring in her. Her entire face and head burned with pain. She inhaled her own blood, swallowed it. He was going to kill her.

She saw her father beating her mother in a drunken rage.

The man was bigger. The man was going to kill her.

Suddenly he threw her back into the kitchen cabinets and stood and released her. Her eyes skittered up to him and thought, *he's crazy, he's gone crazy* because she saw that he wasn't even looking at her now, he was standing over her looking up into the fluorescent lights above. He seemed tranced. Alien. He was panting and his shirt was torn—*had she done that?* He looked like some primitive warrior slipped somehow into modern clothes standing triumphant above his prey, his victim.

You bastard, she thought.

You coward.

He stepped off her and in four long strides was out of the room.

Headed for the stairs.

No! she thought. You are not going to *touch* him!

Her hand slid across a pool of her own blood as she tried to get up and then she was up and running after him, his own half-empty bottle of beer appearing as if by magic in her hand. She was halfway up the stairs when she saw him turn the corridor down the hall to Robert's room and then she missed a step and slipped again, her half-closed swollen eye betraying her. She pulled herself up by the banister, spilling the beer across the wooden stairs but holding tight to the bottle because if he came after her again or did anything to Robert, she'd use it on him, *she would.*

He wasn't in the darkened hall but there was a night light on in Robert's room and she raced toward it, flung herself into the entrance.

Then stopped.

Robert was asleep.

And Arthur was sitting on the bed holding him—his eyes closed. Gently rocking.

I'm living with a madman, she thought.

Dear god. I have been all this time.

"Get *away* from him!" she hissed.

Arthur opened his eyes and looked at her like he was seeing her for the first time all evening and was surprised to find her there.

Madman.

She stepped forward and raised the bottle.

His expression changed from that dazed look of surprise to something that seemed to her like sadness, genuine and deep.

She wanted him out of there.

"Get away!" she said.

He didn't seem to understand at first.

Then he set the boy down gently on the bed and stood staring at her a long second before he stepped slowly forward. She moved aside for him, aware of the bottle clutched in her hand and ready to use it if she had to. He didn't even glance at her as he walked past her out the door.

A moment later she heard the front door slam and a moment after that heard his car start up and pull away.

The dark felt suddenly thick with ozone.

She collapsed to the floor.

She was crying silently and everything throbbed and she couldn't see at all out of her right eye. Somehow she was going to have to clean herself up and get Robert out of there. She was going to have to make up a story for him as to how she got this way so he wouldn't be frightened seeing how she looked. She was going to have to pack a few things and phone Cindy and pile their stuff into her car and then drive to Cindy's house and get him settled in.

And she hoped Cindy had a camera.

Because her next stop was going to be the sheriff's office.

He wasn't getting away with this.

She was not going back to him.

It was her and Robert now.

ELEVEN

DUGGAN

It was late, almost four in the morning. Hell of a time to wake folks up if he was wrong. But he wasn't wrong. The way she described it, there was only one place he'd go after that.

"Officer Welch will take your statement, Mrs. Danse, and then we'll let you go get some sleep."

She nodded.

The woman was one big bruise. He wondered what she'd told her son about that. When they'd picked her up at her friend's house and driven her over to the clinic she was worse. He'd taken one good look at her and insisted she get medical attention right away. You didn't mess with blows to the head.

The photos they'd taken were impressive.

If she decided to go after him the photos alone could probably put the bastard away for a little while.

Privately he thought that would be the best possible thing for Arthur Danse.

He got out of the chair. His back hurt. Everything hurt. The station needed better chairs for guys like him. He was old and it was late.

"I'm going to see if I can't have a talk with Arthur," he said. "Make sure he knows what we know until that restraining order comes along. Okay?"

She removed the ice pack from her face and nodded again. "Thanks."

Tiny little voice. He'd heard its like before. Usually, right after the anger passed. As the realization of what they'd been through, and maybe what they'd escaped, settled in.

Officer Welch—who was *Martha* Welch, thank you very much, and for his money, a credit to both her sex and the badge—stopped him at the doorway on his way out.

"No backup, Ralph?"

"Nah. I know this guy from way back."

"You sure?"

"He's a punk. He beats up women. And maybe cats and dogs."

"Cats and dogs?"

"I told you. We go way back."

The streets at that hour were deserted. The snow had long since given way to snowplows and strong noon midday sun. Still he drove carefully and within the speed limit, aware of his own exhaustion.

With anybody other than Arthur Danse he'd have been tempted to wait until tomorrow. Or maybe hand it over to somebody else. Somebody fresher.

But with Danse, he wanted the news to come from him.

Danse in Duggan's estimation was your basic bad seed. Born bad, raised bad and grown bad. He got slicker as he got older and nobody had any doubt at all about the quality of his intelligence but in people's personalities as well as in bureaucracies, shit always seemed to float to the top.

He wasn't surprised by what had happened tonight. He'd been waiting for something like this to come crawling out of Arthur for a long while.

Too bad it had to hurt the lady.

She was a nurse, she said. Seemed like a decent type. Not from hereabouts.

It always amazed him at what people could overlook in people. Sometimes, he guessed, it was all for the good. You take his daughter, Ginny.

Ginny could look at her own daughter—his granddaughter Stephanie—and all she seemed to see was this happy, simple, loving little girl who was, sadly, very much alone among her peers. Duggan saw what most everybody else saw. Down's syndrome. It made him want to bleed for them both, for all the pain they'd go through all their lives.

But Ginny had found a way to look at Steph that seemed to omit the prognosis for their future and concentrate on what was right in front of her eyes—that happy, loving little girl. She overlooked all the rest of it.

In her case it was probably for the best.

In Lydia, Danse's case it might have turned out lethal.

She was lucky to have gotten out of there.

He was going to try to help her stay out.

He pulled up onto the narrow dirt strip of road that led to Ruth and Harry's place. He was certain that was where Danse would go.

Whatever else you had to say about him, Artie sure seemed to love his dear old mama.

And sure enough, his headlights swept the big black Lincoln right out front.

He pulled up and cut the motor and stepped outside into the starless night. The wind blew chilly up here. He zipped his jacket higher.

The house was dark, silent.

He ascended the steps to the porch and saw a light go on inside and curtains fluttering in the living room window.

He didn't have to knock.

Ruth was right at the door.

"Morning, Ruth."

"Morning, Ralph."

The nightgown and robe looked like they must have been purchased sometime in the 1950's and worn every night ever since.

The grim, almost lipless cut of her mouth told him she knew what he was here for. He said it anyway.

"I need to talk with Arthur, Ruth."

"He's not here."

"That's his car. Right over there, Ruth."

She shrugged. "He went for a drive with Harry."

"With Harry? At four in the morning?"

"That's right."

"Happen to know where they went?"

"Nope."

He looked at her.

It wouldn't do to call Ruth a liar.

Though he'd bet his badge that Harry's car was parked right around back of the house.

"Mind if I come on inside, Ruth? We could do a little talking, you and me. It's awful cold out here."

"I don't mind. That's if you're carrying a warrant, I don't. Otherwise it's like you said. It's four o'clock in the morning. You got me out of bed. We can talk tomorrow. Far as I'm concerned we can talk anytime."

Dammit, count on the smart old bitch to know her rights.

"Ruth, I want to ask you, do you realize what went on over at Arthur's place tonight?"

"Arthur said they quarreled. Decided to spend the night here. That's all."

He shook his head. He could see Ruth knew exactly what had happened. She wasn't nearly the liar her son was. She was just closing ranks, that's all. It was to be expected.

"A whole lot more than a quarrel, Ruth. Arthur beat his wife up pretty bad."

"Her story."

"What?"

"I said that's her story."

"Yes, it is. And she has a hospital record and photos to back it up."

"She going to file charges?"

"I don't know that yet one way or another. But I'm not about to discourage her."

He gave it a moment. The woman never blinked, never wavered.

"Just make sure that Arthur's aware that he's going to be served a restraining order in the morning. He's not to go near his wife or his son under any circumstances till we get this all straightened out. And I'm personally telling you that he'd better be here or over at the restaurant so we can serve it to him nice and easy. No business trips. No *hiding*. Anywhere. Do you understand what I'm saying, Ruth?"

"Uh-huh."

"Good. You have a nice day now. Sorry to have woke you."

He heard her close the door quietly as he stepped down off the porch. He went back to the car and drove a little ways down the dirt road until he thought he was well out of earshot and then stopped and cut his lights.

He jogged back along the road to the house.

The lights downstairs were off again but there was another one burning in one of the upstairs bedrooms. He suspected a conference was in session. He jogged around the row of hedges to the rear of the house. The cold wind made it hard to breathe.

Harry's gray Ford was parked in back. So was his pickup. So they'd definitely been expecting him.

The bastard was right inside but Duggan couldn't get to him. Not yet. And knowing these people, they weren't going to make it easy for him.

One day, though. He'd get to him.

Get to him *good*.

TWELVE

MENDING NO FENCES

"I know a guy," Cindy was saying. "He handled Jeannie Tartelle's divorce back in September. Now that guy, her husband—there was a character. You know he used to let their six-year-old son waltz around the house with Daddy's pistols? Said it was fine as long as he didn't know where they kept the bullets. Anyhow, she liked this guy, her lawyer, said he was good. And I definitely know he got her the settlement she was after. He's also kind of good-looking if you like them sort of bookish."

"I couldn't care less what he looks like. As long as he knows what he's doing."

"Hold on. I'll call her."

Cindy put the beer down and went to the wall phone and dialed.

It was only noon and Lydia wondered about Cindy having a beer that early in the day, but Cindy was being a sweetheart. She'd got Robert fed along with her daughter Gail and then got them out to school, let her sleep so that she'd only just got up, and said Lydia could stay with them as long as she liked. She knew she'd better get back to the house as soon as possible though. Hopefully this evening. She knew that much divorce law from her first one.

You needed to throw the man out and keep him out. You changed the locks and made an appointment with him to pick up his things and when he did, you made sure there was somebody around to watch him.

The son of a bitch.

The swelling had gone down a little in her face and Tylenol with codeine was keeping the pain at bay—though it made her slightly woozy. She guessed she wouldn't be operating any heavy machinery that day. Oh well. She still could barely see out of the right eye.

She sipped her coffee and picked at her cheese Danish and listened to Cindy on the telephone with Jean Tartelle. Happily—and unusually for Cindy—she was being very discreet about it. Not naming names. She just needed the lawyer "for a friend." *Good girl,* Cyn.

She didn't need the world to know.

How stupid she'd been.

She felt like an utter fool for not seeing something like this coming out of Arthur months and maybe years ago, when of course there had been clues and danger signs all along.

She felt furious with herself. Almost as mad as she was with him.

Cindy hung up the phone, smiling and waving a piece of paper.

"Okay. We got the number. Jeannie swears by the guy. You want me to call him?"

"No, I'll do it."

"Hey, I don't mind. Stay there and finish your Danish. Have some more coffee."

Actually she felt relieved. The lawyer might ask for details. And she didn't think she could stand providing them just yet.

Cindy was already dialing.

"What's his name?"

"Sansom. Owen Sansom."

The offices of Owen Dean Sansom, of Seymour, Sansom and Winter, Attorneys at Law, lay in a small relatively new professional building on a quiet tree-lined street a few blocks north of the central square.

Cindy drove her there and dropped her off, saying she'd be back in about an hour, she was just going to do some shopping, but not to hurry on her account. She'd wait.

An hour? she thought. It's going to take me over an hour? Well, of course it was.

She would have to go through everything. Not just last night but everything. The entire marriage. The entire mess she'd made of her life and of Robert's.

She dreaded it. She was actually shaking, dreading it.

She steeled herself and opened the door and stepped inside.

Two hours later she was finally beginning to relax with him and by then the interview was nearly over. Not that he was intimidating.

In fact she liked the look of Owen Sansom and she liked his steady calm in the face of her shame and anger. Cindy was right—he was a little bookish-looking, but she thought that might be all to the good. He didn't look like the kind of man who could be outfaced easily by another lawyer. Nor like the kind of man who was just another hired gun. Like maybe there was some integrity there behind the wire-frame glasses and an actual brain beneath the thinning hair.

"The main question is," he said, "will he contest it? What's your best guess on that?"

"My guess is that he won't. He's a very . . . public man. Well-known in the community. I don't think he'd want anyone to know that he . . . did what he did."

"What about custody? Is he going to fight you?"

"He'll want to see Robert, I'm sure of that. But no, I doubt it. For basically the same reasons. Plus if he thinks about it at all, he doesn't have the time for Robert. I think he'll just want visitation, some vacation time probably. Not custody."

"How do you feel about that?"

"What do you mean?"

"Allowing Arthur to see him. After what he did to you."

"He's never laid a hand on Robert, if that's what you mean. He's been a . . . a pretty good father."

The words were hard to say. And she had to wonder, How could a man be two such different things at once? How was it possible?

"So you think that he's essentially incapable of violence toward your son?"

He was pressing hard on this. Leaning across the desk at her. It was making her nervous all over again.

"I . . . yes, I think he is. I think it's women he doesn't like."

He gazed at her a moment longer, then settled back into his chair.

"Okay," he said. "Here's what I want you to do. I want you to go home right now and . . ."

". . . change the locks."

He smiled. "That's right. Change the locks. I'll phone him and see what lawyer he's using and we'll arrange for him to pick up his belongings at some time when Robert's away from the house, at school maybe. I don't want him seeing your son just yet. And probably, neither do you. Meantime you make duplicates, Xeroxes, of all his and your own accounts and records. We need to see exactly what he's worth and what we're looking at here. All right?"

She nodded. He looked at her. She felt that intensity from him for a moment again.

"You want to go after him for beating you, Mrs. Danse? We could do that. It's a felony. Believe me I'd be happy to help you throw him in jail for a while if that's what you'd like to do."

She'd already thought about this and talked it over with Cindy and by then she'd come to a decision. She wasn't sure it was the right decision, but she thought she'd still stick with it.

"No," she said. "I think it'd ruin him. At least in the restaurant business. And I don't want to do that. Because of Robert. I don't want Robert having a convicted felon for a father and getting grief about that every day after school. I also expect to send him to college someday. And I expect Arthur to help me pay for that. He owes us that much. And he can't do it if he has no business. I want to *keep* him in business, the bastard. For Robert's sake."

He nodded. "That's practical. And I understand your feelings. But if you don't mind my saying so, he *did* beat you, Mrs. Danse. So we've still got yet another wife-beater walking around free out there. You sure you want that?"

In a way she thought it was unfair of him. She felt suddenly close to crying. No, she *didn't* want that. Dammit, she didn't want that at all! What she wanted was to see him punished, put away for as long as the law would allow.

But she couldn't have both. She couldn't have a good strong hold on Robert's future—and maybe even on his sanity, which seemed fragile enough—and still see Arthur hurt too. The two couldn't coexist in the real world and the real world was what she lived in so she'd chosen.

It was *having* to choose in the first place that made her want to cry. Dammit, it wasn't fair.

"I'm sorry," she said. "It's what I've decided. Robert has to come first."

He nodded again. "As I say, I understand. Honestly."

"Besides," she said. Her voice sounded bitter in her ears. She didn't care. "I'm sure Arthur's all very remorseful by now. For whatever good it does anybody. Which is no good. Whenever he loses his temper he's always wonderfully remorseful afterwards."

He looked at her.

"I'm not going to press you, Mrs. Danse. Believe me. I guess that was just my point, though, unfortunately."

"What was?"

"That one word. The word you just used."

He leaned back in the chair.

"*Always*," he said.

THIRTEEN

VISITATION

January 1995

It took until two weeks after Christmas for the divorce to come through, not because Arthur was contesting anything but because the wheels of justice nearly stopped turning entirely that time of year.

The terms were fine as far as she was concerned. She hadn't asked for support beyond however long it took her to get back to work again, just as she hadn't in her first marriage. But the child support was generous and she had little doubt that he'd comply with the order.

If Arthur cared for anyone it was his parents and his son.

At Christmas, Arthur had always gone overboard on presents but this year it bordered on the ridiculous. A new four-speed bike. A basketball hoop and net. Rollerblades. A Sega Genesis Game Gear and six game cartridges at about forty dollars apiece. A TV set for Robert's room to play them on.

If he was trying to buy her son's affection, Arthur was at least going about it in a big way. The only thing she hadn't much cared for was having to send Robert over on Christmas Day to collect all this stuff. It was their day, she thought, mother and son, in the only home he'd known all his life. Arthur was intruding on that.

But the settlement naturally included visitation—one overnight a week and one weekend a month and a reasonable split on the holidays. So Robert sat around his father's Christmas tree in his newly rented house for the afternoon, opening presents with Ruth and Harry. So what. Lydia had him Christmas Eve and Christmas morning. The important times. She guessed she could live with that. She guessed she'd have to.

She'd gotten the house and furniture and sufficient funds to buy a new car. She'd been meaning to buy one in better shape than hers for a long time anyway.

"What we have here, though," she was saying to Barb on the telephone a few weeks later, "is a funny kind of situation."

"How so?"

"Well, half the time he doesn't seem to want to go visit Arthur. Christmas was really an exception."

"Robert?"

"I know. He's always been crazy about his father. But I don't think that's true anymore. It sure isn't lately. You know what he said to me when the papers came through? He smiled and said, 'Mom? *Are we divorced now?*' Can you believe that?"

"So what are you doing?"

"If it were up to me I'd let him do whatever he wants to do. Stay home if he feels like it. But you know Arthur, he's going to insist upon his rights."

"Is he still doing that weird knee-chest thing?"

She sighed. "Sometimes. Yeah, I'm afraid he is."

"And . . . the other?"

"That too. And the stuttering and the nightmares and all the rest of it. Nothing's changed."

"Well, it might be the divorce. He might just be mad at Arthur for breaking up the family. I know it happens with a lot of kids. Or maybe there's just nobody around to play with over at Arthur's place."

"He complains about that. All the kids that live around there are older."

"Maybe that's the problem, then."

"Maybe, I don't know. All I know is I feel terrible having to send him over there when he doesn't feel like going just because the court says I've got to. I mean, Robert should have some say in this too."

"Kids never get say. Kids are still pretty much property. You know that."

"I know. But every time it happens I feel like I'm kicking the family dog or something. I feel like shit."

She heard a car pull up into the driveway.

"That's Arthur, Barb. I gotta go."

"Okay. Phone me."

"I will."

She hung up and called upstairs.

"Robert! Your father's here."

Arthur walked in wearing the blond shearling jacket she'd given him for Christmas the year before. Maybe it was supposed to be a reminder to her, some kind of reproach. That no gifts had passed between them this year or ever would again. She didn't know and didn't want to know.

He was kicking the snow off his boots on the lip of the doorstep, and when he finished that he turned around and she saw that he was also wearing a pistol in a cowboy-style tooled leather holster on his belt.

"What the hell is that for, Arthur?"

"What?"

"You come to pick up your son with a gun on your hip?"

"I'm carrying some cash from the restaurant. It's out in the car. I have a permit, Liddy."

"I know you have a permit. Just don't do it again, Arthur. Ever."

"Oh, for chrissake."

"I mean it."

She called up to Robert again. It was hard keeping the anger out of her voice but she tried.

This time he came downstairs. He was carrying a small box of his plastic guys and some copies of *Cracked* and *Mad*. His boots and jacket were on so he was ready. She was relieved. He didn't look quite so reluctant to be going along this time. Which meant she didn't have to feel so guilty.

"When will you be back?"

"I'll have him back by dinnertime."

"Fine."

She bent down to give him a kiss and a hug. Pretty soon, she thought, she wouldn't be bending anymore. She'd be standing on tiptoe the way he was growing.

"Bye, honey. Have a good time."

"Bye, Mom." He kissed her back. His lips were still wet and smooth. Like a baby's lips.

"Arthur?"

He turned to her.

"Lose the gun, please."

He nodded and they left together out into the lightly falling snow.

Ellsworth, New Hampshire

He'd come here often as a boy. The property was just off his parents' property. There was a hill leading down to a winding solitary stream where you could catch crayfish in summer and which, even now in the dead of winter, slashed its arterial way down the mountain like an open wound, defeating the freezing flesh of ice which attempted to close over it.

You passed the stream, crawled up the banks, and you were in a field of tall brown grass and low scattered scrub. He'd hunted here many times—quail and the occasional rabbit. He wasn't supposed to. But Old Man Wingerter never got down this way very often back then and he was dead now, his property in dispute between his surviving daughters. Nobody was going to give a damn what he did here these days.

"Quiet now," he said to the boy.

They both were breathing hard from the climb up over the banks and the boy was cold, he was shivering. But Arthur could see he was excited too. What kid wouldn't be? Out here with his dad and his dad's brand-new AK-47? Like Cowboys and Indians. Only better. Because the weapon was starkly, coldly real and even the quiet kids like Robert had some sense of its power. Hell, the kid had seen the *Rambo* movies, right?

But it took over an hour of moving slowly and carefully through the grass and brush before they saw anything. And by then it was clear that Robert was getting bored with the game. Kids these days had lousy attention spans, he thought. When he was a kid he could go all day with a pitiful little .22 in his hands. It had all the stopping power of a gnat. But he loved the .22 anyway. You had to have patience to hunt. Patience and desire.

It was obvious his kid had neither.

He heard Robert sigh behind him. Like Arthur was putting him through something.

The kid had no appreciation.

At least he was basically keeping quiet about it. Not tramping around screwing up the hunt like a lot of kids might do. He was good for that much, anyway.

When the rabbit bolted out of the brush not four feet away from them, Arthur was ready, the weapon on full automatic, spraying the ground in a short tight arc that exploded through the bare dry brush, turning it to powder, and exploded the rabbit too—a wet furry brown-and-red mess lying in the snow.

One ear gone.

A leg almost shot away.

"Jesus! Jesus!" Robert was saying behind him.

The kid was astonished. The kid couldn't believe what he'd seen.

Arthur whooped and laughed and held the rabbit up for their inspection. Robert wouldn't think that hunting was boring now. No way. Not anymore.

"Did you see that? We damn near stepped on him! Most times you've got to have yourself some dogs to get one of these guys. We got lucky!"

Jeez, God was all the kid was saying.

Shaking his head. Eyes wide like he'd seen a ghost.

And he realized then that it wasn't just astonishment that he was seeing on his son's face, though that was there too. It was also—inexplicably—horror.

Plymouth, New Hampshire

By 6:45 she was beginning to get mad. Dinnertime was normally 6:00/6:30, and he knew that, and even though the sautéed chicken would do just fine on simmer she still had the rice to make once Robert got home and she still had to steam the vegetables, and the point was, anyway, that he deliver him back on time, not whenever he damn well felt like it.

At just before seven she heard the car pull in, heard its door slam and then heard it pull right out again. That Arthur was leaving quickly was probably just as well. She'd been nearly ready to go out there and make the kind of scene that Robert probably didn't need.

He came in slamming the door behind him and ran for the stairs.

"Robert?"

She smelled it right away.

He'd soiled himself.

He never did this during the day.

"Robert?"

She put down the pan of vegetables and followed him. The bathroom door was closed. His coat lay on the floor. "Robert? Are you all right?"

She heard him crying. *To hell with privacy*, she thought. Even though she'd always been careful to provide it for him. She opened the door.

His soiled pants and underpants were lying on the floor. He was on the toilet.

No. Not quite on it.

He was braced above it, hands clutching either side of the seat holding him up just over it, as though.

She looked at him, tears running down his cheeks.

"It *hurts*!" he said.

. . . as though he couldn't bear to put his full weight down and . . .

She felt the room begin to reel and she knelt in front of him, her hands fluttering out to him, to his arms, to his legs, like the wings of strange trapped birds—she didn't know where to touch him.

. . . and it was impossible for him in that position. She saw the shit slide down his poor little skinny thighs and drop to the floor and it was bad-smelling, dark, abnormal, as though there were something foul inside him, something evil there.

She grabbed some toilet paper off the roll and began to wipe him down, his legs and thighs, and he was crying harder now, so shamed by what he'd done, standing in front of her with his legs spread and shaking with tears and she was saying *it's all right, don't worry, it doesn't matter honey, let's just clean you up*, taking a wet facecloth off the sink and wiping him, rinsing it, wiping him some more, the cheeks of his butt, turning him around, the cheeks red, smelling his shit all the while and thinking that she had never smelled shit like this, it was as though someone had poisoned him.

When she touched him between the buttocks he screamed.

He jumped away, batting at her hand holding the facecloth. He turned and ran for his bedroom. She heard him fall to the bed and heard him sobbing in his pillow.

She knelt there, so stunned that she had to grab the edge of the sink to keep from falling to the tile floor.

The room had come unglued from the universe.

She felt suddenly adrift in an awful ice-cold storm made of sudden insight and a terrible knowledge. Knowledge like a cancer inside her.

It was as though somebody had poisoned him.

Yes. It was.

And she knew.

In a single moment it all made sense to her. She saw into the pattern. She saw deceit. She saw evil. She saw a sickness that was almost beyond her imagining.

The nervousness, the stuttering.

His soiling the bed.

The nightmares. Of course there were nightmares.

He was living one.

Her baby.

Even the goddamn crazy knee-chest thing made sense now. He was telling her something. He'd been telling her something all along.

How could she have been so stupid and blind as to miss it? As to not hear him asking for her help over and over, night after night, in the silent language of his body?

But no. It had been unthinkable until now. Unthinkable that Arthur would do this. Now—anything was possible.

Butt in the air. Head to the pillow.

She'd been there a lot more times than she cared to remember.

Hell, it was Arthur's favorite position.

You sick, cowardly, evil bastard, she thought.

I'll get you for this one.

For this I'm going after you.

I swear to god I am.

She got up off the floor and heard him crying and found that it was possible to stand up and walk again and went to comfort her son.

He wasn't home and he wasn't at his parents'.

Which left the restaurant.

She could have used the phone but she wanted—no, she *needed*— to see his face when she told him. She wanted to be looking right at him when he denied it. She wanted to watch him squirm.

The Lincoln was parked out front. For a moment she considered ramming it. Arthur loved that car. Instead she pulled in right beside it.

She'd driven Robert to Cindy's house once he calmed down. It was still early and Cindy's daughter Gail was still awake, and Robert seemed to like the idea of being in the company of another kid right now. Probably he needed to forget it. To forget everything. It was obvious that Cindy wanted to know what was going on but she didn't pry and all Lydia volunteered was that she had to talk to Arthur right away. Explanations—if she chose to make any, even to Cindy—could wait.

It bothered her that he wouldn't come right out and tell her what Arthur had done to him. She supposed he was ashamed. But she knew it would be a whole lot better if he could get it out and talk about it.

"Does Daddy touch you?" she'd said. "Does he touch you back there?"

He shrugged. "I dunno."

"Tell me the truth, honey. Nothing that's happened is your fault and it's nothing for you to be ashamed of. But I think Daddy's doing something he shouldn't be doing and I think you and I should talk about it."

He just sat on the bed and looked at her. She gave him a moment.

"Do you think you can? Do you want to try to talk about it?"

"Uh-uh."

"No?"

"Uh-uh."

"Do you think maybe you'll be able to talk about it later, then?" She didn't want to press him. Not now.

"I dunno."

"Will you try?"

"I guess."

She'd left it there for the time being.

She had Arthur to deal with. While the wound was fresh.

His bar was crowded. There was a country tune on the jukebox— something about the twentieth century being almost over. *Almost over. Almost over.* She saw him standing at the end of the bar saying something to Jake, his barman. Jake had been with him since the place opened and Lydia knew him and liked him. She also knew he was interested in her in a somewhat less than casual way. She'd caught his glances plenty of times.

Well, this would interest him too.

She walked over.

"I want to talk to you," she said. "Do you want it here or in the office?"

She knew what she looked like. She could barely contain her fury now that they were standing there face-to-face. He simply looked annoyed.

"God, Lydia. What now?"

"You want it here, then? Fine."

She was aware of Jake and of the customers on either side. It didn't matter a damn to her what they heard.

"Look, I know I was late. I lost track of the time. I'm sorry, okay? It won't happen again."

"I'll just bet you lost track of the time! What were you doing that you lost track of the time, Arthur? What were you doing *with my son*?"

He looked at her. Really looked at her finally. And saw in her face what she needed him to see. She watched it dawn on him.

"My office," he muttered.

"No, I don't think so. I changed my mind. I decided I like it here. *Or is Jake too sensitive to hear about you butt-fucking our son!*"

For a moment he looked as though she'd physically struck him. She saw Jake move away down the bar. Giving them space, being discreet. But the men on either side of them had gone quiet.

"You're fucking crazy!"

There it was. The denial.

It wasn't as satisfying as it should have been. She couldn't read guilt on his face and she wanted guilt. Just anger and outrage.

He was too damn good an actor.

She'd never known him.

It wasn't satisfying at all.

"I'm not crazy, Arthur. But you are, if you think you're ever going to see that boy alone again. I'm telling you—you'll never, *never* touch my child again, you perverted son of a bitch! You want to visit? *You want your fucking visitation?* You can have your visitation. You can come to the house and I'm going to be standing right there in the room with you to make sure you keep your goddamn hands off him, you bastard, and won't that be great fun for all three of us?"

"You can't do that."

"I can't? Watch me."

"Look, I never did anything to that boy. Has he said I did?"

Somehow he already seemed to know the answer to that one. She wondered how.

"He doesn't need to."

"Bullshit. He hasn't said a thing, has he? This is all some crap you dreamed up because you're pissed off over the divorce. If you wanted more money why didn't you just say you wanted more money? Why don't you just get the hell out of here and leave me the hell alone!"

"Glad to, Arthur. But you remember what I said. Never. Not once. *Never again.*"

"I'll take you to fucking court, you crazy bitch!"

"Not if I take you first. You're a sick man, Arthur. You need help. I hope you get some. For Robert's sake."

She turned and walked away from him through the bar and out the door.

The cold air, at least, felt good.

Otherwise, furious or not, she felt surprisingly much like crying.

Robert lay in bed and thought, He promised me he wouldn't anymore but he did again anyway and every time he does he hurts me, like he doesn't care, Daddy doesn't care, like he just wants it I think there's something wrong with him, like it's crazy that he doesn't care if he hurts me or not, but if I tell he says he'll do to my mom what he did to that rabbit, and even though he was smiling he absolutely positively meant it, I know he did. I'm sure he did.

I can't tell. I can't make him stop.

I can't do anything right.

I wonder what I did to him.

I wonder what I did.

FOURTEEN

INITIAL RESPONSES

Bromberg was supposed to be the best in the area but that didn't mean she had to like him.

Or even think he was any good.

He sat behind his desk in the toy-cluttered room, wearing a cheap off-the-rack blue suit that made him look more like a balding, middle-aged bank teller than a child psychologist. The white shirt was imperfectly ironed and open at the collar. Patchy tufts of thick brown hair gave his neck an oddly mottled look. His glasses were bifocals. She could see the line.

Right now Plymouth seemed impossibly rural to her. Smalltown, USA. When she needed *experts*, goddammit!

But Owen Sansom said it had to be done today. At the moment she guessed the best in the area was the best she had.

"Your lawyer is aware of all this?" he said when she was finished.

"He's the one who told me to make the appointment. You and a proctologist. What we need is for you to talk to Robert and establish exactly what Arthur did and that Arthur was the one who did it. The proctologist he has to see for the obvious reasons."

"He won't speak to you about it?"

"No."

He frowned and sighed and leaned heavily across the desk.

"You know, he's not saying much to me either. We use a form of play-therapy here as you know and it usually opens them up after a while. A child gets relaxed, he normally starts speaking. But Robert's mostly been playing. Playing period. I got him to address how he feels about the stuttering and he's told me a nightmare or two now and then—though I honestly think he embellishes them—you know, makes up something he thinks might be interesting to just throw in there. Some fantasy. Unhelpful, to say the least. But nothing on soiling the bed and nothing on the diapering."

He got up and started pacing back and forth behind the desk. Tapping his chin with his fingertips. It was his professorial mode. He was going to make a speech now. She'd seen it before and it annoyed her.

"It does fit together, though," he said, "doesn't it. Certainly the nightmares, his generally nervous disposition, the clumsiness, the shyness. It would definitely account for the soiled bed and the position he takes when you try to diaper him. I haven't heard of child molestation leading directly to stuttering before but I suppose that kind of trauma could be a strong causal factor. I'm particularly interested in the clumsiness in light of this. It would be a form of punishment."

He turned to face her.

"To tell you the truth, I'd almost expected as much."

"What?"

"Well, it didn't strike me as whatsoever impossible."

"That Robert was being molested didn't strike you as impossible?"

"I'm afraid I thought it somewhat likely."

"And you didn't *say* something? You kept this . . . this *likelihood* to yourself?"

She could easily strangle the man. Easily.

He sighed again. He seemed impatient with her.

"Mrs. Danse, child abuse is not the kind of thing one discusses lightly. Particularly not—and I must say this to you—with one of the child's potential abusers."

"Wait a minute," she said. "Let me get this right. I bring my son in to see you, with all these questions about his behavior, and you think that *I* might be responsible for abusing him?"

He shrugged. "It's been known to happen. The parent knows the child won't tell, threatens him perhaps. Then, in case it should somehow come to light, brings him to a therapist as a smoke screen. Using exactly the same argument you're using now. *Why would I do this if I were the guilty party?* Or perhaps there is an unconscious wish for the child to reveal the truth, a need to be punished that the parent feels, but he or she is unable to confess directly and hopes the child will do it for him or her. You must admit, Mrs. Danse, that even now, I only have your version of events. For all I know, you may *still* be the abuser. Though obviously I find that highly unlikely. But the key, of course, is Robert. It has always been Robert. Only the child himself can tell me with any degree of reliability."

The man was amazing. The supercilious little shit. It was clear he'd enjoyed his little speech. She wanted very much to walk out of the room and never have to lay eyes on him again.

But she needed him.

Much as she'd like to, there wasn't any point in alienating the man.

That could wait until later.

"When can you see him?"

He made a point of checking his calendar book, peering through the bottoms of his bifocals.

"I can see him at three-thirty tomorrow."

"It has to be today. It can't wait. My lawyer says today." He looked a bit annoyed with her. *Good*, she thought. Be annoyed. Just do it.

"I can slip him in at four-thirty," he said. Then he shook his head and sighed again. "I really wouldn't expect too much, though, if I were you."

"I won't," she said without irony.

For a while after seeing the proctologist they drove in silence, she not knowing what to say, Robert seeming lost in thought.

Dr. Hessler appeared to be a kind man and certainly he was good with Robert, reassuring him right off the bat that nothing he was going to do would hurt him, then changing the subject immediately to whether or not they'd seen *Jungle Book II* yet of all things.

They hadn't seen it. As a matter of fact they'd tried twice already but had been turned away at packed houses. But the doctor had chosen wisely. Since the movie opened it was all the kids talked about. Robert listened, rapt, as the doctor described several scenes in detail—with surprisingly boyish enthusiasm for a man who had to be in his sixties—ushering him into his examining room and closing the door behind them.

Hessler's report was as expected.

But still it hurt her to hear it.

A dilated sphincter and soreness and irritation of the surrounding rectal tissue.

Consistent with anal penetration.

Anal penetration. At age eight. God.

And yes, he'd go to court and swear to it.

They needed to know that. Owen Sansom had outlined the court process to her earlier in his office.

"I've already filed a complaint with the Superior Court to seek termination of all visitation rights which were granted by the divorce, on the basis of child abuse," he said. "You'll be seeing someone out at the house tonight who'll investigate. So you'd better prepare Robert for still more questions. How's he holding up?"

"He cried a little when I told him all we had to do today. I certainly can't blame him for not looking forward to it. He's doing all right I guess, under the circumstances."

Sansom looked somewhat disheveled. Like he'd been running his hands through his thinning hair all morning. There were spots on his glasses. The lapels of his jacket turned inward slightly as though he'd hung it on a chair the night before instead of in a closet.

She wondered what his personal life was like.

The wedding ring was her only clue.

And it wasn't any of her business.

"Based on their investigation the court will issue a summons for Arthur, you and Robert to appear at a preliminary hearing to establish probable cause. If they find probable cause . . ."

"If?"

He smiled. "Sorry. Legalspeak. They will, don't worry. That's what the psychologist and proctologist are all about. I think we've got that part well covered. Anyhow, the statute says that the preliminary hearing has to be held within seven days of the summons. So this will all be happening pretty fast."

"And what about visitation rights? I mean in the meantime. My understanding is that I'm in violation of the terms of the divorce if I don't let Arthur see him at least one more time this week. My God. Is that true? Can he really expect that?"

"He can demand to see Robert, sure, if he wants to. But our complaint will limit visitation until the case is adjudicated. He'll only be able to see him under supervision."

"I don't want him to see him at all for god sakes!"

"Sorry. No can do."

"Why not?"

"Lydia, until we prove the case against him he retains his parental rights."

"Jesus. *Shit!*"

"I know exactly what you mean."

The man looked haggard. He hadn't slept much last night, she was sure of that. She wondered why. Something was bothering him. And she doubted that his losing sleep had much to do with her situation—he was a lawyer after all. No, this was something else. Had to be. Something personal.

And again—none of her business.

"Okay. Go on."

"All right. Within thirty days of the preliminary we go to an adjudicatory hearing before a judge in Superior Court. Unfortunately, it won't be Clarke, the judge who granted your divorce—she's out indefinitely with some kind of heart situation. In any case, we'll be looking for exclusive custody. At the adjudicatory we can present our evidence and call our witnesses. The doctors, you, Ralph Duggan on the beating, your friend Cindy I think, maybe his teacher—and hopefully by then, Robert himself. I've petitioned the court clerk to appoint a guardian ad litem for Robert—an attorney—for purposes of the litigation and to assess his situation and advocate his best interests as he or she sees them. That's who you'll be seeing tonight."

"*Robert* has an attorney?"

"Yes. Hopefully somebody we can work with, someone who'll be squarely on our side."

"And if not?"

"If Robert won't talk then our case is circumstantial. But it's still pretty compelling. You could argue that he could have done this to himself somehow—used some object or something. But it clearly isn't likely. You could argue that someone other than Arthur did it without Arthur's knowledge. In that case they'd have to come up with a likely suspect. Someone with opportunity."

"Like me."

"You?" He laughed.

"Bromberg told me he'd considered it."

Sansom thought about that a moment, drumming his desk with a pencil.

"Maybe that'll change once he sees Robert. If not, I guess we're going to have to have a talk with him. Assess his level of cooperation. Possibly get another opinion. But our best bet is to get your boy to say what happened, hard as it may be for him. You have to really work on that."

She would, but not now. Robert still had Bromberg to see. And then, tonight, the attorney.

What a day for him, she thought.

What a bitch of a day it must be.

She glanced at Robert now, gazing out the frost-melted window beside her, strapped tightly into his seat, hurtling powerless through the wintry streets.

He turned to her, his face unexpectedly alight.

"Mom? Do you think tomorrow night we could maybe just go to a movie?"

She smiled. "Sure."

"Yeah!"

"You got it," she said and reached over and patted his hand.

"And we'll leave real early so we'll be the first ones there so we'll definitely get seats this time, okay?"

"Okay."

"*Great. Neat,*" he said and turned to the window again.

She thought that either he was blocking all this out very successfully or her son had a kind of courage. The former was troubling. The latter, she thought, might be necessary through all the days ahead of them.

She could have her hopes.

He sat on the floor with his back to the television set his mother had turned off before she left the room and listened to Miss Stone. Miss Stone was probably younger than his mother and she was pretty, he thought. Though he thought his mother was prettier. Miss Stone had nice, soft-looking, shiny blonde hair, though, just like Chrissy at school. Her hair was long and straight and that was like Chrissy too.

Chrissy was nice but the one he really liked was Laura.

He found it hard to concentrate on what Miss Stone was saying. More questions. All day long everybody kept asking him stuff. He kept wishing it was bedtime.

And *that* was pretty weird right there.

Then she started on the really bad questions.

"Is there somebody who does things to you, Robert? Who touches you where you don't want to be touched?"

He couldn't help it. He started squirming on the rug. Like the question hit a Nintendo button and from there it was automatic.

How much could he tell her?

He knew he had to say something, that he had to help them somehow. He knew they were doing this just for him, to get his dad to make it stop. He wanted his dad to stop more than he wanted practically anything—but he didn't want his dad to hurt his mom and he would. He knew his dad better than anybody did. He'd hurt her bad.

And it was up to him to protect her.

Maybe he could tell her without telling her, he thought. Sort of like what he tried to do with Dr. Bromberg earlier. "Maybe," he said.

"Somebody who touches you where you don't want to be touched?"

"Maybe."

"Where is that?"

It was getting dangerous now.

"Private . . . parts, maybe," he said.

"They touch your private parts?"

"Maybe."

"*Who* does, Robert?"

He wasn't saying that. No matter what. He couldn't. Even though jeez, he wanted to. If he could only just say my father does, it's my father who does it. But he kept on seeing the rabbit.

He'd wait. Sooner or later she'd leave the question alone and just go on.

The others did.

He watched her write in her book. She seemed kind of nice. She had a nice voice, anyway. He liked that. He waited and stared at the rug.

"You won't tell me?"

He shook his head.

"Why?"

He waited some more. His skin felt itchy. Like he'd been swimming at the beach and his skin was all sticky with salt from the ocean. He rubbed his butt against the rug. It helped a little but not much.

"When this happens, does it hurt you?"

He was safer now. Good.

"Yes."

"A lot?"

He nodded.

"Where does it hurt?"

"Hurts my private parts."

"Front or back? Or both?"

"Back."

"And you won't say who does this to you?"

He shook his head.

"Does it happen often?"

"Maybe."

"Does it happen in this house?"

Careful.

Because it used to. Not anymore but it sure used to happen. *Be careful*. Miss Stone looked smart. It might be the same as saying.

Don't answer.

She leaned forward like she needed to get closer for some reason but didn't want to actually move off the couch to the floor with him.

"Robert, I have to ask you this. It's very important. In a way it's the most important question I'll have asked you all night—and I really, really need you to answer me on this one, okay?"

He shrugged.

But inside she was scaring him. Waiting for it. Waiting for the question.

He'd lie if he had to. And that scared him too.

"Robert, is it your mother who hurts you?" she said.

"Jeez! No!"

He actually jumped.

How could she even *think* something like that? It was like she'd hit him in the head.

People were *crazy* sometimes.

She smiled. Almost laughed. Like maybe she was relieved or something or maybe he just looked funny the way she made him jump. Anyway, he could see it.

But then she got serious again and he knew it was coming. "Is it your father, Robert?"

He saw the rabbit with its leg shot off in his father's hand. He saw him pick up a knife when they were back at the house and pinch the skin and the soft brown fur on the rabbit's back and then stick the knife in and make a slit and then put his fingers into the slit and tear the skin completely around, then peel half the skin all the way down to its feet like maybe you'd take off a sock or something and then saw him cut off its feet. He saw him do the same thing to the top half, except that this time he cut off not just the feet but the rabbit's head and then made a cut in the pink naked chest and reached in and pulled out the guts.

You can do this to a human, too, he said.

Same thing.

Did you know that?

"Is it your father, Robert?"

No. He wasn't going to cry again, god damn it! And he wasn't going to tell her.

Make him stop, he thought. Somehow.

And then he did cry a little.

He wiped the tears away and said nothing.

FIFTEEN

FOREST

Duggan stamped his feet against the cold leeching in through his shoes and lit himself a Newport Lite off Al Whoorly's Winston. He hated Newport Lites more than any other cigarette he'd ever smoked but he was trying to quit so he figured they were good for him.

Years ago there'd been a brushfire out this way. They'd stopped it just about here. You could see the newer growth off to the left, the older stands of birch and maple to the right.

The girl was nailed to maple.

The ME was just about finished with her. The photographs were taken. In a few more minutes the Crime Scene Unit could bring her down and bag her. She'd go with Whoorly and the other state troopers over to the lab in Concord.

"What I don't get," Whoorly said, "is why he left us the IDs. Why make it easy?"

"Considerate," Duggan said. "The guy's got heart."

"You know some of these assholes actually want to be caught. Maybe he's tired of it."

"I don't think you'll prove it by this one."

Her name was Laura Banks—a student at Plymouth State. Her student ID and driver's license were in a brown leather wallet inside her cluttered handbag. The handbag was sitting on top of a stack of neatly folded clothing placed on a rock four or five feet from the tree—coat, jeans, shirt, socks, bra and panties. The girl was the practical type. The shirt was heavy corduroy and the socks were thick red wool.

He thought of how cold she must have been. Unthinkably cold. Before he got to warming her up some.

Silence lay heavy in the still dry morning air. Six of them out here and nobody was saying hardly anything. He guessed they were all a little in awe here. The teenage kid whose big black bastard Labrador had scented her and then run away into the woods while they were out for their morning walk was down at the station for questioning. The kid had a lot to say but it was just the same thing over and over again because the kid was scared. In a way maybe it scared them too.

Lavore walked over and Duggan shook a Newport out of his pack for him. Lavore was trying to quit just like Duggan but the ME's style was grubbing.

"Okay. You can have her," he said.

"Cause of death?"

"You're kidding."

"For the record."

"Sharpened tree limb. Stake through the heart. *Directly* through the heart. I mean pretty much dead center. What you're looking for here is a torture-freak vampire-killer who's pretty good with his anatomy. And you know what? He didn't just shove it into her. He pushed it in nice and slow."

"Time of death?"

"My guess now would be about four A.M. Five, six hours ago."

"Rape?"

"Plenty of rape. Looks like he got her seven ways to Sunday. Vaginal. Anal. I wouldn't be surprised if when we pry open her jaw we find semen there too."

Duggan pointed to an area by a rock about six feet over to their left.

"You see that?"

"What? The gags?"

Two cotton dishrags had been tossed to the forest floor. One was frozen, drenched with saliva. They were bagging them.

"No. Wood shavings. The guy sat there whittling. Putting a good clean point on his stick. You want to bet she was watching him?"

"Sick," Whoorly said.

"What about the rest of it?"

"All happened before she died as far as I can tell. Though some of it might be postmortem. I'll be able to give you a breakdown when we get her on the table."

He looked at her. Lavore was telling him she'd been alive through all of that.

What the guy had done was amazing and god only knew how much time he took to do it. Maybe all night. Maybe longer.

The body was hanging there like frozen meat in a meat locker. At some point he'd thrown water on her. *To revive her? Or just to watch her shake?* There was frost and beaded ice in her long brown hair and in her pubic hair and eyebrows. Small icicles actually hung from her toes where they almost—but not quite—touched the base of the tree.

Her arms were spread three feet apart over her head. Each wrist pierced by a tenpenny nail.

She hung suspended.

Her body was blue-white where it was not a brownish red.

But there was plenty of red.

He'd been at her with a dry stick.

They'd already bagged it. The stick was three feet long and he hadn't peeled too many of the branches off. It was stained with blood and bits of human flesh clung to it, studding its buds and scars.

He'd been at her with matches too.

Duggan was never the type of cop who figured that by now he'd seen everything. He knew that people could always surprise you— that people could be fucked beyond his own wildest dreams. He'd seen the bloody fallout from domestic anger and drunken driving and armed robbery and all kinds of lethal stupidity but he'd never seen anything like this and hoped to god he never would again.

He stepped out his Newport, then picked up the butt and put it in his pocket.

He'd smell like an ashtray now.

Another good incentive to quit.

What he had to try to do now was to find out all he could about the woman in life and in death, and unless he got lucky, unless somebody saw her step into a car with someone he or she knew or unless somebody went strange on him under questioning, to imagine precisely her suffering at the end and then try to construct the person who could be screwed up enough to put her through it. He'd have to look at her, in the flesh and in the photos, over and over again.

How did you imagine a tenpenny nail through the wrist?

Flesh burned black?

Beating somebody down to raw red meat?

How did you imagine that kind of ferocity?

He talked to Whoorly as they left the clearing and pushed their way back through the thick spiky brush to the cars. What Whoorly was guessing at this point was the most depressing of all the possibilities. That it was probably somebody who was just passing through. That somebody had picked her up hitching or something and maybe pulled a gun on her and brought her out here just because it looked deserted enough.

Which meant they'd probably never find him.

"These serial guys are like that," he said. "They just drive around, y'know? Place to place."

"He picked a damn good spot for it though," Duggan said.

"Huh?"

"These woods. Nobody comes here in winter. It's right off the National Forest and people tend to go up there instead if they feel like doing some winter hiking. If that dog hadn't scented her we might not have got her for weeks. Months maybe."

"So you think maybe he knew the place?"

"Could be."

The Danse house lay just over the ridge up there about three quarters of a mile on. He remembered having to go hunt for Arthur the day of the fire and not finding him, the kid showing up that night saying he'd passed out somewhere back of the road to Rumney.

Duggan had never believed him.

But it was possible that Ruth or Harry saw something, heard something. The Hurley place and the Wingerter place were up this way too.

He'd get on it.

"Know what, Al?" said Duggan.

"What?"

"I'm thinking he's local. Obviously we've got to check out everything else but that's what I'm thinking. We know he's no city boy anyhow, he's got some woodsmanship."

"How so?"

"Tenpenny nails driven hard and true. Picked a nice supple birch to use on her. Plus the stake."

"Nice and sharp."

"Uh-huh. Boy knows how to whittle."

SIXTEEN

PRELIMINARY INVESTIGATIONS

Late that afternoon he got a call from Whoorly in Concord. "Computer's spit out two of them over the past two years that are so close it's scary. And two more possibles."

"Where?"

"The close matches are Franklin and Conway. The possibles Munsonville and Tuftonboro."

"Hell, all over the place."

"Yep."

"How close is close?"

"One nailed to the back of an abandoned barn. Tenpenny nails, same position of the body. The other tied to a tree limb, feet off the ground. Both beaten, both burned, both raped. Anal, vaginal, oral. Knife through the heart on the first one, sharpened stick on the second. Close enough?"

"Jesus."

"You want me to send copies?"

"You bet I do."

"How's it going over your way?"

"Nothing. What we've got from the school and what friends we've been able to locate so far is that the girl was a pretty good student, not great but not bad either. Kind of erratic. She was a senior, business major, lived with a girlfriend over on Loudon Road near Livermore Falls who says she has no idea where she was last night. Had no current boyfriend that anybody seems to know of. Liked to hang around the joints, probably drank too much now and then, though nobody's calling her a drunk yet. Definitely smoked a little dope sometimes. Knew how to balance a checkbook, spent almost nothing on clothing, and had two male cats named Scruffy and Simpson. Her parents are both shrinks, psychiatrists, working out of Hanover. They haven't seen her since Christmas."

"Any luck with the neighbors?"

"Nobody saw or heard a thing."

"All right. I'll fax these files on up."

"Thanks."

He hung up, thinking that there was really no point yet in mentioning the one really interesting item he'd learned so far— that Arthur Danse had spent last night at his parents' home. Not his own. He did that now and then, Ruth said, especially since the divorce and this "stupid custody thing."

Ruth seemed to think that her son was going to be charged with smacking his kid around or something, not with abusing him sexually. Duggan didn't bother to enlighten her.

But what was *really* interesting was that Arthur had come in late, without waking them, slept in his bed and then was gone again that morning when they awoke. That too, Ruth said, wasn't unusual. Maybe he just missed his bed, she said. His old room. As though that were perfectly normal in a full-grown man.

She wasn't hiding anything. But she was giving him something to think about all the same.

Arthur Danse. Bad kid. Successful, well-respected businessman who also liked to beat on his wife and had probably been screwing his eight-year-old son. A guy who owned a bar which Laura Banks probably visited now and then. A guy who traveled on business with some frequency.

Franklin and Conway, Munsonville and Tuftonboro.

He'd have to check on all of it.

Duggan sure wasn't putting it past him.

Not by a long shot.

For Lydia the week trudged by in an agony of dull apprehension while she waited for the hearing. She wasn't sleeping, wasn't eating. She was losing weight and there were unattractive circles deepening under her eyes. Her skin felt slack, older.

Owen Sansom said there was little for her to do beyond trying to get Robert to open up to her. Which still seemed impossible. It was all pretty much in the hands of Robert's attorney now, his guardian ad litem Andrea Stone. So Lydia accepted a job offer to do some private nursing. She needed the money. And the distraction.

Her new patient was Ellie Brest, a seventy-three-year-old childless widow who stood no taller than Robert did—and whose problems were enough to make lesser women fold completely. High blood pressure, circulation so bad her legs and hands throbbed all day and woke her up at night, and an advanced case of osteoporosis. The results of which to date were bones broken in the wrist, left foot, and forearm. None of which had healed nor *would* heal completely during her foreseeable lifetime despite the shots of calcimar and the Oscal tablets she received from Lydia daily.

Lydia thought her very gutsy.

She seemed to live with pain as though pain were an old, unpleasant relative, one it was unthinkable to embrace but who had to be tolerated.

It wasn't in the job description but Lydia found herself doing more and more for Ellie—things the woman couldn't do for herself and hadn't the money to pay a maid for. Not just administering the shots and pills, changing the bedding, getting her to the bathroom and back, preparing her meals, exercising her limbs to stimulate her sluggish circulation. Her third day on the job she cleaned out the bathroom: Scrubbed the floors and the tiled bath. The fourth day she cleaned the kitchen. There were cans in the cupboard that must have gone back to the 1950's. A box of semolina supported a small but active colony of tiny flying insects. She threw out all of it.

Ellie was delighted. It had been years since she'd had the health and vigor to clean like this.

She kept trying to offer Lydia money. Lydia kept declining. It did her good to feel as useful to Ellie. What did the Jews say? It was a *mitzvah*, a blessing. And though she knew it was silly she couldn't help thinking that maybe by helping this woman who so clearly needed help, she was making some kind of rent in the fabric of things, a breach in the karmic wall around her through which she and Robert might slip—in danger no longer.

"The court finds sufficient cause to proceed with an adjudicatory hearing.

Until then the father shall see the child only under supervision. I'll hear opening arguments . . . let's see . . ." Judge Burke consulted his docket. ". . . we'll hear them Wednesday, February twenty-second. Court's adjourned."

It had happened so quickly it was practically shocking.

Andrea Stone had twice been to her home and had talked with both Bromberg and Dr. Hessler. Today she presented her findings. That there was indeed sufficient evidence to suspect abusive behavior by the father in this case.

"*Not* the mother?" asked the judge.

"No, Your Honor. Not the mother," Miss Stone said. "You're certain of that?"

"I'm morally certain, Your Honor."

"*Morally* certain?"

Owen Sansom had warned her about the Honorable Thomas J. Burke. He'd been on the bench so long nobody could remember when he hadn't. He was a member of the Board of Trustees at Plymouth State College, Chairman of the local Republican Party, and a power in practically every professional and civic organization in the area. He would not like hearing this particular case in his courtroom. Arthur was a businessman. He would not be happy listening to testimony about a businessman abusing his kid.

"Then can't we get a different judge?" she asked.

"Luck of the toss," said Sansom.

Miss Stone wasn't backing off from Burke now, though.

"I've talked to Robert at length, Your Honor," she said. "He considers the notion that his mother might be abusing him a very bad joke."

"I see," he said. "All right. Then we can keep the child in the home. I'd prefer to do that anyway. And obviously your office will be responsible for monitoring the situation there."

"Yes, Your Honor."

And then he made the ruling.

And that was that.

She stood waiting in the hall while Sansom talked privately with Miss Stone a few feet away.

She saw Arthur leave the courtroom with his lawyer, Edward Wood.

She knew Wood. He dined often at the restaurant and even more often held his own kind of high-profile court toward the back of the bar. It figured that Arthur would hire him. And in some ways she thought that unfortunately it was a pretty good decision on his part.

Wood knew everybody. Lawyers. Professionals. Politicians. He bought drinks for them all too, although he was very discreet about it. His tab was enormous. His secretary paid it out on a regular monthly basis.

He was smooth and he was intelligent. She had never seen him drink even the slightest bit too much while at the same time managing to get half the men around him loose-lipped and half-soused.

She guessed there were things to be learned that way. Arthur always said Wood knew where the bodies were buried.

As they stepped out into the hall he smiled at her.

It was a *tolerant* smile. Poor Lydia.

Poor woman.

Screw you, she thought. We'll see if you're still feeling sorry for me two weeks from now. We'll just see.

Arthur noticed her too.

In the courtroom she'd avoided looking at him. Only enough to note the new blue pinstriped suit—nearly a ringer for Wood's own. Now she saw that his face looked thinner, drawn, pale.

Good, she thought. If I'm not sleeping you sure as hell shouldn't be.

He stopped and for a moment she was afraid he had it in mind to approach her. He looked as tired as she'd ever seen him and almost as anxious as she was. His jaw was set so tight she thought it must hurt. The dark eyes glared at her. She took an involuntary step backward, heard the click of her high heels echo in the corridor.

The eyes softened. He mouthed something to her and then he turned away.

It took her a moment to register what he'd said.

And then she did. The hall began to spin.

Mine, he'd said.

SEVENTEEN

CRIMES AGAINST THE PUBLIC

It was only a couple of lines in the Manchester *Union Leader*'s weekly courts summation.

"Arthur W. Danse, Plymouth restauranteur, was charged by his ex-wife, Lydia Danse, in State Superior Court on Tuesday with abuse of a minor. Hearings begin February 22nd."

It was a rainy evening but still it was a Friday and The Caves was crowded. Everywhere he looked he seemed to see the newspaper. At the tables in back, sitting on top of briefcases, one of them folded beside a woman's elbow at the bar.

He kept thinking they'd all read it. Everybody. Of course they had. They were all snickering at him behind his back.

Bastards.

"I'll be back in the office if you need me," he said to Jake.

Jake nodded and gave him a wave. The second barman, Billy, just glanced at him.

Jake at least was loyal.

Not like the rest of them.

He made his way through the loud party of office workers and college kids to the back of the bar. Normally he'd have taken his time, greeting familiar faces, stopping to talk. He was good at that. Now he just cut his way through. To hell with them.

At least business hadn't fallen off yet.

He closed the door behind him and sat down at the big mahogany desk. The desk was practically empty. He kept it that way. Neat and tidy.

He listened to the sounds filtering in from outside. Happy voices, lots of them, male and female. Laughter. Music. The tinkle of glasses. These sounds had always pleased him. They meant money and success and status within the community. Things he'd always known he'd have someday. Things he deserved and needed.

And now she was threatening to take them away from him.

Child abuser.

If she made it stick they'd be gone.

Let's go eat at that place, you know the one I mean, the guy who owns it fucks his kid. You know the place.

It would all be over. Finished. Even if he didn't go to jail, which was still a possibility despite what Edward Wood said, he'd still have to sell The Caves eventually—a place he'd built from nothing, sell it probably for a song—and then move on.

Again.

Damn her, he thought. Goddamn them all.

He poured himself a short Glenlivet and belted it back. Then another, larger one, sipping it slowly.

He sat back in the heavy brown leather chair and listened and stared at the walls. Hung there were images from his past. A framed poster from a Who concert at the Boston Garden. A bronze plaque from the State Chamber of Commerce and another from the Rotary Club. The first painting he'd ever bought, right after The Caves began turning a profit—a painting by a New York artist named McPheeters of a slouched, exhausted man walking the beach at night under a blood-red moon, a smiling figure riding on his shoulders, somehow blending into him. A photo by Ansel Adams depicting a dark road through deep woods at the end of the day.

He could picture packing up none of these.

He'd leave them there.

No. Smash them. Leave her nothing. Nothing.

There was a knock at the door. Then it opened.

Billy. Fucking Billy. Jake would have waited for him to say come in.

"Someone to see you, Mr. Danse."

"Tell them I'm busy."

"It's Ralph Duggan, Mr. Danse."

Like that was some big fucking deal to him.

"Jesus Christ. All right. Okay. Send him in."

Duggan. The ending to a perfect day. The guy had been on his case since he was a kid and showed no signs of stopping. What the hell was it with these cops? All this holier-than-thou shit. Even the courtroom bailiff had looked at him as though he'd crawled out from under a rock somewhere.

Duggan was the worst of them. Duggan thought he was so damn smart. But he wasn't smart.

If he were smart he'd have learned a lot of things long ago.

I'm going to enjoy this, Duggan thought.

"Arthur," he said and sat down.

Danse nodded. "You still on duty or would you care for a whiskey?"

"No thanks."

He poured a glass for himself. Duggan doubted it was his first one. The hands were far too steady.

"You saw the paper, I guess," Danse said.

"Nope. Heard you made the records section, though."

"Here." He tossed a copy across the table.

Duggan just let it sit there.

"I know what's in it, Arthur. Besides, I'm not really much for the *Union Leader*. Are you?"

"Is that what you came to talk about?"

"The Union Leader?"

"No. This custody thing."

"Seems to me it's a good bit more than a custody thing, Art. But no, that's not why I stopped by. You know I was out to see your mom and dad the other day, had a kind of talk with them. Your dad looks awful tired, Art. How come he doesn't just retire?"

"He still likes the work, I suppose. They told me you were by. It's about this thing over on the Wingerter property, right?"

"Right. Pretty bad business, Art. Ugly."

"I heard."

"What'd you hear?"

Duggan watched him drink his scotch. Playing for time? Could be.

"That it was a murder. A girl from Plymouth State."

"That all you heard?"

"I heard she was raped."

"Oh, she was raped all right. And then some. I'd give you all the details but you know how it goes, we got to hold on to those best we can, eliminate the cranks. Mind if I smoke?"

"Go ahead."

He lit a Newport Lite. Arthur opened a drawer and took out a clear glass ashtray and put it in front of him on the clean empty desk.

"Ruth tells me you were over there that night. That you came in pretty late and slept at the house. That correct?"

"Yes."

"You hear anything? See anything?"

"I was coming from a party here. Opening of that new office building over on Prospect. To tell you the truth, I got a little loaded. I doubt I'd have heard or seen anything if it jumped out and bit me."

Duggan clicked his tongue. "Drunk driving, Arthur? Shame on you."

"I shouldn't have been on the road, I admit."

"What time'd you arrive?"

"Oh, about one-thirty. Two o'clock."

"Alone?"

"Of course alone."

"Listen, Art. Tell me something. How come you went to your folks' place? I don't get it. Why not to your own?" Danse put down the drink.

"It's . . . it's actually kind of embarrassing. Since the divorce I get . . . well, it gets sort of lonely sometimes."

"You? Really? That surprises me, Art. With all these people out there? With all these *ladies* out at the bar? Damn! I wouldn't think that at all."

Danse smiled slightly. "I suppose it *would* surprise you. But I've found it isn't smart to mix business with pleasure. I don't date the customers."

"Never?"

"Rarely. Very rarely."

"Too bad. Must be awful tempting, I mean. All those young pretty college kids. It'd sure tempt me. Listen, do you remember this Laura Banks? She used to come in here pretty often I understand."

"I don't remember that name at all."

"Maybe if I showed you her picture."

He dug in his jacket pocket for the snapshot they'd taken from her apartment. That and the other one. The *after* photo. He'd had the lab reduce it down to snapshot size. The face only. That was bad enough.

He made a point of not looking at them as he handed them over.

He saw Danse wince.

He didn't look like a guilty man.

He looked like any citizen would. Faced with that.

Could he maybe be wrong about this?

He took the "after" picture back from him.

"Sony," he said. "I don't know how that one got in there. Take a look at the other, though, will you?"

Danse appeared to study it.

"Maybe," he said. "She looks familiar. But she's not somebody I know, really. Did you try Jake? He's a whole lot better at faces than I am."

Duggan doubted that. "I will," he said. "One other thing, Art, and then I'll leave you to go back to your business."

He took back the second photo and then made a show of rooting through his pants pockets until he found a small piece of folded paper.

"These places mean anything to you?"

He read directly off the paper. Playing the dumb country cop with not much memory to speak of.

"Franklin, Conway, Munsonville, Tuftonboro. Mean anything?"

Danse looked puzzled. He shrugged.

"Towns. Towns in New Hampshire. I don't get it."

"You do any business there?"

"Near there, sometimes. I distribute to Wolfeboro, which is near Tuftonboro, and Keene, which is over by Munsonville. And there's one store in Conway. But my stuff's all over the state these days, everywhere there's tourists. I go all over. Up into Vermont. Why?"

"No reason." He turned to go. "Thanks for your help, Art."

"Whenever."

He stopped at the door and then turned back to him.

"How do you think it's gonna go, Art? Just between you and me now. I mean, you think you'll beat these charges?"

And he finally saw the coldness there like he wanted to see it, just beneath the thin veil of honest-businessman sincerity.

"I know you don't like me, Ralph," Danse said. "I'm sorry about that. But I didn't do this.. . this thing she says I did. My wife's a goddamn crazy woman. And that's the god's honest truth."

"I guess she was crazy when you smacked her around that time too then," he said.

"You won't believe this but yes, she was. If you'd heard what she said to me, if you'd seen the way she was acting, you'd probably have lost it and smacked her too."

Duggan smiled. "I kinda doubt that, Art," he said. "But I suppose you never know. There's always an edge. And always somebody ready to push you right on over."

Happily he found after a while that it was possible to dump Duggan's visit like the sack of shit it was and get some work done.

When he was ready to leave it was well past eleven and the room outside was still going strong. He didn't relish walking through it. The article in the paper was still on his mind. He could leave through his private entrance but that would be like admitting something.

To hell with it. He'd run the gauntlet.

When he was halfway down the bar he was glad he did. Edward Wood was standing there drinking his usual Absolut martini with another, older man who Arthur wasn't able to recognize at first. Not until he was standing right next to him. And then he was shocked. The man was Tom Modine, another lawyer. The last time Arthur'd seen him here Modine had probably weighed a good two hundred and fifty pounds. Now it looked like he'd shed a hundred of it. The man had a wasted sickly yellow look. *Cancer*, he thought. Had to be.

His handshake, though, was still firm.

"It's good to see you, Arthur," he said. "Edward was just filling me in on your problems in the courts these days. I hope you won't feel he was talking out of school. You've got to trust your lawyer."

"Of course. And I do."

"Excellent." He drained the last of what looked like a whiskey soda and set the glass down on the bar.

"The fact is," he said, "that I really think things are going to work out for you. I honestly do."

"From your lips to god's ears, Tom."

He laughed. "Don't worry. You've got the best in the county. Thanks for the drink, Edward. I've got an early tee-off in the morning or I'd stick around and let you sell me on having another one."

"Next time," said Wood.

"Next time." Modine patted Arthur's shoulder. "Don't worry, Arthur," he said. "You'll be fine. See you soon."

"See you soon, Tom."

They watched him walk away.

"Sad," said Wood.

"Cancer?"

"Yes. He's in remission now but you can see what it's done to him."

"Too bad. Tom's a good guy."

"The best." He ordered another drink. "You didn't like my talking to him, though. Did you?"

Wood was nothing if not perceptive.

"Listen, I feel funny about *anybody* knowing about this. Jesus! What a thing to have people saying about you. And now with this damn newspaper thing . . ."

Wood held up his hand, smiling. "Guess who's part of Tom's foursome tomorrow, Art."

"Who?"

"The Honorable Thomas J. Burke, that's who. They play together all the time. Same club, very old friends. They went to law school together. And Tom's a big contributor to Burke's campaigns. You still think I did the wrong thing talking about your case?"

"You mean you think he'll talk to Burke?"

"I know he will."

"How? I don't get it. How can he do us any good?"

"Modine can't try to influence Burke directly, if that's what you mean. He's an officer of the court. It's illegal. Not to mention unethical. But he can plant the seed."

"What seed?"

Wood laughed again. He knew how he looked.

Anxious as a kid on a blind date.

"That *I* can be trusted, Arthur. That he's known me for nearly as long as he's known Burke. And if I say that there's more to this than meets the eye, that no way are you guilty on this and that your wife's just an angry hysteric who's out to get you, then that's very probably going to be the case."

He sipped his martini. "*That* seed," he said. "That's the one he can plant out there on the golf course tomorrow. It will go a long way, believe me. Then all we have to do is follow up. Hell, Burke's dealt with me before any number of times and doesn't know her man from Adam. He's already halfway there."

Arthur understood. There was a network to everything. And a good ol' boy behind half the deals in the state of New Hampshire.

He liked it. He liked it very much. For the first time in a week he thought he might just whip this thing.

It would be a good idea, he thought, to join Wood in a nightcap. To stand there at his own bar in front of patrons and god and everybody.

He felt better than he had all day.

"Jake, Glenlivet please," he said.

EIGHTEEN

VISITATION, PART TWO

Andrea Stone hadn't graduated first in her class at Emory Law in Atlanta in order to come north and babysit. Ordinarily she'd have passed this particular chore on to some assistant. In this case, though, she thought she'd like to make an exception.

It was an opportunity to see who Arthur Danse really was and how his son responded to him.

And it turned out that Robert was really no trouble. Since his mother dropped him off at her office twenty minutes ago, they'd talked for a while and then he'd sat playing quietly with his Game Boy while she tried to clear her desk of some long overdue paperwork. She glanced at the clock on the wall overhead.

Arthur was now fifteen minutes late.

Form of protest? she wondered.

He'd requested of course that the meeting take place either at his house or at his parents'. Preferably at his. As far as Andrea was concerned both were out of the question. She didn't even bother to put the idea to Lydia Danse or her attorney, both of whom certainly would have rejected it in any case. Her own concern was both moral and practical.

The way she figured it Arthur Danse was a user and a pervert. Robert might not be willing to say so but she'd bet her job on it. So why should she give him even the slightest consideration?

Why put yourself out for a man like that?

And how in god's name did he have the temerity to think he deserved it?

No. Edward Wood could complain to her all he wanted.

Unless the judge said otherwise any visits between Robert and Arthur were going to be here at her office. Or they were going to happen nowhere at all.

She was signing a release form for some evidentiary property on a case that was already two months settled now when her assistant announced his arrival. She let him wait a minute or two just on principle. Robert didn't seem to mind. Then she let him in.

"I want you to know," he said, "that I think this stinks." Speaking first to her and not to Robert.

"Noted," she said.

"How's it going, Robby?"

"Fine."

He barely glanced up from his Game Boy.

"How's school?"

"It's okay."

"Just okay?"

"I got another perfect in spelling."

"Good. That's good."

He sat down next to him on the couch but not particularly close and crossed his legs and folded his hands.

"Kind of rough, isn't it?"

"Huh?"

"We don't get to see very much of one another, do we? Not like the old days."

"I guess."

Robert frowned and sighed, concentrating. Clearly he wasn't doing real well this time on his Super Mario Brothers. "Robert, put down the Nintendo for a minute, okay?" He turned it off but held onto it. With both hands. *He's almost clutching it*, she thought.

I think he's afraid of him.

"You know I care a lot about you, right?" Arthur said. He nodded.

"And you know that I want to do what's best for you too."

Robert nodded again, more slowly this time. Like he didn't exactly know where his father was going on this. Arthur looked at him for a moment as though he was wondering about something too and then went on.

"So you realize that's why your mom and I are having this . . . this kind of fight . . . we're doing this because . . . *oh, for god's sake!*"

He turned to Andrea and threw up his arms.

Low flash point, she thought. Slick but quick to burn.

"Look," he said. "This is impossible! How can I have a personal conversation with my son with you sitting here? Could you have one with *your* kid if *I* were sitting in the room? You're a stranger, for god's sake."

"I don't have any children, Mr. Danse. And I'm not exactly a stranger to Robert."

"You know what I'm talking about. In *theory*. Listen, I haven't seen my son in *weeks*. Couldn't you just do the decent thing and leave us alone for a while? A few minutes?"

"I'm afraid not. Court order."

"For five *minutes*?"

"I'm sorry."

"Five fucking *minutes*?"

She saw Robert flinch at the word. Visibly flinch. And she wondered, not for the first time, if Danse had ever hit the boy. Or had threatened him. It would explain why he wasn't talking. She'd asked Robert both those questions before and got nothing but mute denials.

"Mr. Danse, I want to explain something to you. It's going to be important for you to remember that until this case is closed I am Robert's legal guardian. My function is to carry out the orders of the court and to make certain that Robert's rights are respected by everybody concerned. *You do not have the right* to see Robert alone. The court took away that right. Is that completely clear? I'm sorry. But that's the law."

"This is *bullshit*."

He stood up and reached for Robert's hand.

"Come on," he said, "we're leaving. We're out of here. I'm your father and I say we're *gone*."

Robert looked first at her and then at him. He didn't seem to know what to do.

But what he didn't do was take his father's hand.

Why's he being so insistent about this? she wondered. Exactly what did he want to say to the boy?

"Mr. Danse."

"I am his father!"

"Mr. Danse, may I speak with you in private for a moment?"

"No you may damn well not speak with me in private for a moment! Not if I can't speak with my own son you can't!"

"In that case listen to me—you take one step out of this office in Robert's company and I'll have you thrown in jail so fast it'll make your head spin. I'm sorry to have to say this in front of Robert but you leave me no choice and I urge you not to test me on this. I urge you very, very strongly."

She watched the man deflate. Watching him deflate did not displease her one damn bit.

"I'll see you, Robert," he said quietly. "I'm sorry we couldn't . . ."

"Sure, Dad. It's okay."

He turned on his Game Boy again.

Danse glanced at her once and then opened the door and left the room. She followed, closing the door behind her. "Mr. Danse."

She spoke quietly so that Robert wouldn't hear. The walls were thin.

He turned.

"Mr. Danse, if I ever hear you use the word 'fuck' again in Robert's presence I will personally bring an action against you for the verbal abuse of a child—a second, independent action—before the Division of Children and Youth Services. And that action will land you in district court no matter how this custody case turns out. Are we very clear on that?"

He smiled. "He can't hear us now, though, can he?" he said. Now he was speaking softly too.

"No."

"Then go screw yourself, Miss Stone. You fucking tight-assed bitch."

She felt she had the measure of the man.

Lydia was deep asleep when the phone rang. She looked at the clock.

4:45.

"Hello?"

"You'll never prove it," he said.

She was instantly awake.

"He won't tell," he said. "So how are you going to prove it if he won't tell, huh? You can't."

"How do you know he won't tell, Arthur?"

"Because I know my son. I know my kid. He's loyal to me."

"You think so?"

"I know so."

"We'll see."

"You'll never prove a goddamn thing you stupid cunt!"

"Gee. *Cunt*, huh? Would you rather I was a little boy, Arthur?"

It felt good to say it to him. To taunt him.

"Fuck *you!*" he yelled and slammed down the phone. She was shaking when she replaced the receiver, but in a way the call was far from unsatisfying. She looked again at the clock. Nearly five in the morning, she thought.

It looked like Arthur was losing it a little.

Too bad.

She thought about that. And after a while, she slept.

NINETEEN

THE MOST IMPORTANT THING

Two days before the hearing, she was finishing the lunch dishes over at Ellie Brest's house and worrying why Owen hadn't called back yet so she could tell him about this phone-call-in-the-night thing when Ellie asked her to come into the living room.

Normally this was nap time.

Ellie was usually completely predictable. She'd fall asleep in the middle of one of the soaps and then all afternoon she'd wonder what she'd missed. If Lydia happened to hear any of it while she was going about her business she'd fill her in.

She turned off the tap and dried her hands, and walked into the darkened room. Ellie kept the lights off in there unless Lydia was cleaning. Saved a dollar or two on electricity, she said. Though the television was on all day and well into the night.

Now she wanted it off, though.

"During your soaps, El?"

"Yes."

She walked over and turned it off, thinking how it was such a little thing—but knowing the enormous and painful effort it would have taken for Ellie to get up and do it for herself.

"Sit down, Liddy. Please."

She sat across from her in the big overstuffed armchair that nobody ever used anymore now that her husband was gone.

"I know you're going to be away for a few days," she said. "And I just wanted to tell you while I still have the nerve to go butting into other people's business that I admire what you're doing, Liddy."

She didn't know what to say. She couldn't have been more

surprised if Ellie had got up and danced.

In the past she always seemed embarrassed by Lydia's . . . situation. She'd ask a question now and then—but always seemed to shy away from actually listening to the answer. She'd never expressed approval before—or disapproval either for that matter—just an infrequent, hesitant curiosity.

"Thanks, Ellie," she said. "That means a lot to me."

"I know a lot of women would have just let it go on and on, would have turned a blind eye, so to speak. Wouldn't want the publicity or be too frightened of him or whatever."

She hesitated. This clearly wasn't easy for her to say.

"Willie and I never did have children and there are many times I've regretted that. But regrets don't get you much in life, do they? The point is, I want you to know that I think you're doin' your duty by the boy. The important thing's the boy. That nobody hurt him. A child and the good decent life of a child is the most important thing in the world. I think I missed out on something. But I'm glad that a woman good as you are, Liddy Danse, I'm glad you didn't. Nothing I can do but pray for you. But I want you to know that I'll do that for you."

She saw tears in the old woman's eyes. She was shaking with the effort of holding them back. And then there were tears in Lydia's eyes too as she stood and stepped over and gave her the gentlest and most delicate of hugs, her body so frail between her arms and against her cheek, smelling the good clean old-lady smell of her and feeling the warm wet tears pressed between their faces, and she thought, I love you old woman, I had no idea, it happened so quickly, I didn't know it could happen so quickly, but I do.

Just look. Just look at what you've given me.

TWENTY

VISITATION, PART THREE

When she pulled into the driveway after school with Robert the Lincoln was parked outside.

"Go on into the house," she said to him.

He didn't hesitate.

She walked over to the car. Arthur was slumped low in the seat. If he was trying to look inconspicuous sitting there it wasn't working. Not in the big black Lincoln.

He rolled down the window.

"Arthur, what are you doing here?"

"Nothing. Waiting."

"You know you're violating a court order being here."

"I wanted to see him."

"Why? You saw him the other day."

"That was nonsense."

It was a cold, gray damp afternoon. She could feel the heat wafting out of the Lincoln. She wasn't about to stand here talking to him.

"Well, you saw him," she said. "Good-bye. You can leave now."

"Lydia?"

"What."

"When did you get to be such a bitch?"

He was smiling. She didn't think it was funny.

"When I found out who you really were, Arthur." She turned to go.

"Lydia?"

"What?"

The smile was still there. In his hand, poking out of the window and held so low that only she could see it, was the magnum.

"Bang," he said.

"You go to hell, Arthur."

"Bang," he said.

"You go play your damn games somewhere else."

She hoped she didn't look or sound as scared as she felt. Who knew what he would do? After what he'd already done? He was crazy enough, anyway, so that she'd bet the gun was loaded.

She turned and walked quickly toward the door.

She was shaking.

"*Bang, bang,*" she heard behind her.

It was only when she was in the house, peering out through the window to see that the Lincoln was gone, that she realized there was a week's worth of groceries in the trunk. She walked out to get them like a soldier looking for sniper fire and wondered if things would ever be anything like normal again.

TWENTY-ONE

THE HEARING: FIRST DAY

The room was old and dark as the day was dark outside beyond the three long tiers of windows—and empty but for the lawyers, judge, bailiff, stenographer and Lydia and Arthur. Child welfare cases were closed to the public and press, and she was glad of it. More and more so as the day progressed.

It started badly. After brief opening statements from the attorneys, Judge Burke ruled on a motion by Edward Wood to disallow testimony and evidence regarding Arthur having beat her in November, finding it irrelevant to the matter at hand despite Owen's argument that it went to show potential for violence. So they couldn't use Ralph Duggan or the officer who'd examined her. Or the photos or hospital records.

For their side it was a major disappointment. Wasn't violence an issue here?

Apparently Burke thought it wasn't.

Things got better with Andrea Stone.

Stone's role here was unusual. She was both attorney representing Robert's interests in the case and available for questioning, as investigator of the case, from either party.

She told Owen Sansom how she'd spoken with Lydia Danse at length, with Hessler and Bromberg, and visited Robert alone at home on three occasions. That she found him seemingly quite content there, and hesitant but open to speaking to her in what she called guarded terms about what had happened. Until she asked him who'd done it.

He still wouldn't talk about that. Or about his father.

"Which leads you to conclude what, Miss Stone?" asked Sansom.

"Objection."

"Miss Stone is in the *business* of conclusions, Your Honor. Mr. Wood's aware of that."

"Overruled. The witness may answer."

"Which leads me to believe that his abuser and his father are one and the same."

"Is he willing to talk about any *other* man? His grandfather, for instance? Or me?"

"Yes."

"It's just his father he doesn't want to speak of."

"Yes."

Over Wood's repeated objections Sansom led her through the incident at the office.

"And do you remember his exact words when he lost his temper?"

"He asked if he could see Robert alone and I said no, that he was legally barred from doing that. Then he said, shouted really, `Not for five fucking minutes?'"

"In front of Robert?"

"Yes."

"And did you see a reaction to that from Robert?"

"He flinched."

"Flinched?"

"Actually moved. As though somebody were about to strike him."

"And what did you make of that?"

"That the word upset him. The word 'fuck.'"

"And did Mr. Danse use that word in your presence again that day?"

"Objection. Irrelevant."

"I'll allow it."

"Yes. Outside my office. He called me a 'fucking tightassed bitch.'"

"His exact words?"

"Yes."

Sansom paused, went back to their table, and sorted through some papers. He found the ones he wanted and walked back to

Andrea Stone and handed them to her.

"Miss Stone, is this your report, your recommendation to this court? Is this your signature?"

"Yes."

"Could you give us the gist of it?"

"I'm recommending that exclusive custody be given to the mother, Lydia Danse. And I'm recommending termination of all visitation rights for Arthur Danse, the father."

"On what basis?"

"I believe Arthur Danse sexually molested his son. I believe he's been doing so for quite some time now."

"Thank you, Miss Stone. Exhibit A for us, Your Honor. And no further questions for this witness."

"Mr. Wood?"

Wood got up slowly and approached her. He was smiling as though they were old close friends and for a moment Lydia could actually believe they were—even though she knew better. He was that good. He consulted his notes.

"Miss Stone, your testimony is that you asked Robert if there was someone doing things to him that he didn't want done, and he said, 'Maybe.' Is that right?"

"Yes."

"And you asked if someone was touching his private parts and he said 'Maybe' again. True?"

"Yes."

"But he didn't say yes or no exactly to either question, did he?"

"I felt he was avoiding a direct answer, that he was in effect trying to tell me without telling me."

"How do you know he wasn't just playing with the notion of telling you?"

"Excuse me?"

"It's been known to happen that a child, angry with one parent or another, or for that matter, angry with any adult, will use an accusation of this kind—often a thoroughly false accusation— against them. How do you know Robert wasn't just experimenting with the possibility of doing that? And then decided not to?"

"I've been at this profession quite a while, Mr. Wood. I knew. He was saying that someone had molested him."

"You say you spoke to Lydia Danse at length and she told you all about the night she made her . . . observations regarding Robert. Is that true?"

"Yes."

"And did you also speak with Arthur Danse?"

"Only that one time at my office."

"Why only then?"

"He declined to see me. On your advice, I gather."

"So you never did hear his side of this. Meaning you'll be hearing it here for the *first* time, am I right?"

"I suppose that's true. Yes."

"Yet you've already made your recommendation to the court. Interesting—let me ask you something. You say that Robert was willing to answer your questions about other men, but not about his father, is that correct?"

"Yes."

"And you asked him *specifically* about other men?"

"Yes."

"Why?"

"I wanted to exclude the possibility that he didn't want to talk about men, period. About men in general. In an abuse case, when the abuser is of one sex or the other, that's always a possibility."

"Which men did you ask him about, specifically?"

"His grandfather, Harry Danse. Ed, Cindy Fortunato's ex-husband. Dr. Bromberg. Owen Sansom."

"Did you ask about their next-door neighbor? I believe the name is Collins?"

"I may have. I don't really remember. I asked Mrs. Danse to suggest a few men he'd be likely to know. I don't recall all of them."

"You asked Mrs. *Danse* to suggest them?"

"Yes."

"So she orchestrated this, ah, list of suspects?"

"Objection!"

"Mr. Wood, please rephrase your question."

"There were a lot of men you *didn't* ask Robert about, weren't there? Men who weren't on this list that Mrs. Danse gave you? A lot of men in the neighborhood perhaps? Male teachers at school? Isn't that true?"

"I suppose so."

"So how do you know he wouldn't have wanted to talk about one of *those* men, either? How do you know it's just his father he doesn't want to talk about?"

"I wasn't going after his abuser here, Mr. Wood, if that's what you mean. I wasn't looking for suspects. I was only eliminating a possibility. I thought it was a fair sampling."

"You weren't going after his abuser, as you say, because you were already convinced that his abuser was Arthur Danse, am I correct?"

"Basically, yes. From the evidence it seemed quite clear to me."

"This is an investigation?"

"Objection."

"Sustained. Move on, Mr. Wood."

Wood consulted his notes again.

He walked back to their table and stood directly behind Arthur Danse.

"My client called you . . . what was it? A tight-assed . . .?"

"Fucking tight-assed bitch, Mr. Wood."

Her voice had gone hard now.

He smiled. "Didn't endear him to you very much, did it?"

"No. It didn't."

"In fact you don't like my client, do you, Miss Stone?"

"My likes or dislikes have no relevance here whatsoever, Mr. Wood. As you know very well."

"No more questions, Your Honor."

She thought that Cindy did wonderfully. Wood wasn't able to shake her for a moment and hardly even tried. She was there for the most part as a character witness—as was Olive Youngjohn, Robert's teacher—but also to establish Lydia's conduct the night of the incident. Dressed in a tailored blue suit, her long blond hair pulled back in a tight knot, carefully and sparingly made up, she radiated calm and respectability. It was as though she did this every day. Lydia was proud of her.

"Mrs. Danse was obviously angry when she came to the house that night, wasn't she, Mrs. Fortunato?" Wood asked her.

"She was angry, yes, and I'd say she was deeply shaken."

"Would you say that her anger was under control?"

"Objection. Calls for an opinion," said Sansom.

"I'll allow it."

"Yes. Under the circumstances."

"But you weren't aware of the circumstances at that time, were you?"

"No, I wasn't."

"Were you aware where she was going when she left your house that night?"

"She said she had to talk to Arthur, right away."

"But she didn't tell you why."

"I didn't ask."

"You're best friends and you didn't ask?" He looked incredulous.

Cindy smiled. "Best friends know when not to ask, Mr. Wood—that's why they stay that way. But you already know that, I'm sure."

Mrs. Youngjohn was a little rockier. She *looked* the part perfectly—middle-aged, somewhat plump, glasses, sensible cotton print dress belted at the waist—and spoke with assurance and determination as she told them about Lydia's habit of keeping in very close touch with her and Robert's other teachers about his problems. It was those problems, however, that Wood finally managed to use against her.

"You say he stutters?"

"Yes. Has trouble getting the words out."

"And he's receiving therapy for this?"

"Yes. We have a speech therapist working with him right at school."

"And you're aware that he's seeing Dr. Bromberg, a psycho-therapist."

"Yes."

"And he's shy?"

"Yes."

"But his work is good."

"Yes."

"Do other kids *like* him, Mrs. Youngjohn?"

"Oh, Robert's a very nice boy."

"I'm sure he is—but that's not what I asked. As a teacher of what, twenty-two years is it? I'm sure you're aware how cruel kids can be. I mean, he stutters, he's shy, he goes to a therapist for one thing and a second therapist for another. He's different. He's an outsider. Isn't that the case here?"

"Robert has friends."

"But he does get teased, doesn't he?"

"Well, yes, he does get teased."

"And do they tease him about wearing a diaper too?" Sansom was on his feet. "Objection! Irrelevant. Council is going nowhere with this."

"If you'll give me a moment, Your Honor, I'll show where this is going."

"I'll allow it—for the moment. Witness may answer."

"I . . . I honestly wasn't aware that he *did* wear a diaper, Mr. Wood."

"He wears one every night to bed, Mrs. Youngjohn. I'm surprised you didn't know. Since you and Mrs. Danse are working so *closely* together on all of Robert's problems."

"Objection. Now he's making a speech!"

"Sustained."

"Can you think of any reason Mrs. Danse *wouldn't* tell you about Robert wearing a diaper?"

"Not really, no. Unless she thought it would embarrass him somehow."

"And would you consider this important for you to know? Despite the potential for embarrassment? To understand his problems?"

"I . . . maybe. I don't know."

Lydia saw a prissiness in the woman that she'd never seen before. On some level, she was offended that Lydia hadn't confided in her. His next question made it clear that Wood hadn't missed it either.

"So how do you *feel* about Mrs. Danse concealing it from you? Personally, I mean. Your feelings concerning Mrs. Danse's reliability, her cooperativeness. Does this change things in any way?"

Youngjohn saw where he was going on this and recovered, thank god. But Lydia was afraid the damage was done already. A character witness was supposed to come down firmly on the side of character.

"I have no feelings about it at all," she said. "I'd have to talk with Mrs. Danse. I'm just surprised to hear it, that's all."

"I'm sure. So to make a judgment on it, though, you'd have to talk with her further?"

"Yes."

"So it's an open question for you. How you feel personally about her concealing this from you, I mean."

"Yes."

Wood paused for a moment and walked back to his table.

"One final matter, Mrs. Youngjohn. Did Robert ever appear in school with cuts, bruises, scrapes? That kind of thing?"

"Occasionally."

"Would you say he's clumsy?"

She smiled. "I'm afraid he is . . . a little."

"You know this firsthand?"

"I've seen him fall a few times, outside playing." She smiled. "I've seen him fall over his own two feet."

"A few times?"

"Yes."

"Would that account for all these cuts and bruises?"

"No, not really. Most of them I think happened playing outside of school."

"Did you and Mrs. Danse talk about his clumsiness?"

"Yes."

"Did she tell you how he got this or that bruise, this or that scrape?"

"Yes. Sometimes."

"But not always."

"No. Of course not. Not always."

"And you felt she was telling you the truth?"

"Yes."

"You didn't think she might be *concealing* anything on this subject either, did you?"

"Objection, Your Honor!"

"Overruled. Witness may answer the question."

"No. I didn't."

"Nothing further for this witness."

"Redirect, Your Honor," said Sansom. He walked over to her, looking like a man who wanted to get this over and done with in a hurry.

"Mrs. Youngjohn, do you have any reason to believe that Mrs. Danse ever *lied* to you about Robert?"

"No."

"Or about how he hurt himself on any given occasion?"

"No."

"And wouldn't you say that Robert's clumsiness at home or wherever was completely consistent with what you saw of Robert at school?"

"Absolutely."

She was firm on that much, anyway.

Hessler, the proctologist, came off like someone's kindly grandfather. For all she knew he was. Dressed in a neat gray suit and conservative blue tie, he spoke with quiet authority. Wood could do almost nothing with him on cross-examination.

"You say this is *consistent* with anal rape, Dr. Hessler," he said. "Yet you found no semen. So couldn't it have been something else then? Some other form of penetration? An object other than a penis? The boy's own *finger*, perhaps?"

"Very unlikely. I've indicated the degree of dilation. The boy couldn't do that with his own finger. I doubt that an adult's finger alone could do it—and even if it could, that's still abuse, isn't it? Or if it were done with any other object you care to mention."

"So you rule out self-infliction."

"Yes. Particularly since it was clear the muscle and the surrounding tissue had been damaged repeatedly, and over time. As I said, there was scarring. One could imagine the boy doing this to himself *once* for some reason, perhaps, with some foreign object. Unlikely but not impossible. Children, I suppose, will experiment sometimes in very odd ways. But not repeatedly and not over time. This caused *pain*, Mr. Wood. I would say a great deal of pain. So unless you conclude that the boy's a masochist . . ."

"I see," said Wood. "No further questions."

Andrea Stone stood up, eager to eliminate even that possibility from the judge's thinking.

"Dr. Hessler, did any of Robert's behavior indicate to you that he indeed might be a masochist?"

"Quite the contrary. He was very timid about being touched. He is not a young man who enjoys pain."

"Thank you, Dr. Hessler. I have nothing further."

The bedroom was cold, though she'd already turned up the thermostat. Something wasn't working properly. She lay in the dark beneath the covers and considered getting another blanket out of the closet. Exhaustion kept her lying there instead and perversely, kept her awake as well. Worrying.

She thought that despite a few setbacks the day had gone fairly well, all told. So did Owen Sansom.

Tomorrow was the problem.

Tomorrow it was her turn.

If only he'd tell them, she thought. If only Robert would say.

She'd tried once again in the car, picking him up after court and driving him from Cindy's house back home. She'd tried to reassure him. Said that she'd protect him. That if he told nothing would happen to him.

She was losing patience, though.

It was impossible to understand his reluctance in the face of what was going on.

She'd pressed too hard. She'd made him cry.

It wasn't the first time.

It wasn't just worry but guilt that was keeping her awake nights.

She phoned Barbara afterwards as soon as they got home. She'd been somewhat out of touch with her sister lately. It was hard for her to talk about this over and over again, even with her. Barb had wanted to go to court for her as a character witness, but Sansom said that with Barbara being family it would carry little weight. Besides, she'd only just started a new job. So they'd decided she should stay where she was. Cindy was always there for her if she needed somebody.

But at that moment for some reason she needed family. She told her sister how guilty she felt.

"You're doing this for *him*," Barbara said. "Not for yourself. You're doing it to put a stop to what Arthur's been doing and you've got to remember that. Of course you're frustrated. How else could you possibly be?"

It was good advice. But Lydia knew she was also doing it *to* him. *To* Robert. There was no getting around that. Badgering him to say the most terrible things about a man he'd always loved. And probably, despite everything, still loved.

If he can't then he can't, she thought. Leave it alone. Make it happen without him.

You do it instead.

And the day to do it for him was tomorrow and that was keeping her awake.

She needed another blanket. The room was too damn cold.

She got up and walked to the closet. The floorboards felt freezing under her feet. She took a heavy quilt off the shelf and spread it out across the bed and then slipped between the sheets. Better.

Something bumped into a table downstairs.

She heard movement. A floorboard squeaked.

She thought about the cold. Maybe it wasn't the thermostat.

An open window?

They'd been closed when she went to bed. It was winter. They'd been closed for months.

An intruder.

Arthur.

She got up and moved back to the closet as quietly as possible. The Ladysmith .38 he'd bought for her was in a shoe box behind some shoes and linens. She hadn't looked at it once since he'd left. But she knew he kept it loaded. Safety on, bullet in the chamber.

The metal grip felt icy in her hand.

There was a choking sensation in her throat and her heart was suddenly pounding—as though the gun carried an electric current that traveled up from her hand and jolted her.

She moved to the stairwell. The urge was strong to check on Robert but his room was down the hall and the door was shut and whoever was down there was bound to hear the latch fall if she opened it.

If someone was down there.

If it wasn't just her imagination.

No, she thought. You heard something.

Maybe you heard Robert. Sure, that's it. It's him down there.

But she wasn't exactly sure she believed that.

She took the stairs slowly, holding tight to the banister with one hand, tighter to the gun with the other. By now the hand that held the gun was sweating.

On the landing she heard the sound of metal brushing ceramic. The chain on the table lamp by the window.

She peered around the corner, leading with the .38.

She saw him kneeling on the couch. Motionless. His elbows leaning against the back of the couch. He was staring out the window. She slipped the gun into the deep pocket of her nightgown hoping he wouldn't notice its dark heavy mass through the thin cotton.

She walked over and touched his shoulder.

"Robert?"

He didn't acknowledge her at all. Just kept staring. *Sleepwalking?* she thought. Please, god. Not that too.

"Robert?"

"He's outside," he said.

"Who?"

But she knew.

"Do you think he wants to get in?" he said.

"Daddy?"

He nodded.

She looked out the window. The lawn, all the way down the hill to the street, was empty.

"Where do you see him? Where is he?"

"Over there."

He pointed to the old elm tree near the center of the lawn. "I woke up and saw him from my window and I came downstairs."

He sounded calm enough. But his eyes were wide.

"He's hiding," he said.

"Wait here."

In the hall closet she found a pair of boots. She took a coat off the coat rack and slipped it on. Robert remained staring out the window. She transferred the gun to her coat pocket, unlocked the door and stepped outside.

As quietly as possible she closed the door behind her.

She stuffed both hands into her pockets and walked toward the tree. The boots and coat were no match for the cold but her face felt flushed and the hand on the gun felt greasy now with sweat. She approached quickly at first and then as she got closer slowed her pace.

She walked wide of the tree to the right until she could see around it to the other side.

Nothing.

To be absolutely certain she walked all the way around it. Circled it.

She felt limp with relief.

He wasn't there.

She wondered what she'd have said to him or done to him if he had been.

She walked back to the house remembering what Robert had said.

He's hiding, he'd said.

It wasn't true, not literally, not this time. Robert had imagined him out there behind the tree, dreamed him there no doubt and then come downstairs still frightened and half asleep. But in a less literal sense it was completely true.

Of course he was hiding.

And Robert saying that, acknowledging that, was probably as close as he was ever going to come to telling the truth about his father.

And accusing him.

TWENTY-TWO

THE HEARING: SECOND DAY

Waiting for Owen Sansom in the courtroom, sitting across from Andrea Stone, she tried to read a newspaper. It had been days since she'd seen one but now her attention kept slipping away. The stories took on the patchwork quality of a dream, one slipping into the other, none of them coming to any real conclusion.

One story managed to hold her though. In New York, a twenty-seven-year-old suburban woman had been arrested for leaving her children at home unattended while she drove to a nearby town to engage in acts of prostitution. The woman had been abandoned by her ex-husband—a lawyer—over a year ago and since that time had received no child-support payments from him and had no training and was unable to find a job. Her two boys, aged seven and nine, had been placed in foster homes following her arrest. The woman said she had involved herself in prostitution only to support them.

She thought how horrible it must be to become so desperate as to feel that this was your only option. That if her story were true then this woman had felt backed into the kind of corner in which responsibility and irresponsibility were all but indistinguishable.

The story troubled her.

"*Where is he?* Where's Owen?"

Andrea Stone was standing over her.

Lydia was aware of her cologne. *Georgio*, she thought. She was dressed in a dark blue tailored suit and white blouse, wearing a single string of pearls. She looked keyed-up, nervous.

Lydia put the paper aside.

"I don't know," she said.

"Burke'll be here any minute."

Lydia looked at the clock. It was ten after nine. Where the hell was he?

Andrea Stone turned abruptly and walked back to her desk.

"The Honorable Thomas J. Burke. All rise."

Burke crossed to the bench just as the double doors flew open behind her and Sansom appeared hurrying down the aisle.

The fact that he was late wasn't lost on Burke. He didn't comment.

Sansom looked awful.

His suit didn't exactly look as though he'd slept in it, but it did look uncomfortably close to that. The tie was crooked, the collar in need of pressing. His glasses were water-spotted again.

She glanced at Edward Wood standing next to Arthur. She didn't like the contrast she was seeing.

"Are you all right?" she whispered.

He nodded. "Late start," he said. "Sorry if I worried you."

You're worrying me now, she thought.

"Be seated," said Burke. And so the day began.

Bromberg seemed ill at ease, shifting in his seat and sipping from a glass of water as Sansom questioned him about Robert's symptoms. His shyness and his stuttering, his clumsiness, his incontinence, his dreams.

"And are all these consistent with what you'd see in a case of child abuse, Doctor?"

"At Robert's age the onset of stuttering's somewhat unusual. Otherwise I'd say yes."

He took him through an explanation of his treatment—the "play therapy" that was designed to open Robert up. "Would you say he's responding well or badly?"

Bromberg smiled. "Not too well, sorry to say."

"He's uncommunicative?"

"Yes, mostly."

"And is this consistent, in your opinion, with a child who's . . . with ah, with an abused child?"

"An abused child would tend to be secretive and withhold information, especially from adults. Yes."

"Doctor, based on your knowledge of him, do you believe it

likely that Robert's been abused?"

"Likely?"

"Yes. Couldn't these symptoms all be accounted for by some other means? His parents' divorce, maybe?"

She saw what he was doing. He was heading Wood off at the pass with that one.

Bromberg thought it over.

"No, I'd have a problem with that explanation. It's what we've been calling his clumsiness, you see, which isn't really clumsiness at all. The boy's hurting himself—and he's doing it frequently. To me, that's the most significant indication that someone else is hurting *him*. That and his incontinence, of course."

"So you'd say it *is* likely."

"Yes."

On cross-examination Wood took him carefully over the same terrain—at first going nowhere in particular that Lydia could see. But Bromberg seemed more relaxed now and she had to wonder to what extent the two men had talked together prior to the hearing.

Then that became apparent.

"So this is your conclusion, Doctor. That Robert's been sexually abused."

"Yes."

"And did you also conclude that the abuser was definitely his father?"

"No, I did not conclude that. Not necessarily."

"Couldn't it just as likely have been his *mother*, then? Didn't you in fact *tell* Mrs. Danse that you hadn't yet ruled her out on that?"

"I did mention the possibility, yes."

"Exactly what did you say?"

"I said I had suspected abuse for some time. She asked why I hadn't reported it to her. I told her that one did not discuss this sort of thing casually, especially when it had been known to happen that a parent would bring his or her child in for therapy as a kind of smoke screen, to disguise their culpability in the abuse or perhaps even, subconsciously, in the need to be discovered."

"And how did she respond to that?"

"She became . . . quite angry."

"How do you know she was angry?"

He smiled. "You only had to look at her, Mr. Wood. Or listen to her."

"She was hostile toward you?"

"She became quite curt with me, yes. And I'd say, sarcastic."

She was aware that Andrea Stone across the aisle was glancing at Owen Sansom. Her expression seemed puzzled. And Lydia thought she had a pretty good notion why.

"Shouldn't you be objecting to this?" she said. "I mean, isn't he calling for an opinion or something?"

He waved her off and continued writing whatever he was writing in his pad. "Means nothing," he said.

He was starting to scare her.

"Let me ask you this, Dr. Bromberg. Have you ruled out Mrs. Danse as the boy's abuser *to this day*?"

"How could I? The boy won't say."

"Nothing further, Your Honor."

She looked at Sansom.

"I have nothing for this witness, Your Honor," he said.

No, she thought. *Get up. Do something* for god's sake.

Sansom just kept writing.

What in the hell was wrong with him?

Was she overreacting? She felt suddenly as though she were drowning. Bromberg had just told the court that there was every possibility that *she* was the one who was hurting Robert—a lie as outrageous as it was frightening.

She saw a look of displeasure cross Andrea Stone's face as she glanced at them once again and then stood up.

"Doctor," she said, "do you have any reason to seriously *believe* that Mrs. Danse is the abuser here?"

"Objection."

"I'll allow it. Objection overruled."

"No. I have no real reason to believe that at all."

"Do you find it likely?"

"One can't be certain. Not without the boy's saying."

"But do you find it *likely*, Doctor?"

"Not really. No, I tend to doubt it."

"And her response to you. Isn't an angry response from a worried mother completely within the scope of what you'd call perfectly normal behavior under the circumstances?"

"I suppose it is, yes."

"I should think so. Thank you, Doctor."

"We call Lydia Danse, Your Honor."

There was never any question that she'd have to go through with this, but knowing that didn't make it any easier. She had nothing in her experience to compare it to. Both divorces had been relatively easy, uncontested. Now she felt a sick hollow empty feeling in her stomach and her hands were shaking as she walked to the witness stand, her mouth dry and sour-tasting. She asked for a glass of water and drank it down immediately.

She began to relax a little as she felt Owen more or less regain control of the situation, questioning her carefully but gently about Robert's symptoms in general and his behavior up to the night he'd come home from Arthur's fouled and hurting. He referred to the notepad frequently. He took a good deal of time going over the once-mysterious knees-to-chest position, getting her to describe it in detail and estimate its frequency and finally, over Wood's objections, establishing its meaning.

"You had seen this position before, then, is that right, Mrs. Danse?"

"Yes"

"You had personal experience of this position?"

"Yes."

"Tell us what that experience was."

"With Arthur. It was Arthur's favorite position. When we were having sex together."

She felt herself flush.

"Anal sex?"

"Yes."

He took her through the night in question. Her discovery of what had happened, packing Robert up and taking him over to Cindy's, going to the bar and accusing Arthur to his face. And then the following day, taking Robert to see Bromberg and Hessler. When she got to the part about cleaning him up that night she began to cry, remembering her helpless pain for him. Otherwise she thought she got through it well enough and calmly.

And then Wood stood, smiling, and walked over.

"You were angry with your husband that night. Weren't you, Mrs. Danse?"

"Yes."

"Furious?"

"I suppose so, yes."

"Hysterical, would you say?"

"No. Angry."

"And you let him know that you were angry in no uncertain terms."

"Yes I did."

"In public. At his bar."

"Yes."

"Within earshot of others?"

"I wasn't paying attention to who might be listening, Mr. Wood."

"Understandable. As you say—you were furious."

"Objection." It didn't come from Owen but from Andrea Stone.

And Judge Burke seemed annoyed with her.

"Ms. Stone," he said, "you are not Mrs. Danse's lawyer, you are *Robert's* lawyer. Try to keep that in mind, all right?"

"*I* object, Your Honor," said Sansom.

"Fine. I'll sustain that objection. Please move on, Mr. Wood."

"You didn't mind making a scene, then."

"You didn't see my son, Mr. Wood. If you had, you'd know that making a scene or not making a scene was not something you'd consider at the time."

"It didn't bother you, Mrs. Danse, that you were accusing your husband of a terrible, heinous crime there in his place of business, at the establishment in which he earns his living, in front of patrons, possibly friends, even business associates?"

"He raped my son, Mr. Wood!"

He smiled again. "That is what we're here to determine, isn't it? Were you speaking loudly?"

"To Arthur?"

"Yes."

"I don't know. I suppose so. Probably."

"Loud enough so that others might easily have heard you."

"Yes. Probably."

He paused, looking at his notes.

"Do you recall saying to him at that time that from now on you were denying him visitation?"

"I recall saying that he was never going to see Robert alone again, not if I could help it. And that if he wanted visitation he could see Robert while I was in the room and only then."

"But that was not your legal arrangement with him at the time, was it?"

"No."

"Were you aware that in denying him visitation you might be breaking a law?"

"Excuse me?"

"Were you aware that by denying your husband the right to see his son without a hearing on the matter or at the very least, a report to the DCYS, that you were breaking the law?"

"I did report it. The following day."

"But not at that time. Not at the time you told him he was never going to see his son alone again if you could help it. Am I correct?"

"Yes, but . . ."

"Are you willing to comply with the decision of this court, Mrs. Danse?"

"Of course I am."

"Even if the court's decision is to allow my client to see his son exactly as he had been, alone, unsupervised?"

"That's not possible."

"Certainly it is, Mrs. Danse. This hearing isn't concluded yet. Anything's possible."

"How could you . . . how could anyone allow that when a man molests his child?"

"Again, that's not been proven. My question to you is, simply, could you comply with the decision of this court if that decision was to allow visitation to continue according to the previous terms of your divorce? Please, just say yes or no."

She felt trapped, spinning dizzy and out of control with fear and anger. She knew what the bastard was trying to do to her yet she felt powerless to stop it. Where was Sansom?

Where was *anybody*?

"Shall I repeat the question for you, Mrs. Danse?"

"That man will *not* hurt my son again, Mr. Wood!"

It was the first she'd looked directly into Arthur's eyes since he'd pointed a gun at her from inside his car. This was not the same man. The man she saw now was bland, quiet, at rest. Incomprehensible.

"Meaning that you would not comply?"

"How can you even ask me that? Do you have any children of your own? *What kind of man are you?*"

"Mrs. Danse," said Burke, "I'm instructing you to answer Mr. Wood's question. Answer it with a simple yes or no. Could you comply with *any* order handed down by the court, however disagreeable to you personally, or could you not?"

She saw a way. Maybe. A possibility.

The thinnest of thin ice.

"I don't know," she said.

"You don't know?" said Burke.

"Asked and answered, Your Honor," said Andrea Stone. Burke ignored her.

"You realize, Mrs. Danse, that your answer runs perilously close to being in contempt of court."

"I'm sorry, Your Honor," she said. "I have nothing but respect for this court and I don't mean it to be. I only hope that you'll find . . . that everyone will do the right thing here. I hope to god that I'll never have to make that decision. Ever."

The judge studied her. Don't back off, she thought. And don't exactly fight him either. Meet his eyes. Be careful.

Burke sighed. "All right, Mrs. Danse. We won't press this any further at this time. Mr. Wood, please continue."

Wood seemed to feel he'd won his point. She wasn't sure. Burke was hard to read.

"This position you've made so much about. Did your husband ever force this position on you, Mrs. Danse?"

"Physically, you mean?"

"Yes."

"No. Not physically."

"He never raped you then, did he?"

"No."

"But you think he raped your son. Forcing him to use the same position."

"Yes. I do."

"Because your son would assume that position or a similar position."

"Yes."

"How do you know he wasn't just copying what he saw?"

"Excuse me?"

"How do you know your son wasn't just copying a position he'd seen you and Mr. Danse use while the two of you were making love together?"

"Robert never saw us have sex together."

"Never? Surely you mean not to your knowledge."

"I mean never."

"How could you possibly know?"

"I'd know."

"You consider yourself a good mother, don't you?"

"Yes, I do," she said.

"You're considerate of Robert's feelings, aren't you?"

"I think so. Yes."

"What about Robert's feelings the day following this . . . incident you speak of?"

"What do you mean?"

Suddenly Wood went all theatrical, heaving a sigh and pacing the floor with the appearance of a man who had finally grown impatient with some recalcitrant naughty child.

"Come on, Mrs. Danse. You pull him out of his house in the middle of the night, you leave him somewhere while you go out and have a public row with your husband, then in the morning you pile him into a car for a round of visits to doctors' offices, a proctologist he's never met before, an unscheduled visit to his psychotherapist, all of them asking questions, prodding him for information—*about his relations with his father*—then that night there's Ms. Stone here asking him some more questions. It goes on all day long! Is putting him through all that what you'd call being considerate of his feelings? Wouldn't you say that this particular day was a little *upsetting* to him?"

"Of course it was. But it couldn't be helped. How else was I supposed to . . .?"

"It couldn't be helped? You couldn't have waited one day or two days after this alleged incident for things to return to normal for the boy? You had to put him through this instantly?"

"That was my attorney's advice. To get this done right away."

"But you *wanted* to get it done right away, didn't you? Personally you wanted to."

"I thought it best."

"So the answer is yes?"

"I personally thought it best to get it done right away." Wood sighed again and shook his head.

"Was Robert crying when he left Dr. Hessler's office?"

"A little. It didn't last. A few moments."

"And when he left Dr. Bromberg's office?"

"No."

"And that night? After the interview with Ms. Stone?" She looked at Andrea Stone. She couldn't lie. Not with her sitting there.

"He may have been crying during the interview, I don't know. I thought he might have. But not afterwards. Not when I put him to bed."

"So this was a long day of interview after interview, basically a wonderful, happy trail of tears for Robert, wasn't it?"

"Objection."

Finally Owen Sansom was actually doing something. But this was a question she *wanted* to answer. Because how could you compare that day to the previous one with his father? How could you compare what she'd put him through to what Arthur had been doing to him that day and all along before that? You couldn't and it wasn't fair.

"Sustained," the judge said.

"Isn't it true that this is *personal* with you, Mrs. Danse? That you'd have done pretty much the same *without* the advice of counsel?"

"I don't know what you mean by personal. But I'd probably have proceeded along the same lines on my own."

"Even down to the proctologist?"

"I'm a nurse, Mr. Wood. I'd probably have thought of that, yes."

"A proctologist. Whose examination caused your son to come out of his office crying."

"Yes, Mr. Wood. Dr. Hessler was very good with Robert. Very kind. But as I said, it couldn't be helped under the circumstances.

None of this was comfortable."

"What if I said it *could* have been helped, Mrs. Danse, that the actions we're describing here are the actions of an angry, vengeful, probably hysterical woman who did not take the time or bother for one instant to consider her son's feelings in the matter, who did not . . ."

"Objection!" said Andrea Stone. A pencil clattered to her desk.

"Objection," said Sansom.

She thought, better late than never.

Burke sustained it.

"No further questions for this witness at this time," Wood said.

"We rest," said Sansom.

They adjourned for lunch and Lydia and Sansom walked two blocks down to a small family-run greasy spoon across the street from the courthouse. It was a beautiful New Hampshire day, one where you could feel spring not far away. The air felt cool and crisp to the lungs but the sun was so warm and bright that she took off her coat and folded it over her arm as they walked. It felt wonderful after the stale cloying heat of the courthouse.

They ordered eggs and coffee.

"What's going on?" she said.

"What do you mean?"

"With you. What the hell's happening, Owen?"

His smile looked pained. He let his spoon drift slowly through his coffee. "I guess I wasn't exactly one hundred percent in there sometimes, was I?" he said.

"One hundred *percent*?"

"I don't think he hurt you at all, though."

"It didn't feel that way where I was sitting, Owen. I felt pretty damn pushed around up there. Jesus! He came *that close* to getting me to admit I wouldn't let Arthur see Robert, even if it meant going to *jail* over it, for God's sakes!"

"There was nothing I could do with that. Honestly. They were all perfectly admissible questions."

He seemed to slump forward as though finally admitting something to himself he'd have preferred not to.

"Look," he said. "I'm sorry. Really. I am."

She believed him. For what it was worth. He stared down at his coffee.

"You know nothing about me," he said. "And usually that's the way it's supposed to be."

She waited for him to go on.

"A week and a half ago my wife went into County General. She had some intestinal blockage, that's all. We thought that basically it was going to be a whole lot of nothing. Then she developed fluid . . . in the lungs . . ."

"God. She went wet on you."

"Right. Wet. That's the word the nurses used. Somebody screwed up. For three minutes she was off relief systems and that's how long it took for her to go into a coma. It lasted nearly all last week. Fever of a hundred and two through the whole goddamn thing. When she finally came out of it Saturday the fever had . . . her mind was . . ." He shook his head. "Shit. I've been going over there every night. I sit there and I talk to her, trying to get her to remember the smallest things. How to use a knife and fork. How to shuffle a deck of cards. I don't even think she knows who's sitting there. I show her pictures of her mother and father, her brothers and her sister. I don't think she knows them either."

He pushed the coffee away from him across the table and looked at her.

"It's no excuse. I know that. I'm really sorry. I've got to do better by you and Robert in there and I will do better. It's just hard to put it away, you know? To find a place to put it all."

"I know."

On impulse she covered his hand with her own and left it there a moment aware of the heat of the palm of her hand against the cool of the back of his and then she removed it. Their food arrived.

There was no replacing him now. There wasn't time. They both knew that. She'd have to trust that he could do what he said he could do. Put his personal life aside and fight for her. It wasn't fair but they were committed.

They ate in silence.

Jake Whalen, Arthur's barman, was his opening witness.

He'd got himself a haircut that in her opinion was actually

too short to look particularly good on him and a brand-new suit. Probably Arthur had picked the suit out. Jake was a good-looking guy and popular with the women but he was never much of a dresser.

He didn't look at all happy to be there.

She'd always got along well with Jake and thought him a pretty decent sort, despite the occasional inappropriate sidelong glances, so probably that was why. He was here because Arthur wanted him here, but he didn't have to love it.

Wood got his name, address, and occupation out of the way and then went right to the night she'd stormed into the bar.

"Did she talk to you?"

"No."

"To anyone else?"

"No. Just to Mr. Danse."

"And she was speaking loudly? Loudly enough so that you could hear?"

"I heard some of it, yes."

"What exactly did you hear her say?"

"I heard her accuse him of doing something to her son, to Robert."

"Doing what?"

Jake looked very uncomfortable. She almost felt sorry for him.

"Do you remember the exact words she used, Jake?"

"She said he was butt-fucking him."

"Butt-fucking? And she said this loudly?"

Jake nodded. "Yeah. Pretty loud."

"And what did he say?"

"He said she was crazy. He said he'd never laid a hand on Robert."

"And did she *act* crazy, Mr. Whalen?"

"Objection," said Sansom. "The witness is not a psychoanalyst."

"I'll rephrase it, Your Honor," Wood said. "How would you characterize her attitude toward him at the time?"

"She was mad. Real mad at him."

"Violent, would you say?"

"She didn't hit him or anything if that's what you mean but I guess it looked like maybe she wanted to."

"Where were they standing? Were they standing close together?"

"They were about three or four feet to one side of me over across the bar. Yeah, they were close together. I mean, she was sort of right in his face."

"Shouting. Swearing at him."

"Yes."

"What else did she say, Jake?"

"I remember her saying she was never letting him see Robert by himself again. That she'd have to be there if he did. Mr. Danse said she couldn't do that. She said something like you just go ahead and watch me. Then he asked if Robert had actually said anything about Mr. Danse doing something bad to him."

"And what was her response?"

"She said he didn't have to say something. Like she just knew."

"So she didn't actually say that Robert had told her *anything*."

"Not that I heard."

"Jake, do you *like* Lydia Danse?"

"Sure."

"So you're not here to do her any personal harm, are you? I mean, you have no problems of your own with her do you? No grudges? No mistreatment?"

"No. I always thought Mrs. Danse was a pretty nice person."

"Thank you, Mr. Whalen."

Sansom stood and approached him.

"Mr. Whalen, you've said that Mrs. Danse was very angry. Was Mr. Danse angry too?"

"Not at first. He got real angry though."

"Did you hear him say, 'I'll see you in court, you bitch'? Or words to that effect?"

"Something like that, yes."

"And when he said that, was he in *her* face, as you put it?"

Jake smiled. "I guess he was, yeah."

"So what you were listening to was two people shouting, swearing, am I right? Not just one."

"Right, yes."

Wood followed Jake Whalen with someone Lydia knew only slightly—Harold Milford—a short stocky man she'd seen sometimes at the bar. Milford owned a siding business in town. As it happened he'd been sitting next to them that night. Wood took him through pretty much the same paces he'd taken Whalen. In the beginning, anyhow.

"She was acting hysterical," Milford said.

Sansom objected. The man was not a doctor. Burke sustained him.

"Did you hear Mr. Danse respond to all these accusations?"

"I did."

"What did he say?"

"He said this was all just something she'd come up with because she was angry about the terms of their divorce. That if she'd wanted more money she should have just said so and he'd have given it to her."

"And did she deny that money was her motive?"

"No."

"And then did she at any time threaten Mr. Danse?"

"Yes, she did. I heard her say that if he ever came near Robert again she'd fucking kill him. Those were her words. That he was a sick man and if he ever came near Robert she'd fucking kill him." He turned to the judge's bench. "Sorry, Your Honor," he said.

"That's all right, Mr. Milford."

Owen Sansom looked at her.

"He's lying," she whispered. *"Jesus, Owen, I never . . .!"*

"It's okay," he said.

"Your witness."

Sansom got up slowly and walked over to Milford and then stood there a moment gazing at him. The impression was of someone who was contemplating a tree and wondering if it was worth bothering to climb it. Lydia felt frozen to her seat. How damaging was this lie and could he shake it? She thought back to their conversation over lunch. He'd come back well since then. But she knew that Sansom was hurting.

"Mr. Milford, you said that Mrs. Danse didn't deny that money was a factor in this, correct?"

"Yes."

"Did she affirm it?"

"She just ignored the money comment, am I right?"

"Pretty much, yes."

"And you say she threatened to kill Mr. Danse."

"Yes."

"And you were sitting at the far end of the bar close to them and you could hear them."

"Yes."

"They were yelling at one another at this point, true? So that it was pretty easy for you to hear them?"

"It was very easy. Sure."

"So presumably others heard her threaten Mr. Danse as well. Wouldn't that be reasonable to assume?"

"I . . . well, sure. I guess so."

Milford seemed to feel he was on ground that was not quite so firm anymore. He was right.

"You're an old friend of Arthur Danse's, aren't you?"

"Sure. I've known Arthur a long time."

"Are you good enough friends to lie for him?"

"Am I . . . hell no, I don't lie for anybody!"

Milford puffed up, full of indignation. Sansom only nodded.

"That's good, Mr. Milford. Because a lie in court can result in perjury charges—as I'm sure you're aware. And I'm sure you're aware that I can call in others who were at the bar that night and ask them what *they* heard. So I want to be absolutely sure of one thing here. I want to be absolutely certain that you heard Mrs. Danse use the word 'kill.' Before I ask anybody else about it. That it wasn't some other word. So, was that the word she used? 'Kill'?"

His bluff was working. The little man looked worried.

"I heard . . ." he said. "I'm pretty sure I heard her say that, yeah."

He was trying to have it both ways. Sansom wasn't letting him.

"Pretty sure?"

"Yes."

"But not completely sure?"

"Listen, they said a lot of things."

"Who was sitting next to you at the bar that night, Mr. Milford? I'd like a name, please."

"I didn't know the guy. Sorry."

"How about somebody sitting near you, then. A few seats away, maybe."

"I don't know."

"You didn't know *anybody* in the bar that night? Not a soul? How about Jake Whalen, the bartender? You knew him, didn't you?"

"Sure, but . . . look, Jake was there. He might've heard, he might not. But the others . . . hey, I wasn't paying attention. I was there to have a couple of drinks, that's all."

Sansom gave him a look of disgust.

"No more for this witness, Your Honor," he said.

That night she was struck by a cold unreasoning fear.

She kept hearing Wood's words. Judge Burke's words.

Could you comply with the decision of the court if that decision were to continue visitation rights according to the previous terms of your divorce?

That meant private visitation.

That meant Robert raped again.

And no way for her to stop it.

Anything's possible.

She tried listening to music over a glass of white wine, hoping it would relax her and calm her down but music only seemed to open up her heart, to make her feel soft and yielding, and she needed to be hard now and not feel sorry for herself or Sansom or his wife or even for Robert because sorry wasn't the answer. Winning was the answer.

The alternative was unthinkable.

The wine helped a little. She poured another and got into bed. She lay sipping it in the half-dark, staring out her window into moonlight. The sheets felt cool and soothing against her legs.

Could it happen?

Could they actually do such a thing?

When the telephone rang it didn't really surprise her. It was as though the telephone's ringing was going to be part of the answer for her.

"Hello?"

"I didn't think it went all that well for you today, Lyd. Did you?"

"Arthur, I don't need this. What do I have to do, change my phone number?"

"Don't bother. I won't be doing this often. I was just curious. So. What do you think?"

"It doesn't matter what I think."

"Sure it does. It matters to me."

"I can't imagine why."

"Because if you thought it was going badly for you, you might do something stupid. That's why."

"Stupid like what, Arthur?"

"Like packing Robert up and trying to make a run for it. That wouldn't be smart."

"You think?"

"Yes, and you know why? Because you have to work, Liddy. You're a nurse—and nurses need to be registered. So no matter where you went, no matter what state or how far away, I'd find you. You realize that? And I could probably get you thrown in jail when I did. I mean, what a great guarantee of your basic stability, you know?"

"I'm happy you're happy, Arthur. Now do you mind if I go back to bed?"

"No problem. What're you wearing, Lyd?"

"Fuck you, Arthur. Sheet metal."

She hung up.

The call made her angry. And not just his last comment.

Am I really that easy to read? she wondered.

Because she'd considered running.

And rejected it for exactly the reason Arthur cited. It boiled down to money. If she had money of her own she might have run already.

But he was right. She had to work. And nursing was the only way she knew of keeping them both somewhere above the poverty line. There wasn't much choice but to stick it out in the courts and pray it would all come out for the best.

Could they really be so insane as to give him what he wanted? Unlimited, unsupervised visitation?

And if they did—what was she going to do?

It took two more glasses of wine to put her to sleep

Restless sleep. Full of unremembered dreams.

The kind that provide no clues and answer no questions.

TWENTY-THREE

THE HEARING: THIRD DAY

They led with a pair of character witnesses, local businessmen who did nothing more than establish that Arthur was reliable in financial matters and business practices. Neither Stone nor Sansom even bothered to question them.

Next was Arthur's mother.

She hadn't seen much of Ruth since the divorce except around Christmas time and she certainly hadn't missed her. Even decked out in her Sunday best—again, she suspected, selected by Arthur—there was something basically unattractive about the woman and always had been, some meanness of spirit that worked its way through her flesh like a subtle but distinct aroma.

She's give her this much, though—she was loyal.

"My boy wouldn't hurt a soul," she said. "If you ask me it's nonsense. And he sure wouldn't hurt somebody *that* way, let me tell you. My Arthur's had more nice girlfriends over the years than you could count on your hands and toes. Fact is I used to confuse the names of 'em."

"Thank you, Mrs. Danse," Wood said. "Nothing further."

"Mr. Sansom?"

"Nothing for this witness, Your Honor."

He looked better today, she thought. Tired. But that haunted look was gone.

"I have a few questions for Mrs. Danse, Your Honor," said Andrea Stone, "purely of a formal nature."

"Proceed, Ms. Stone."

"Mrs. Danse," she said, "when I visited you at home you indicated to me that, in the event that the court should find for neither Arthur *nor* Lydia Danse in this matter, you would be willing to offer Robert legal adoption. Is that still your position and your husband's position?"

"Absolutely."

"Your husband's too?"

"Absolutely."

"And would you be able to comply with the court's instructions regarding visitation?"

"How do you mean?"

"Well, suppose the court said Lydia Danse was allowed to visit Robert twice a week, take him on vacations, have him for a given number of weekends every month, that sort of thing. Would you be all right with that?"

"Sure I would. She's his mother. Whatever I might think about her and what she's doing to my boy personally have no bearing on it."

"And then suppose the court *limited* Arthur's visitations. Suppose the judge ruled that Arthur could only see Robert under structured, supervised conditions. Or even permitted no visitation at all."

She hesitated only a moment. But Lydia wondered if she was the only one in the room who was able to recognize the sly secret look that passed over her face and then was gone. She wondered if you had to have seen it before—as she had many times—to notice it.

"Well, I have to be honest," she said. "I wouldn't like it. I wouldn't think it was fair to Arthur. But if that's what you folks decided then I'd be duty-bound to honor the law, and that's what I'd do."

"Thank you, Mrs. Danse. Nothing further."

"We call Arthur Danse, Your Honor."

She studied him as he turned to face them on the witness stand. If I were the judge, she thought, would I be inclined to believe this man?

I might. Dammit, he looks good.

His face contrived to show nothing other than to register the seriousness of the moment—kind of intelligent concern. No guilt, no shame. No nervousness. The face of a man who wished nothing more than to clear this up once and for all and leave it behind him. She decided he'd missed his calling. The camera would have loved

Arthur. He met her eyes for a moment and didn't seem to need to look away.

Wood made quick work of the preliminaries. So that the lies and half-lies weren't long in coming.

"Mr. Danse," he said, "can you describe for us in your own words the events of January eleventh of this year?"

"Yes." He leaned forward intently. "I picked up my son at his mother's house at around noon. We drove to the McDonald's out on 93 for lunch. Robert likes the Chicken McNuggets there, though I try to keep our visits down to one or two a month. We ate in the car. After that we drove to Ellsworth, near where my parents live. We went hunting. I'd just bought a brand-new shotgun—a Remington over-and-under—and I wanted to give it a try."

"Robert didn't have a gun, though, did he?"

"No. He's got a couple of years yet before I'd consider letting him handle a weapon."

The responsible family man. Sure.

"How long were you out there hunting?"

"I'd say about two and a half hours. I think it was about three-thirty by the time we got back to the car. Something like that. I could see Robert was getting pretty tired and I'd managed to bag a rabbit, so a couple of hours out there was plenty."

"And then what did you do?"

"I had some business to take care of so we drove back to my house and Robert watched a movie on HBO and then played one of the Sega Genesis games I keep for him over there, while I got to the paperwork. And I guess we both lost track of time. Because the next thing I knew it was quarter after six and I thought, oh my god, I was supposed to have had him home fifteen minutes ago already. She's going to be furious."

"She?"

"Robert's mother."

"Why didn't you call? To say you were going to be late?"

"I tried. The line was busy. So I just hustled him out into the car and got him over there as fast as I could."

"Mr. Danse, did you notice if Robert appeared to be in any discomfort at all while you were driving him back to his mother's house?"

"Yes, I did. He seemed . . . antsy. Like he was having a hard time just sitting there in the car seat. And I remember that once we hit a pothole that was pretty deep and my head practically hit the roof even though I had my seat belt on. So I looked at Robert to make sure he was okay. He had this odd kind of look on his face. Like he was hurting. Though he also had his seat belt on too."

"And did you ask him what was wrong?"

"Yes."

"What did he say?"

"He said nothing was wrong. That he was just worried that his mom was going to be mad at him and punish him for us being so late. I reassured him. I told him it was my fault and I'd tell her so. So he didn't have to worry."

"Mr. Danse, when you were doing your paperwork, were you sitting in the same room as Robert?"

"No. I was in the study. Robert was in the living room."

"For about how long, approximately?"

"About two hours, maybe a little longer."

"And were you aware of him getting up and going into the bathroom at any time?"

"Yes. To get to the bathroom from the living room in my house you have to walk right past the study. He came in after the movie was done. I asked him how it was. He said it was pretty good. Something about killer clowns from outer space. We laughed at that. Then he went on in the direction of the bathroom and I went back to work."

"Were you aware of him coming out of the bathroom again?"

"Not really, no. I was pretty absorbed in what I was doing."

"Mr. Danse, did you sexually abuse your son that day?"

"No. Absolutely not."

"And have you *ever* abused your son, Mr. Danse? Sexually or otherwise?"

"God, no. I'm amazed that I'm even being asked a question like that. Robert is . . ."

His brow furrowed. His chin fell to his chest and he slowly shook his head. When he looked up again his eyes were full of tears.

"Robert is the single most important thing in my life," he said. "I would never hurt him. Never."

You bastard, she thought.

"Do you have any idea then, Mr. Danse, why Lydia Danse should be bringing this charge against you now?"

"Objection," said Sansom. "Calls for speculation."

"I'm going to allow it, Mr. Sansom. I think the witness's opinion on the matter is relevant."

"The only way I can think to explain it," Arthur said, "is that she's never forgiven me that the marriage didn't work. To say I'm surprised is the understatement of the year. I'd thought our divorce was amicable. Now I guess it wasn't. Not from her point of view, anyway."

He looked at her directly, unflinchingly.

"Lydia," he said, "I swear—I'm sorry. I really am."

"Objection," said Sansom.

"Sustained. Strike that," said Burke. "Do you have any further questions of this witness, Mr. Wood?"

"No, Your Honor."

"Mr. Danse," said Owen Sansom, "I believe you just told us that you noticed in the car that Robert was acting as though he had a hard time sitting there, and that then when you hit this pothole you thought he was actually hurting. Am I right?"

"Yes."

"And you asked him what was wrong and he said nothing, that he was only concerned about being punished by his mother for being late."

"That's right."

"And you believed him on this?"

"I didn't see any reason not to. Yes, I guess I did believe him."

"Didn't you say you thought he was actually *hurting*? *Physically* hurting?"

"Yes."

Sansom was sweating. She could see it from here and so could the judge. She knew the effort this was costing him with what was going on in his own life, but she thought that so far he was managing to do this right.

"And isn't there an obvious difference between what a person would look like if he were simply worried about the loss of a few privileges, say, as punishment for being late, and what he'd look like if he were physically in pain?"

"Speculation, Your Honor. My client's neither a doctor nor a trained psychologist."

"Sustained."

"Let me put it another way, then. Why did you so quickly dismiss the notion that his discomfort was physical, after seeming to observe exactly that?"

"I believed what he told me."

"You observed what appeared to be a physical discomfort in your son, and then dismissed it, said to yourself, fine, no problem, he's just worried about his mother punishing him for being late—you dismissed these observations simply because you believed what he told you. Is that correct?"

"Asked and answered, Your Honor."

"This conversation didn't occur at all, did it Mr. Danse? Nor these 'observations.'

"Objection. Argumentative."

"Sustained. Please, Mr. Sansom, get on with it."

"What sort of paperwork were you doing in your office that day, Mr. Danse?"

Arthur shrugged. "Bills. Orders. Shipment records. The usual."

"And were these very . . . engaging?"

He smiled. "I wouldn't say *engaging*. Pretty dull stuff, actually."

"But they were absorbing enough so that you never heard Robert leave the bathroom. All these boring bills and orders had that much of your attention."

"Sure they're boring. But they still take concentration."

"Were you aware of hearing the toilet flush? Water running in the sink? The bathroom door opening and closing?"

"No. Not really."

"You have hardwood floors over there, don't you?"

"Yes."

"Was Robert wearing shoes?"

"I don't remember."

"But this is a hall we're talking about, correct?"

"Yes."

"What else is down that hall?"

"Excuse me?"

"What else is down the hall aside from the bathroom?"

"There's a deck leading out through a door to the backyard, and then if you turn the corner and go around the other way you're in the dining room and then beyond that in the kitchen."

"So you don't really know that he went to the bathroom at all that day, do you? You heard nothing. Saw nothing. He might have been going to the deck, or to the dining room, or to the kitchen."

"He was jiggling."

"He was what?"

"He was jiggling. Standing there jiggling. You know, the way kids do. When they've got to go to the bathroom."

"So you assume he went to the bathroom because he was jiggling."

"Yes."

"You didn't tell us that earlier, though, did you?"

"It didn't occur to me."

"Isn't it true that it didn't occur to you because this is just another *lie*, Mr. Danse? Like your conversation with Robert in the car and your observations in the car?"

"Absolutely not."

"Did Lydia Danse ever tell you or give you any reason to believe that she was unhappy with the terms of her divorce prior to this incident?"

"No."

"Then why would she now?"

"I don't know."

"Mr. Danse, you're aware that there are penalties for perjury, right?"

"Yes."

"Good. Then I'll ask you once again. Did you, on that day or on any other day, sexually molest your son, Robert Danse?"

"Listen . . ."

"Yes or no. *Did you?*"

"If you don't believe me, why don't you just ask him? Ask Robert. No, I did not. Ask my son."

Wood requested a sidebar and the three lawyers approached the bench. Whatever they were talking about went on for a while and, Burke aside, drew heat from all of them. Finally Burke said something and they turned away.

As he returned to their table Owen Sansom was shaking his head.

"What? What's happening?" she asked him.

"We'd like to recall Lydia Danse to the stand, Your Honor," Wood said.

"That's what's happening," said Sansom. "Try not to strangle him, all right? Try to stay cool up there."

Cool was not the operative word. She felt frozen. Afterwards she could barely remember walking across the room to the witness chair and sitting down and then being reminded that she was still under oath. It was as though something had locked down inside her, frozen into gear like a cog on a wheel that still ought to have been spinning.

Wood didn't waste a minute.

"You stated earlier," he said, "that you didn't know if you could comply with any order that would permit my client free and unrestricted access to Robert. I'm talking about perfectly normal visitation rights. You've had time to think it over, and we're wondering now what your position is on this."

"My position?"

"Yes."

She wasn't stupid. There were danger signs everywhere.

She knew what he was after. She just couldn't believe that Judge Burke was allowing it.

Careful, she thought. There's got to be some way to deal with this.

"My position is that my ex-husband is a rapist," she said.

Wood looked stricken. It was pure phony melodrama, playing for the judge. But she thought maybe it actually might give her an opening. Maybe she could put him off balance for a change.

"Is it the *word* that bothers you, Mr. Wood?" she said. "Maybe you'd prefer something like 'morally challenged'?"

"Unresponsive, Your Honor."

"Please answer the question, Ms. Danse," said Burke.

It hadn't worked. She'd have to scramble for some other way. She needed time.

Think.

"I'm sorry, Your Honor. What was the question again?"

"What is your position regarding Arthur Danse receiving free and unrestricted visitation rights, if that should be the decision of this court?" Wood said.

"That he absolutely shouldn't have them and that the court shouldn't order it. Not under any circumstances whatsoever."

"But if that should be the *case*, Ms. Danse."

"I don't believe it will be, Mr. Wood."

"But if it *is*."

"Mr. Wood is badgering the witness, Your Honor!" said Sansom.

"Overruled. The witness will please respond."

Get control, she thought. Tear it off him. Tear it away from him. One last time. Rage simmered hard in her just below the surface. *Use it. But get control.* Turn this around on the son of a bitch.

"You're asking me, Mr. Wood," she said, "if I could comply with an order that would give a child molester, a rapist, access to an eight-year-old boy who also happens to be my son. Is that right? I don't understand. Why would you want to do that?"

He smiled as though to say, *pretty good*, and then covered it immediately.

He sighed dramatically. "Ms. Danse, your ex-husband, my client, is not a rapist until this court *finds* him a rapist. Hasn't everyone made that clear to you from the beginning?"

"Yes. But your client's sexual proclivities ought to be clear to you by now too, shouldn't they?"

Wood turned to the bench, arms spread wide, imploring. "Your Honor . . ."

Burke leaned down to her.

"Ms. Danse," he said, "the issue here is strictly a question of compliance with the law. Mr. Wood is attempting to determine your willingness to uphold the law as a citizen of this county and this state, as that law is handed down to you. We are not now addressing the question of what Mr. Danse may or may not have done to your son. We are not addressing his guilt or innocence. Only this single issue. So I am ordering you now to answer Mr. Wood's question with a simple yes or no. Could you comply with any judgment the court may arrive at in this matter, *whatever that judgment might be?*"

You're not going to scream, she thought—though she wanted to out of sheer frustration. And you're not going to cry. She looked at Owen Sansom. She thought she'd never seen a man look quite so tired, and certainly never a lawyer look quite so sad.

She looked at Andrea Stone. Her eyes seemed hard and angry and compassionate all at once—angry at the unfairness of this and compassionate with her in its inevitability.

She drew herself up.

If this failed because of her, if they lost this now, she would have to find other ways.

"Not if it hurt Robert," she said. Her voice was clear and unbroken.

"No, Your Honor. Not if it hurt my son."

TWENTY-FOUR

CRIMINALS: SOME FOILED, SOME NOT

It was 5:45 and Duggan was nursing a headache that aspirin wouldn't budge, wishing he were already home an hour ago with Alice lying on the sofa in the living room while Alice fussed around him, getting hot towels for his forehead and cups of tea. She wouldn't bother him about being behind on the mortgage. She wouldn't complain about the work hours. Alice was great when you were sick. The mother-mode kicked in and everything was all of a sudden you name it, you got it.

He sure could wish for that.

But this arrest he had in front of him here was a doozy.

The guy's name was Elmo Lincoln—his mama had named him after Tarzan, no less. He'd held up a convenience store out on route 3A. Emptied the cash register, pointed his .22 pistol at the owner and told him to hand over his car keys. At some point the owner—a scared old guy of sixty-five with glasses thick as hubcaps—had managed to hit the silent alarm. But Elmo didn't know that. He went outside and started up the car.

Then realized he couldn't drive it.

The car was a '63 Chevy. Fully and lovingly restored. Cherry-red and polished to perfection.

With a manual shift.

And Elmo couldn't drive manual.

Realizing that made him mad at the owner so he went back inside and started yelling at the guy, what the fuck was he doing with a car that was practically older than he was, and Elmo knew the owner had another car, a real car, sitting somewhere the fuck around so where was it? He pulled the owner outside to look.

Elmo badgered the old guy and shook his pistol at him for ten whole minutes.

When Duggan arrived Elmo took one look at the squad car and then just dropped the gun into the dirt and shrugged.

"I coulda got away," he said.

No shit, Duggan thought.

Duggan was doing the paperwork on this idiot and musing through the dull throbbing headache on the amazing clarity of the criminal mind—*I coulda got away*—when the phone rang.

"I got another one here," Whoorly said.

"Oh shit. Where?"

"Canaan. Dumped her off the side of the road this time, but the coroner says the MO's right on the money. Raped, anally and vaginally, nail holes in the palms of her hands, beaten, burned . . ."

"And staked through the heart."

"You got it."

"This asshole's got women all fucked up with Dracula."

"What?"

"Nothing. He place the time of death yet?"

"Last night. Somewhere between three and four in the morning. You want the file?"

"I want the file."

He hung up the phone and wondered where Arthur Danse was last night.

He wondered how his custody hearing was going.

He wondered if it was maybe making him angry at somebody.

He filed away the great Elmo Lincoln auto-theft caper for tomorrow and got up to check it out.

He talked to the bailiff and then drove out to Arthur's place.

Arthur wasn't pleased to see him. He opened the door and rolled his eyes and said, "What, Ralph? I've had a long day."

"Not the days I'm interested in, Art. It's the nights."

"What?"

"Tell me how you spent last night, Art."

"Went to the restaurant, stayed until about ten and then came home, watched TV, and went to bed. Why?"

"All alone, I guess."

"I'm afraid so, yes."

Duggan peered in through the doorway. From what he could see the place was spotless, the furnishings practically Spartan.

"How 'bout inviting me in for a quick cup of coffee. I really could use one."

"Another time, Ralph. Like I said, it's been a hell of a day."

"Sure. How's the hearing going?"

"Fine."

"Must make you mad, doesn't it?"

"What?"

"I mean, mad at your wife. What's 'er name. Lydia. Hell, at women in general. I'd be mad."

"The important thing is winning."

"Think you will?"

"My lawyer says we will."

Duggan smiled. "Course, you know, her lawyer's telling her the same thing. Lawyers'll do that."

"Naturally. I have to go, Ralph. Really. I still have to get over to the restaurant yet tonight."

"I understand. G'night, Art. I'll stop by again sometime."

He shut the door and Duggan heard him throw the lock.

No alibi. But no way to bring him in either. And no good reason to search the place. He'd talk to some of the people over at The Caves tomorrow. Shake the tree. Maybe find out nothing. But maybe it would make Danse a little nervous, a little angry, help him slip somewhere. Right now he was a little too cocky for his own damn good.

He pointed the car back toward town and home and couch and Alice. The headache, he realized, was gone.

Maybe thinking about Danse behind bars had a tonic effect on him.

One slip and I'm on you like flies on dogshit, he thought.

He lit a Newport Lite. I bet I could even quit smoking.

Lydia woke to the sounds of screaming.

Robert, she thought, and was out of bed and halfway across her room when she realized that the sounds were coming from outside, not in. She crossed to the window.

In the moonlight she could see them, gray and colorless against the spiky grass, a cat and two dogs, the dogs of no particular breed but big, heavy, dwarfing the cat, the cat stuck between them not far away from a big blue spruce tree, hissing and clawing at them and backing away and then screaming again, trying to angle his way toward the safety of the tree, the dogs lunging repeatedly, snapping, not even barking, deadly serious, they were concentrated on a kill here—so concentrated it was scary. She could see their eyes wide and glinting like polished stones.

She flung open the window, found a shoe on the floor and threw it at them yelling *"get out of here!"* at the top of her lungs, not feeling the slightest bit silly about the cliché shoe, wanting the cat to live. Her aim was lucky and the shoe hit the bigger of the dogs at the shoulder and for a moment everything stopped except the cat started backing away the way they did, almost in slow motion. It was as though the dogs were waiting to see if more and bigger was forthcoming. A shoe or a boot wasn't going to do it. So more and bigger it would have to be.

Beside her on the wall there was a framed English sampler, *Remember Now Thy Creator In The Years Of Thy Youth, Hannah East, Aged 14, In The Year 1863*. She had bought it back in Boston when she was married to Jim. She pulled it off the wall and leaned out the window screaming "Fuckers! *Get! Out!*" and hurled it at them, wincing as it almost hit the cat and then smashed in front of him, glass flying, the dogs startled and the cat taking his advantage and dashing for the tree. And then up the tree.

Perched on a branch. Calmly looking down.

"Mom? What's . . ."

Robert was standing in the doorway, eyes almost as wide as the cat's had been.

Her heart was pounding.

She felt wonderful. Terrific.

She laughed. Wonderful, she realized, to finally find herself able to *do* something. Something positive.

Something that made a difference.

"It's all right," she said, smiling. "I just saved a kitty with somebody's old heirloom."

"What's an heirloom?"

"Come on. We'll go downstairs and get it off the lawn and I'll explain it to you over a glass of hot cocoa, okay?" She followed him down.

TWENTY-FIVE

FOURTH DAY: JUSTICE

He knew almost instantly how it was going to be. So did she, the bitch. He could see it on her face. The courtroom was silent, not a sound but Judge Burke's deep flat voice and the stenographer's fingers on the keys.

Arthur listened, and felt the power rise.

"I cannot find with absolute certainty that there has indeed been sexual abuse in this case," he said, "despite Dr. Hessler's remarks as to its probability, Dr. Bromberg's suspicions, or Ms. Danse's own contentions. Nor do I find that Robert's 'maybes' constitute compelling testimony. It seems to me that a troubled boy, as it has been well established by all who have interviewed him that Robert is indeed troubled, may have inadvertently or even intentionally harmed himself in this fashion. And it would be ill-advised for me to assume differently until further proof is provided or until Robert himself says in a far more clear and straightforward manner that he has indeed been abused by his father.

"That said, I must also admit that I am distressed by the mother's actions here."

He looked at Lydia.

"Ms. Danse, I'm sorry to tell you that I believe you've acted against Robert's interests in some very serious ways here. There is evidence of a kind of hysteria in your behavior. A tendency toward which you displayed, I believe, by marching into your ex-husband's bar and accusing him loudly in front of anyone who cared to listen. But more to the point, you have continued to insist on his guilt despite the lack of credible evidence against him. And in order to further those beliefs, in the course of a single day you paraded a troubled boy to a lawyer's office, a proctologist's office, a psychologist's office, and then encouraged yet another interview by Ms. Stone—all in the possibly paranoid suspicion that Mr. Danse had done something to your son that Robert wouldn't affirm he'd done nor that you'd had any concrete proof he'd done.

"If this is your notion of helping Robert, I don't share it. And I fear a recurrence of this kind of unstable behavior.

"Finally, I am *deeply* distressed and saddened at your stated unwillingness to adhere to the guidelines of law in this matter. Frankly, I have to wonder how you plan to bring up the boy, with this kind of an attitude. I see far too many youngsters in here as it is who couldn't care less about the law. It is and has always been part of the function of our court system in this country to promote respect for and compliance with the laws of society whatever they may be, and I would not be doing my duty as an officer of the court if I didn't take this into consideration here.

"Consequently, given your own stated recalcitrance in the matter of continuing unrestricted visitation by Mr. Danse, and given the absence of proof of the allegations against him, I am transferring custody of the child, Robert Danse, *to* Mr. Danse. I expect the three attorneys to work out a plan for visitation rights for the mother and submit that plan to me. And I expect, Ms. Danse, that you will proceed expeditiously to comply with this order of custodial transfer or else I will hold you in contempt of court, that I promise you. Dismissed."

The gavel rang in his ears like a sudden clap of thunder.

He was the storm. Unstoppable. The wind that blew them all away and out of here like autumn leaves. It was better than he'd ever expected. He shook his lawyer's cool smooth hand and smiled.

His son was his again.

TWENTY-SIX

CHANGE OF HEART

"I won't do it. I'm running. That's all there is to it. His school's two blocks away. I'm taking him out of there right now and we're getting out of here."

They were walking through the parking lot, Lydia flanked by Sansom and Andrea Stone. The day was warm and sunny. Her hands felt like ice.

"You don't want to do that, Lydia," Sansom said, "believe me. For God's sake, they'll *arrest* you. You'll go to jail. You think the courts are going to look at you any more favorably as a custodian for Robert with a jail sentence hanging over your head? You'd risk never seeing him again."

"Listen," said Andrea Stone, "I can buy us some time. Let me appeal the judge's decision as Robert's attorney and guardian ad litem. I can get him into a foster home within a day or two at most, and in the meantime . . ."

"A *foster* home?"

". . . and in the meantime I can go over Arthur's house with a fine-tooth comb, find reasons—*make* reasons if I have to—why Robert shouldn't stay there. You can hire an investigator, see what you can dig up on him. We can draw this out for a long time, believe me."

"She's right, Lydia. Do it our way. Do it through the system."

"The system stinks," she said.

She got to the car and fumbled the keys into the door, aware that they were watching her, as though they were afraid for her. Well, she was afraid for herself. And Robert.

She'd run if she had to.

She'd whore the streets.

For all their good intentions, fuck them. They were the system and the system was shit. The system was nothing but betrayal.

There was one more card to play.

"You sure you don't want me to drive you?" said Andrea Stone. "I'm fine," she said and started the car. "I'm going to Robert's school. I'll call you."

When she saw him at his desk through the window of the school-room door she almost cried, almost lost it. The class was silent. Taking a quiz. The shifting in seats. The scuffle of shoes. And that was all. She took a deep breath and walked on in.

He glanced up and saw her and she managed to smile at him and then whispered her intentions to Mrs. Youngjohn, who nodded—trying, she knew, not to show concern and not to pry. Mrs. Youngjohn walked over to Robert and spoke to him and pointed to his mother. He collected his books and quietly got up and she put a hand on his shoulder as she walked him out the door.

She knew he wanted to ask her what was going on, but he didn't dare—not here. There was something about the quiet of the empty hall which was denying him permission with each echoing footfall, urging him outside where it was possible to speak in the open air.

She led him to the car.

The air felt even warmer to her now. She was sweating. She felt empty inside, as though being with Robert had calmed her but somehow at the same time had blocked off all emotions but the simple feeling of being alive and in his presence.

She was aware of him staring at her.

She started the car and began to pull away.

"You going to tell me, or what?" he said. His voice was a little angry with her—and frightened.

She braked and turned to him and then turned off the ignition.

"The judge said that you have to go and stay with your father, Robert," she said.

She could think of no other way to do this than to say to him directly.

She was trying not to cry and she could see that so was he. She could feel the tension running through him electric with fear and uncertainty.

"When? For how long?"

He didn't understand. She had never hated anything more than this.

"Robert, the court said you have to go and *live* with him."

It was as though she'd slapped him. He flung himself back against the car door, he was halfway up on his knees. He looked like something trapped there.

"No!"

"Robert . . ."

"I won't! They can't make me! *Why won't you help me?*"

And now she *was* crying. Because it was true. She hadn't helped him. Not enough. Not nearly.

"Robert, I *can't* help you. None of us can. Not if you won't say what he does to you. Not if you won't tell."

"I'll tell! I swear I will! I *can't* go live with him! I can't."

He was terrified. Pressed back against the door and trembling, sobbing.

She slid over on the seat and reached for him, put her arms around him and held him, rocked him, both of them letting the tears come freely, her breast wet and warm with them, the musky scent of tears filling the car until finally after a good long while they subsided.

She whispered, "Why not before, Robert? I know you love your daddy but . . ."

"I don't love him. I *hate* him."

She looked into his eyes and saw that it was true. "Then why . . .?"

". . . going to kill you," he murmured into her blouse. He was clutching at the blouse in back, holding onto her like he wanted to burrow deep inside her.

"What? Say that again?"

And then it all came out in a rush.

"He had this rabbit, he killed it. He pulled off its skin and cut off its head and its feet and he said that's what he'd do to you if I told and I knew he wasn't kidding and that he'd do it because he hates you, really *hates* you and now I *am* telling and he'll . . ."

"Hey," she said, hugging him close.

His fear was a kind of ozone in the car and she felt she could barely breathe as what he'd said sunk in. She hugged him tighter.

So that was it.

He'd been telling the truth when he denied to her and to Andrea Stone that his father had threatened to hurt him. It was her he was protecting.

Not his father. Or himself.

He'd been doing what he thought he had to do all along. Protecting her life by coming within an inch of destroying his own.

"He's not going to kill me, Robert," she said. "He's not going to hurt me or you at all. I don't care what he said. He's a liar and a coward and he's never going to hurt either of us ever again."

He looked at her. *He wants to believe me*, she thought.

He almost—but not quite—does.

"Do you know how much I love you?" she said. "Do you know how brave I think you are? I love you, Robert. And we'll go through this the two of us together, and then we'll see. Then we'll see who does what to whom, okay? Okay, big guy?"

His smile wasn't much but at least it was there.

She smiled too. Because now there was something to do. Now there was somewhere to go with this.

She needed to get to Owen Sansom and Andrea Stone immediately.

Everything's changed now, she thought.

We sprung the trap.

We can beat this goddamn thing. We can win.

TWENTY-SEVEN

TRANSCRIPT

"Here's what we're going to do," Sansom told her on the phone. "We're going to drive him down to Concord. I know one of the police psychologists there. I've already spoken with Andrea and she knows another. She's arranging things with them as we speak. These guys are good, Lydia. We'll have him go through it with both of them, run it through twice, and we'll get it all on videotape. Let Edward Wood argue with *that*."

"God. Thank you, Owen."

"We'll be over in about an hour. Until then don't let him out of your sight, you hear me?"

"I won't."

She hung up. She looked out the window and saw that the sun had slipped behind a cloud. It was going to be hard for Robert, she thought, very hard. But to her mind the day was growing better and brighter by the second.

Concord, New Hampshire
February 25, 1995
4:45 P.M.

Excerpt from the transcript of a videotaped conversation between Lt. D. A. Sweeney, Ph.D., of the New Hampshire State Police and Robert Philip Danse, age eight, resident of 145 East Cedar Street, Plymouth, New Hampshire

Q: What do you call this part, right here? (Points to rag doll, penis area.)

A: The private parts.

Q: The what?

A: The private parts.

Q: The private parts. (Turns doll.) What would you call this part right here?

A: The rear.

Q: Now you told me that you didn't like your dad messing with you. Can you show me, using these dolls, what you mean? What he does to you?

A: He messes with me back here (pats buttocks, ignoring doll) with this (pats penis).

Q: He does what?

A: He messes with me back here with his privates.

Q: He messes with your rear with his privates? And who does this to you?

A: My dad.

Q: Your dad. And what's your dad's name?

A: Arthur Danse.

Q: Only your dad?

A: Uh-huh.

Q: Nobody else?

A: No.

Q: What else does he do? Can you tell me more?

A: Well . . . that's what he does. That's all he does.

Q: How does he mess with you, Robert? What do you mean by "messes" with you?

A: He puts his thing in. Back here.

Q: He puts it in? Puts it in where? Do you have a name for it?

A: Rear. (slightly inaudible)

Q: What?

A: The rear.

Q: He puts it in your rear. Is his thing hard or soft?

A: Hard.

Q: Hard. And does that hurt?

A: Yes.

TWENTY-EIGHT

THE GOOD NEWS AND THE BAD NEWS

"We can't release him to you."

Lieutenant Sweeney lit a cigarette and blew the smoke out away from her. They were standing in the gray hallway outside the cubicle where Robert had been interviewed. He was still inside and she could see him there sitting with Cindy, who'd come down with her to provide moral support.

"What do you *mean* you can't release him?" she said.

"Dammit, I was afraid of this," said Sansom. He looked at Andrea Stone, who sighed and shook her head. "Edward Wood called you, didn't he?"

"That's right," said Sweeney, "reminding us that the boy was under a court order giving custody to his father and removing it from his mother."

"*What are you saying?*" She felt dizzy. Like she'd fallen down into some insane eat-me drink-me rabbit hole again.

Was this ever going to end?

"Well, there's no way we're giving him back to his father. Not after this. But I can't hand him over to you, either, Mrs. Danse, much as I'd like to. I'm sorry. Best thing we can do now is put Robert up in a shelter for a few days, until the judge can view this evidence."

"A shelter? Jesus! Hasn't he been through enough?"

"Just for a couple of days. It won't be long, I promise."

"Oh, Christ. He's barely gone on two overnights in his entire life. Much less a shelter."

"Don't worry, Mrs. Danse. They're not exactly snake pits these days."

"Will I be able to see him?"

"Whenever you want."

"Will *Arthur* be able to see him?"

"Only under supervision. I'll make absolutely sure of it." She looked helplessly at Sansom and Andrea Stone. "Isn't there something . . .?"

"It's the law, Mrs. Danse," Sweeney said gently.

The law. She was beginning to hate the words.

She felt suddenly very tired. She sat down on wooden bench opposite the window. She could see Robert smiling inside the cubicle. Cindy had said something funny to him. It helped to have Cindy there.

"Give me a minute, will you? A minute alone, I mean. I just want to sit awhile. Then I'll go in and . . . I'll tell him."

"Take your time. We'll go get some coffee," Sweeney said. "If you need anything we'll be right down the hall here."

"Thank you. You're . . . very kind."

She saw the psychologist wince. Obviously he was dealing with his own feelings on this and didn't feel particularly kind.

Right now neither did she.

Arthur, she thought, you've got an enormous amount to pay for. Hurt all around.

She wondered if he'd ever pay.

Most of them didn't.

"He's evidently stated that you had anal intercourse with him on several occasions. Including the afternoon in question," said Wood. "He described it in detail. And what's this business about a rabbit?"

Arthur gripped the phone like he wanted to squeeze it in half. He was glad Wood wasn't around to see the face that stared back at him from the office minor. Wood wouldn't like what he was seeing there.

"He's lying," he said.

"It doesn't matter if he's lying. It only matters whether the psychologists, and ultimately the judge, believe him. And from what my source at the troopers' station tells me, he's been pretty convincing."

"Christ! So now what do we do?"

"We wait. I'll obtain a copy of the tape and look it over. There'll be another hearing in a couple of days to see if the judge wishes to amend his ruling. Just the lawyers present. I'll argue coercion on the part of your wife and—if, from the look of the tape, I feel I can get away with it—leading on the part of the psychologists. I'll talk to Robert and see if he might not recant his testimony. Then we see what happens. In the meantime it might be a good idea to go visit him. It'll look good for you. I'll call with the shelter's address first thing tomorrow. Try to get some sleep, Arthur. You looked awful in court this morning. No offense."

Wood said good night and hung up the phone.

He'd visit him all right, he thought. He'd visit the little bastard.

And the goddamn fucking little piece of gash was going to seriously wish he hadn't.

TWENTY-NINE

FOREST NIGHT

It had only happened to her because she'd done the right thing.

The party had lasted from nine till two in the morning and by then even though she was only nursing white wine spritzers she was really too high to drive, she didn't drink much, and because she came to the party alone and as usual was going to leave alone she decided it was better and wiser to walk back home—and she was over halfway there with nobody around anywhere when the man pulled up in his big black car opposite, going south to her north, and stopped the car and got out and walked over and pointed a gun at her and said, *get in.*

By now he'd raped her twice on the woodland floor at gunpoint and Marge Bernhardt was pleading for her life. It wasn't much of a life.

She knew that.

Four months ago nearly to the day the man she was going to marry was killed in his car, sideswiped by a drunken sixty-year-old man. She thought of it as murder. Dean was an electrician and made good money and they were going to have kids. Maybe two or three kids. They had already looked at a house. She'd never quite put herself back together since. Her life was work at Denny's and the gym after that and her three cats Beast and Vinni and Zoey and then at night reading or watching television.

She didn't date. She didn't party. Deciding to go to Mary's twenty-fifth birthday party was an aberration, an act of will compounded by longtime allegiance to her best and dearest friend, who had comforted her and kept her sane since the night they pulled Dean's blackened body, cut practically in half by the smashed-in driver's side door, out of his 1994 Mazda.

It wasn't much of a life but it could be more someday and now maybe it would never be anything, nothing, as Dean's had become nothing that night and she realized what that truly meant now and she pleaded with him.

She was tied by her wrists to the limb of an oak tree, each wrist tied separately to the limb for some reason and the lengths of rope slightly uneven so that she was standing canted on tiptoe and all she could think to say was *please please please* as she watched him in the moonlight. He was walking back and forth in front of her looking up, searching for something, and the gun was in his pocket but instead he held a knife which he'd taken from the shoulder bag.

He reached over her head to the left and cut a branch away and then stripped it of leaves using his gloved left hand. The gloves too had come out of the bag.

He walked over and popped the top button of her blouse with the knife. He'd raped her with her clothes on, cutting just the panties away. They lay in front of her like a patch of snow in the moonlight.

He hadn't even removed her Reeboks.

When the buttons were gone he cut the neck of the blouse at the back and tore it down and then cut through each sleeve. She could feel the cold blunt edge of the blade travel along her arms. The blouse fell away and the cold night air on her flesh made the trembling even worse.

He used the knife on the button of her skirt and then unzipped it and pulled it down and off her. He stepped back and looked. He swung the branch back and forth. Once. Twice.

It whistled in the silence.

He put it down on the ground and reached into the bag again, and took out two thin white dish towels. He balled one up and approached her.

"Open," he said.

She shook her head. "Please," she said. "No." The thought of the gag was terrifying to her. If she couldn't talk to him then there was no possibility of stopping him. None.

She couldn't have him use the gag.

"Open!" he said and placed the point of the knife against her bra, unerringly finding the fear-hard tip of the nipple, and pressed in. The pain was electric. She licked her lips and parted them, aware of the salt taste of tears.

He shoved the cloth into her mouth and tied the other towel over it, catching long thin strands of her hair in the double knot behind her head.

She saw him reach into the bag again and heard a soft tinkling sound as he took something from the bag and placed it in his right front pocket and then turned and put something else into his back pocket as he did so. Then he walked over.

He reached up and she watched him as he pulled the knot free of her right wrist. The knots he'd used were some sort of trick. She'd been tugging at them so hard her wrists were raw, but all he did was pluck the center of this one and it fell right off her.

The hand and wrist throbbed with returning circulation and it seemed to affect her entire body. She saw bright yellow spots in front of her eyes in a surrounding, shimmering blackness and then as it cleared saw him reach into his pocket and take something out, so that whatever it was, was still in his hand when he grabbed her wrist and held the back of it flat and open to the wide thick trunk of the oak tree and she felt the sharp point of something against her palm, his powerful wrist against hers, holding it in place.

She felt a stab of pain against the center of her hand as he reached into his back pocket and suddenly she knew what all of this meant. Knew what he was doing.

"No!" she screamed beneath the gag and just as the hammer came down she pulled hard from the shoulder for all she was worth. The hand moved just inches, and she felt the thickness of the nail pierce the delicate web of flesh between her third and fourth fingers and thud deep into the tree.

She heard him curse and reach into his pocket for a second nail.

It was the only chance she'd get.

She screamed again and pulled.

The flesh tore away with a surprising, terrifying resistance. She was aware of blood pouring from the wound as she reached up and grabbed the rough limb of the tree with both hands and hauled herself up and swung back, kicking at him while he still fumbled in his pocket for the second nail, felt a moment of elation as her shoes connected solidly with his chest that was as frightening as anything that had happened to her all night long because now there was hope.

She reached up with bloody slippery fingers and tugged at the second knot exactly as he had done.

And suddenly she was free.

She saw that kicking him she'd sent him flying into a stand of white birch opposite. He had fallen, was trying to stand, but his fall had wedged him into the low, four-limbed bole of one of the trees and he couldn't find sufficient purchase at an angle that would allow him to haul himself up.

And maybe she'd hurt him. Maybe he was dazed.

It gave her that moment. That precious second to run.

She didn't know which way he'd taken her through the woods but that didn't matter. She was young and he was not. She had fear and need on her side and he did not. She'd find the road or she'd find a place to hide but either way he was not going to take her. Not again.

Not Marge Bernhardt.

She had too much to live for.

Ignoring pain and cold and blood she sprinted free into the dense forest night.

THIRTY

VISITATION, PART FOUR

It wasn't as bad as he thought it would be in some ways.

But then in some other ways, once he knew it was real and really happening to him, it was worse.

The shelter wasn't a kind of prison the way he'd imagined it. It was a normal-looking house though old and bigger than any he'd seen and it sat on a quiet, tree-lined street somewhere up into the hills away from town, with a big lawn and trees in back so that if it weren't for the high chain-link fence you'd think just anybody could live here—not just a bunch of messed-up kids waiting for something to happen to them. Inside there was a big comfortable living room on the first floor with a fireplace they said nobody used anymore, a kitchen and dining room with a huge table, and upstairs were the bedrooms, four of them, six boys to a room assigned to bunk beds.

His roommates were all pretty much his age except Willie something, who was just a little kid and had the bunk down under him and David Fosch, who was maybe two years older. So that was okay.

David seemed to think he was pretty tough but he hadn't started pushing anybody around or anything.

He was worried about tonight, though.

His first night here.

What if he messed his pyjamas again?

It wasn't happening *every* night, thank god, not since he hadn't been seeing his dad so much but it still was happening often enough and what if he shit his pants in the middle of the night and everybody smelled it and somebody woke up and said, jesus what's *that?*

Everybody'd know.

And he wondered if David Fosch would just act tough after that.

Mrs. Strawn and Mr. McKenzie said that they all had chores to do every day and his that afternoon was peeling carrots and potatoes for supper. They'd shown him around and got him unpacked and settled in to his room and then as soon as his mom left with Mr. Sansom, Mrs. Strawn handed him the peeler.

He didn't mind. It was something to do.

Though he wasn't real good at it.

He kept remembering his mom crying as she left and trying to smile, Mr. Sansom's hand on her arm leading her out the door. And thinking about that made him want to cry because why was she crying if she wasn't scared for him again?

I told, he thought.

I told on my dad. Is that why this is happening?

He kept worrying about tonight. About going to bed and sleeping and doing . . . whatever.

He kept wondering what was going to happen to him next—how long he was really going to be here, whether he was going to get picked on eventually by some kid or maybe a whole bunch of kids and when it was going to happen. It almost had to happen.

They said it was only for a day or two.

He wasn't dumb. He knew a lot could happen in a day or two.

A lot of things he didn't want to happen.

So he wasn't too great at the peeling. He kept gouging holes out of the potatoes trying to get at the dark spots and breaking off the thin tops of carrots.

They smelled good, though. The carrots and potatoes did. They smelled like home and his own kitchen.

When? he thought. When will they get me out of here?

He listened to some of the other kids playing out back on the lawn outside through the kitchen door, the screams and the laughing. At least he knew you could laugh here.

Somebody out there could. Maybe that meant he could too. Eventually.

There were still a couple of hours before supper time. He wondered if, when he finished, he'd have the guts to go out and join in.

"Robert?"

Mrs. Strawn was standing in the doorway. There was gray in her hair and she wore thick black-rimmed glasses and her hips and belly were too big for the tight skirt she was wearing but his first feeling about her was that Mrs. Strawn was okay, that she was pretty nice.

"You have a visitor," she said. "Go rinse off your hands and you can finish up later."

He did as she said and stepped outside, following her through the hall into the living room.

He sat in an armchair with his back to them as they walked in so that Robert could see only his head and shoulders, but he knew who it was way before he turned and when he did turn his father was smiling.

That was wrong. He felt a wave of terror. *Why was he smiling?*

Didn't he *know*?

His father stood up.

"Hi, Robert," he said.

"Hi." It was all he could do to manage to get the word out.

"I'm sorry, Mr. Danse," said Mrs. Strawn. "But you know I have to stay here with you."

"I understand. That's fine. I just wanted to stop by and say hello and see how Robert was doing." He smiled again, bigger this time. "This is really quite a nice place you have here, Mrs. Strawn. You sure wouldn't know there were . . . how many boys living here?"

"Twenty-one at the moment. We have three beds open right now."

He shook his head as though he couldn't quite believe it. "Well, you run a tight ship," he said. "It's amazing."

She smiled. "We try. Thank you."

He turned to Robert. "So. How you doing, son? I know this is a . . . big adjustment for you. God knows it's got to be. I know it's not easy. I know it can't be easy."

"I'm . . . I'm okay."

"Really?"

Robert nodded. Why was he asking all this?

Did he really care?

What was he doing here—and didn't he *know*?

"Anything I can do for you?"

"No. I mean, no thanks."

"Anything I can bring? You got your Game Boy? Stuff like that?"

He nodded again. He noticed that his father was scratching at his thumb with his index finger. Otherwise he looked completely calm, like nothing was going on here at all. It was weird. It was like this happened to him every day, going to visit his kid in some home.

"Well, if there's anything you need, you know where to phone me. He can make phone calls, can't he, Mrs. Strawn?"

"I'm afraid not, Mr. Danse. The bills would be a disaster. You'll have to phone him here. And then because of the court order . . ." She looked embarrassed. "Because of the court order I'd have to be on the extension. You understand, I hope."

He seemed to want to ignore that last part.

"Sure, I understand," he said. "Twenty-one kids could make a lot of phone calls. I'll phone him, then. Any particular time of day?"

"Not before nine, please. And not after nine in the evening."

"Fine. No prob . . . oh, *damn* it!"

He held up his thumb, turning it over and cupping it with the palm of his hand. Blood was flowing off it, running fast and hard down over his wrist.

"Oh, my Lord!"

"Could you . . .? Where's the bathroom, Mrs. Strawn? I'm sorry . . . I did this this morning putting in a new razor blade but I thought . . ."

She pointed. "First door to your left."

"Could you get me something . . . some paper towels maybe? Have you got a first-aid kit around or anything?"

"I'll be right back."

She hurried down the hall to the kitchen. His father took one step in the direction of the bathroom and then stopped and turned, pulled a handkerchief out of his pocket and wrapped it around his finger, striding toward him, reaching over and grabbing Robert's arm with the other hand, squeezing his bicep hard, that nice easygoing look on his face slipping away and sliding into a fury he had never seen on anybody's face, ever.

He'd been scratching at the finger.

Robert had seen him.

It was just to get him alone.

He tried to pull away. Arthur jerked him roughly back.

He tried to cry out to Mrs. Strawn but his voice wouldn't work and then his father's words were a whispered rush washing over him like a cruel wind.

"You think I'm fucking stupid, Robert?" he hissed. "I told you what I was going to do and now I'm going to do it—unless you say you lied, Robert. You think I can't? You seriously want to fuck with me? Unless you tell them you lied and you tell them fast I'm going to skin your fucking mother while she's still alive and then I'm coming after YOU! You understand me?"

He squeezed the arm and then released him just as he thought the arm couldn't take any more, just as he thought he was going to break it, and then he moved off quickly to the bathroom.

Robert heard water running.

His legs were about to give way. He sat down trembling on the couch. Fell into it.

Mrs. Strawn came in from the kitchen with some paper towels and a first-aid kit and she didn't give him a glance. She walked to the bathroom and he heard the water go off again and then he heard them talking.

Nobody could protect him.

The realization was final.

His father could do what he wanted to, to both him and to his mother because his father could always outsmart them whenever he wanted and his father didn't care. He'd do anything.

He was the only one who knew that.

In spite of what his mom said, he was alone.

When they came out of the bathroom his father was smiling again holding up the thumb with a band-aid on it like it was some kind of thumbs-up thing and Mrs. Strawn was smiling too, completely fooled by the phony look on his father's face and the phony cut he'd made this morning just to get to him.

"All fixed," he said. "Thanks again, Mrs. Strawn. It's really good of you. I've got to go, Robbie. But I promise, I'll be in touch. Okay?"

And Robert knew he would. He'd be in touch. Forever and ever.

He always would.

THIRTY-ONE

THE BURDEN OF PROOF

"It's for you." Cindy held out the phone. "Owen Sansom."

Lydia took the telephone and Cindy went back to what she was doing—simultaneously preparing them a meal of chicken cacciatore, green beans and pasta, clearing her daughter Gail's toys and books off the kitchen table and sipping her second bottle of Miller Lite.

"I thought I'd find you here," said Sansom. "God, Lydia, I hate to have to tell you this. But Robert's recanted."

"He's *what*?"

"He's recanted."

"Oh God, *no*!"

Cindy stopped everything, stood there with casserole dish in hand and stared at her.

"I just talked to Andrea Stone. She got a call half an hour ago from Lois Strawn at the shelter. Robert told her that everything he said to the state police was a lie. That he made up *everything*."

"I don't understand. Why? Why would he *do* that?"

"I don't know for sure but I've got a pretty good idea."

"Why?"

"You're not going to like this. Lois Strawn says he had a visitor earlier. Arthur. All very civil, she says—but Andrea had a bad feeling about it anyway. She asked if Strawn had left the room at any point. Seems that while they were talking Arthur opened up a cut on his finger and she went out to the kitchen for some towels and a Band-Aid. She was only gone a minute or two but hell, how long does it have to take? I can't prove it, but I'd bet anything Arthur threatened him."

"I'm going over there."

"That's a lousy idea. Even if you could get him to admit that Arthur threatened him, at this point it's going to look like coercion on *your* part. Like you're exerting undue pressure. Andrea Stone's over there right now, taking his statement to submit to Judge Burke. Let's see what she comes up with. And I don't care what he's saying now—those videotapes are still very convincing. Burke's going to have a damned hard time overlooking them. These were police experts doing the questioning and Burke knows it."

"So what am I supposed to do? Just sit here and hope and pray that he believes my son's first confession and not his second? Jesus!"

She felt Cindy's hand on her shoulder. Only then was she aware that she was shaking.

"I don't like it any more than you do, honestly. But . . ."

"Arthur's not playing by the rules. Why the hell should we have to?"

She heard him sigh. "Lydia, I think you already know the answer to that. Think about it. You already all but admitted in court that you were willing to break the law in order to get what you wanted out of this. That's the way Burke sees it, anyway. He also sees you as prone to hysteria. Given that, the only way to do this is to go about it calmly and correctly and keep a low profile until we hear from him. Believe me, it's the only way."

"I'm taking him. Goddamn it! I'm . . ."

"*No, you're not.* We haven't come this far so you and Robert can become a pair of fugitives! Listen to me. I want you to calm down. I want you to tell Cindy to pour you a drink—a stiff one—and I want you to stay there and hang tight until I hear from Andrea. Okay? I'll phone you right away as soon as I do. Promise me."

"Owen, I . . ."

"*Promise* me, Lydia."

She felt old and weary, defeated—and sick with shame for feeling that way. She couldn't afford to feel defeated. Probably he was right. She had to summon the patience somehow and the strength and faith in some kind of future for them that would allow her to do this one more time.

"All right," she said. "All right, Owen."

"I'll call you as soon as I know."

She hung up the phone.

"Oh, honey," Cindy said, both hands on her shoulders now, not even knowing what was going on but getting it right, knowing somehow exactly how she was feeling and putting it perfectly— quietly and perfectly and succinctly into words.

"You do get the shit, don't you?"

Andrea Stone thought the instruction was unusual to say the least. When she returned to her office there was a message on her desk from Judge Burke, saying that he wanted to hear the tape of her interview with Robert Danse immediately. That he would still be in chambers.

And that he intended to make a ruling in the morning.

She phoned Owen Sansom and gave him the gist of it and then walked across the street to the courts building. The street was dark. She saw that one of the streetlights was out and it gave her a strange uneasy feeling as though someone had vandalized the light, knocked it out purposely, as though typical urban street crime had reached this far north into the boonies and from now on was going to be part of the lives of all of them.

When it was probably just a burned-out bulb.

She presented her ID to the guard and walked the dimly lit hall to the judge's chambers.

She found him sitting at his desk, turned to a VCR and television monitor, listening to Robert say, *"He messes with me back here . . . with this . . ."* She closed the door quietly and saw him push a button on the remote. The screen went black.

"Ms. Stone," he said.

She handed him the small voice-activated tape recorder. "The tape's inside?"

"Yes."

He handled the recorder as though unfamiliar with this kind of gadget, turning it, frowning, looking at the control panel on the side and then putting it down in front of him on the big oak desk.

"So?" he said.

"Excuse me?"

"So how did it go? With the boy. How did you find him?"

"Upset," she said. "Nervous. Scared."

"Scared of what?"

"You're asking my opinion?"

"Yes, I am."

"I believe he's scared that he'll never see home again at this rate. And I believe that he's scared of his father." Burke nodded.

"I'll speak candidly, Ms. Stone. This doesn't surprise me. This videotape . . . I've watched it half a dozen times . . . both these interviews with him tend to be convincing."

"He recants it all on my tape, Your Honor."

"So I understand. After seeing his father."

"And according to Mrs. Strawn, seeing him alone. For a minute or two at least."

"Unfortunate. And this tape of yours—is this convincing too? Objectively speaking?"

"I have a problem with it."

"What's that?"

"He won't say why he supposedly lied to the psychologists in the first place. Why he would want to implicate his father. It doesn't make a lot of sense to me."

"Could it have been the mother? Coaching him?"

"I doubt it, Your Honor. I doubt it very much. I think he told them the truth down there."

"At this point I tend to agree. Despite what my feelings are regarding the mother's actions in the case, I . . ."

"Your Honor . . ."

He stopped her. "I understand that we don't agree on this, Ms. Stone. It's not the point. The point is, right now, the father."

"Yes, Your Honor."

He sighed. "I'll listen to the tape. Thanks for delivering it at this late hour. These cases demand a lot of all of us, it seems to me. Trying to do the appropriate thing for a child such as this, trying to prevent further damage." He smiled ruefully. "Late hours are the least of it. Anyhow, thank you, Ms. Stone. I'll see you tomorrow."

"Thank you, Your Honor."

As she stepped outside and quietly closed the door she heard her own voice coming from the other side, tinny and thin-sounding, from the tape.

The man was willing to do his homework, anyway.

She realized that despite what the judge had said about the credibility of the videotape she was still afraid for Robert Danse. Preventing further damage was a tricky thing. When there had been so much already.

She thought not for the first time that child abuse was a kind of parasite, one that digs in deep and painfully at first so that you can see its effects quite clearly if you happen to be looking. But then sometimes after a while the symptoms almost seemed to disappear. The insidious thing about a parasite was that you got used to it, the pain notwithstanding. The feeding of the abuser. The slow starvation of the victim. Both became routine. Part of the organization of the internal structure of life.

While all the time the thing inside grew and grew, the sheer *need* of it constantly expanding. And eventually—if it ever did come to light—leaving its famished, wasted host to fend for himself as best he could in order to seek whoever and whatever else had come in contact with it. Family, friends, marriages.

Getting inside them too.

Even courts. Even lawyers and judges.

The parasite didn't think. It fed.

And nothing was exempt.

There was no reason involved. No intelligence to speak of in the organism.

Only hunger.

It was up to them, to the social services system and the courts, to apply reason like a poultice to a wound made by long seasons of the lack of it—while they themselves already had the thing inside them too, had already been affected.

Some of them, like herself and Judge Burke, over and over again.

It changed them. One way or another.

She wondered if any of them were really up to the job. And how the judge would find tomorrow.

She walked to her car across the darkened street. An hour's drive from home, she thought, another hour maybe to get to bed. Already she wished for sleep.

There were times she'd thought she'd like to have a husband and kids of her own someday but this was not one of them. Not with this thing inside her.

I hope they get that goddamn light fixed by tomorrow, she thought.

We need some goddamn light here.

THIRTY-TWO

JUDGMENT

She saw the door open and Sansom, Wood and Stone emerge from the judge's chambers and got up from the bench. None of them looked happy. Wood paused and said something to the other two and then walked off alone down the corridor. Sansom and Stone glanced at her and then seemed to avoid her eyes as they approached her.

My God. How bad was it?

How much worse could it be?

She sat down again, unwilling to trust her legs a moment longer. Sansom sat to her left, Andrea Stone to her right.

"Nobody wins on this one," Sansom said. He shook his head. "God."

"Tell me." Her voice sounded strange to her, hoarse, as though she'd been shouting.

"The good news is that Arthur gets no unsupervised visits whatsoever. None. Apparently the judge believed the videotape, not the recant. For my money that's the only decent part of any of this. It gives us far more leverage on appeal and . . ."

"On appeal? Oh, Jesus. What do we need an appeal for, Owen?"

He glanced at Andrea Stone.

"Because you don't have custody, Lydia. I'm . . . I'm really . . . I'm very sorry."

She couldn't speak. She couldn't even ask him why, how it had happened. It was as though for a moment her soul had led to some safer ground than this—leaving only the shell of her sitting empty between these people. She could almost view herself seated there, her face pale in the ray of bright warm sunlight streaming through the narrow window.

"Burke's worried about what he called 'a recurrence of the mother's emotional instability.' I can't believe it, but those were his words exactly. He's still hung up on us taking Robert to those damn doctors and your denying Arthur visitation if he happened to decide to order it—even though he *didn't* order it. So what we'll have to do, what we'll have to prove, is that you're anything *but* unstable. I'm afraid that's going to take some time. I've got to be honest with you, it could be as long as six months before we can make a go at this again. In the meantime you do have visitation. Unrestricted. And Arthur doesn't. We'll document every facet of your life, round up employers, former employers, relatives, friends. One big push in, say, six months' time, and I think we can break this thing for good. We don't have to worry about Arthur anymore, only the judge. That should make things easier."

"Six . . . months? Where? In that place . . . that shelter? Some foster home?"

Sansom glanced at Stone again.

"No. I know you're not going to be happy with this. Certainly we're not. But Burke's given custody to the grandparents. To Ruth and Harry. To Arthur's parents."

"He can't *do* that!"

She was aware of Andrea Stone's cool smooth hand on her forearm.

"He's done it, Lydia. With the strict provision that Arthur cannot be living with them or even be allowed to stay there overnight. I still think a foster home would be preferable and both Andrea and I argued that. But it's not at all unheard of when a judge has questions about each parent's fitness for custodianship. He'll prefer, if possible, to keep a child in the extended family. There's plenty of precedent. We argued for Barbara. But Barbara's a single working woman. I think if your own parents were alive, he'd have . . ."

She felt sudden rage.

"Ruth and Harry brought up a goddamn *child molester,* Owen! What the hell is he thinking? Is he *out of his fucking mind*?"

Sansom glanced toward the judge's chambers across the hall.

The door was closed but Burke was still inside there and the walls were thin.

"I think we'd better get out of here," he said. He looked up and down the empty corridor. "Go get a cup of coffee or something. This is . . ."

"I don't *want* a fucking cup of coffee!"

"*Lydia!* This is exactly what we need to avoid right now! Jesus! We need to avoid it for the next six months. Do you understand me?"

She had heard of people going crazy and killing strangers out of sheer frustration and she thought she knew what they felt like now. She would have liked to walk in through that door and break a chair over Burke's face, pummel him until his mouth ran red with blood. She wanted to scream. She wanted to hurt somebody. For the first time in her life she could almost want for a gun.

"You've got to stay in control," Andrea Stone said softly. "Lydia, you *have* to."

She almost laughed. *In control.* She hadn't had control of anything since the whole thing began.

Andrea was right, though. She would have to do it for Robert.

It was all for Robert and always had been.

If the rage did not subside she at least could bank its fires for the moment.

"Let's go," she said. "Before I walk in there and tear his goddamn eyes out."

"Good idea," said Stone, "before I start thinking about helping you."

They walked out into morning sunlight. The sun felt good on her body and for a moment she was almost comforted. Then a thought occurred and she felt her stomach churn.

"Harry and Ruth," she murmured. "What does 'supervised visitation' mean, Owen? I mean, who does the supervising? Who arranges the meetings?"

"As Robert's legal guardians, they do."

"I don't trust them."

Hell, after all these years she felt she still barely knew them. But she knew they were devoted to Arthur.

"Come on, Lydia. I don't think they'd stand by and let Arthur molest their grandson," Sansom said. "The judge'll inform them that they'd be open to criminal charges if anything remotely like that happened. And after all this . . . commotion about it, I'd think they'd be pretty careful. Wouldn't you?"

"I don't know what they'd do."

What she did know was that another measure of power had just passed out of her hands. She felt its loss immensely—a loss that matched but in no way exceeded that other loss, the loss of intimacy with Robert, with her son, which would inevitably follow, the loss of all the days and nights—at least for the time it took to return him to her. She felt almost resigned to these losses. Almost, though not quite, cold enough to play the hand being dealt to her.

That didn't mean that she was resigned to being powerless. She'd watch them. And if anything happened to Robert . . . *anything* . . .

They'd wish they'd never met her. Ruth and Harry. Arthur. All of them.

THIRTY-THREE

SURVIVORS

For a day and a half now Duggan had been looking for Arthur Danse and his big black Lincoln—ever since the Bernhardt girl came in off the highway the night before last wrapped in a trucker's blanket, raped and bruised and bleeding from a deep gash in the hand. Ever since she described a car that could easily have been Arthur's Lincoln and sat down with a troopers' composite artist to arrive at a face that, except for the softer rounded shape to the chin and the slightly higher forehead, looked remarkably like him.

He'd been looking. And coming up with nothing.

Not at Arthur's house. Not at his parents' house. And not at The Caves. There was an APB on the Lincoln but nothing had come of that yet either. His lawyer hadn't even been able to reach him with the results of the latest hearing.

Arthur Danse had disappeared.

And that wasn't like him.

Jake over at The Caves said that the business could pretty much run itself at this point, at least for quite a while, but Arthur was a hands-on guy when it came to his restaurant. He was in there almost every night. So why the sudden change of habits? Stress over the court's decision—which had practically branded him a baby-fucker? That was Ruth's pinion. The lady was bitter. Was he unable to show his face around town because of the publicity?

It was possible.

But just as possible—*more* possible as far as Duggan was concerned—it was because of Marge Bernhardt.

Maybe his first survivor.

He got a list from Jake on the distributors and retailers for the product line and called each of them, but they hadn't heard from Danse either.

Without a car to search or a suspect to question he was left with going over the minutiae of the victim's story. There was no doubt in his mind that whoever grabbed her was the same guy who'd killed the rest of these women. Anal and vaginal rape, bondage, the peeled switch which—lucky for her—he didn't get around to using, and finally the nail to the hand. Practically his signature.

That and the Van Helsing bit. Which he hadn't got to either.

Trouble was that the girl didn't know cars or guns or knives or tenpenny nails for that matter.

All they had was her composite.

In case he was wrong about Danse they were running that through the computers down in Concord for a possible match. Whoorly'd suggested that maybe he'd sold the car and they were working on that angle too.

He had plenty of other work to do right here on his desk but none of it was holding him and he had to fight the urge to just climb into his car and go cruising, go hunting for a big black Lincoln. Maybe drive by Harry and Ruth's place again. Hell, he'd do that every hour on the hour—be glad to—if he thought it would do any good.

Got to have patience, he thought. Police work is patience. You know that.

But he didn't like having Arthur among the missing.

He wanted him in a lineup with Marge Bernhardt sitting there in front of a two-way mirror.

And what if the disappearing act meant that Arthur was totally losing it? Losing the handle on what passed for his fucked-up life. There was no way of knowing what he'd do. Because the guy was dangerous. Whether he'd done the women or not he was dangerous.

He was certified now. The system had already judged him a man who was dangerous to others, at least to his son. Though Duggan hadn't needed the system to tell him anything about Arthur Danse and hadn't for a long time.

The hell with it, he thought. It's a pretty nice day for a ride. Get your butt out to the car.

So he did.

THIRTY-FOUR

VISITATION, PART FIVE

Ellsworth, New Hampshire

It kept nagging at her.

She'd been to Ruth and Harry's every day, twice over two days with this afternoon being the third time. Her reception was cold and distant but that was to be expected. That didn't bother her. What bothered her was Robert.

He acted as though he were hiding something again.

She pulled into the pitted dirt driveway, got out of the car and walked toward the house. It was just after three and the day was gray and chilly and felt like rain. She'd gone back to work for Ellie Brest but Ellie had thrown her out early today, saying she didn't want to see her get caught in a rainstorm—even though the woman was in pain, having broken yet another of the small bones in her wrist while Lydia was away.

She knew that rain had nothing to do with it. She'd voiced her concerns to Ellie about Robert's behavior and as a result she thought it possible that Ellie was nearly as worried about him as she was. She'd phoned ahead from her house and Ruth said begrudgingly that it was all right for her to come over.

Harry's getting sloppy, she thought—or else he's just getting old—because the wooden porch badly needed fixing. The broad gray plank of the second step was cracked through most of its length. All the way across to the rusted tenpenny tail on the right-hand side, and it gave beneath her foot.

At the door she knocked and waited.

It was yesterday, mostly, that disturbed her. It was nothing specific, nothing she could put her finger on. Just a silence about him which she didn't feel could be accounted for by the situation he was in, away from her and all the familiar aspects of home, not even by the uncertainty of his future.

Because two days before, on Thursday, he'd seemed to have adjusted more or less. He had a room of his own and all his things were there, including his television and all his toys and books and video games. He seemed to accept what was going on as best as you could expect him to. For his sake she'd been happy to see it.

And then yesterday, complete sullen silence.

As though he blamed her.

She'd asked when they were alone if it was something that had passed between him and Ruth or between him and Harry but all he did was shake his head no and continue working on the math homework she was helping him with. She'd asked if he'd seen his father. No again. So what's the story then? she said. What's the matter? You mad at me?

No, he said. Nothing was the matter. But he said it too loudly so that it felt as though he were annoyed with her. No. As though she ought to have *known* that something was wrong. As though she were stupid for asking.

She asked if he'd even heard from his father and got another denial.

He wouldn't talk again.

He wouldn't open up again.

That was what was bothering her.

She was about to knock a second time when Ruth appeared at the door. Behind her the first drops of rain were falling. She realized she hadn't rolled up the window on the driver's side.

"Wait," she said. "One minute."

She dashed for the car. Suddenly the rain was coming down for real. So she'd gotten caught in it after all. She rolled up the window and slammed the door and ran back toward the house, glancing up just before she hit the porch to see a lace curtain close in one of the bedrooms on the second floor. Ruth's room, she remembered. She and Harry had separate rooms. Had for years now.

Her blouse was soaked by the time she made it past Ruth and

through the door, her thin white lace bra showing.

She flushed seeing Ruth glance down at her breasts.

"I'll get a towel," Ruth muttered. "Boy's in the kitchen, workin' on a puzzle."

"Thank you," Lydia said.

I'll be unnerved by this woman forever, she thought.

The puzzle was really something. He had it about halfway done. She was rusty on her art history but it was either Bosch or Brengel. Angels wielding swords and spears against a fleeing horde of surreal-looking monsters—toad-things, fish-things, things being hatched out of eggs. She picked up the box and read the cover and looked at the completed painting. Breugel. *The Fall of the Rebel Angels.* Brussels, 1562. Musees Royaux des Beaux-Arts.

Pretty wild stuff.

She kissed him on top of the head.

"Hi, Mom," he said.

"Hey, you're doing pretty good there."

"Yeah, but it's taking forever."

"So? No rush, right?"

"I got one more hour and then Gramma wants the table back."

"We'll transfer it to something, don't worry. Where'd you get this, anyway?"

"Dad . . . Gramma . . . um, it was Daddy's."

It was as though he'd said too much. He blushed. He went back to fiddling with the puzzle.

"It was Daddy's when he was a boy?"

He nodded.

"What'd they do, pull it out of the attic for you?" He nodded again.

Silence. Silence once again.

Dammit. What the hell was going on?

Ruth walked in with the towel.

"Here," she said. She glanced at the puzzle and smiled thinly and then she left the room.

Lydia toweled dry her hair. The towel had an unpleasant musty odor. She wondered when it had last been washed.

Whether all Ruth's towels smelled like that or if this one had been specially selected for her.

"Have you heard from your father?"

He shook his head again, staring down at the puzzle, turning a piece of it between his fingers, looking for a place to fit it in.

"Everything okay?"

He nodded.

"You sure?"

He nodded again.

"Hey. I miss you. You know? The house is pretty big and awful quiet without you."

She saw him draw a quick breath. The piece of the puzzle stopped turning in his hand. The tip of his thumb went white where he was holding it.

For god's sake, she thought. What are you doing? Torturing him?

"We'll get you back there real soon, I promise."

She ran her hands over his shoulders and kissed the top of his head again.

"Want some help with that?"

She pulled out a chair and sat down.

They stared at the puzzle and at the pieces of the puzzle. An hour later it was still not finished and they had said barely ten more words to each other.

When she went outside it was almost dark and the rain had stopped. It lay in shining black puddles on the pitted drive. She stepped around them and got into the car and started it.

As she pulled away she gazed again at the second floor window. The curtain was still. The room was dark.

But something about it felt wrong and it took her only a moment to realize that it could not have been Ruth at the window earlier because Ruth was at the door and it could not have been Robert either.

So if Harry was still at the store—as he usually was until just before dinnertime—who was at the window?

She drove by the store to check and pulled into the parking lot in front of it. She could see Harry's young assistant inside sitting alone at the register but not Harry. His pickup wasn't there. But then it hadn't been over at the house either.

She didn't like what she was thinking.

What she was thinking could make her crazy.

But it was possible. It would not be smart and arguably not even sane but it was possible.

It all depended on exactly how arrogant these people actually were. On how much they thought they could get away with.

She was going to watch this carefully. Watch it like a goddamn hawk.

Starting tonight.

THIRTY-FIVE

ONLY CHILD

She asked Cindy to drive her there, then kill an hour and a half somehow and return to pick her up. Owen Sansom's words kept coming back to her—*what we have to prove is that you're anything but unstable*—so she didn't want to risk anyone recognizing her car parked somewhere along the side of the road and wondering where she'd got to or some stranger reporting it abandoned to the police. She wanted to be in and out of there undetected, completely invisible. An hour and a half seemed plenty of time to find out what she needed to know.

She changed into jeans, sweatshirt, running shoes and a dark blue jacket and made herself a bowl of soup in the microwave and drank a cup of coffee while she waited for Cindy to drop Gail off at Ed's house for the evening. When she heard the horn outside she was ready.

Cindy's car smelled like potpourri deodorizer and something like vinegar. The vinegar smell came from a glass of apple juice Gail had spilled down into the backseat a couple of months ago. Cindy said she kept on meaning to pull out the seat and clean it up and then she kept forgetting. A pair of Styrofoam dice dangled from the rearview mirror. The ashtray was full to overflowing with the filters of Virginia Slims.

Cindy was too fast a driver and probably drank too much beer for her own good. And she wasn't the neatest person in the world god knows. But she'd dropped everything for this. She was a damn good friend.

On their way out of Plymouth and up the mountain Lydia filled her in on Robert's behavior and the figure in the window.

"You don't really think he'd be crazy enough to . . ."

"I can't tell what he'd do. Who'd have thought he'd have done all this?"

"You remember at your sister's wedding? You remember it was me who encouraged you to . . . Jesus! I could kick myself in the face for that!"

"You didn't know him then. Or me."

"I thought he was cute and I heard he had money. Turns out he's about as cute as a pet sewer rat."

"He did have money, though."

"Oh, yeah. I got that part right. I'm a genius. Yenta the shithead matchmaker."

"You've made up for it a billion times, Cyn—and you know it. Just do me one more favor?"

"What's that?"

"Slow down to about a hundred-eighty, will you?"

"Just for you, doll."

They climbed up into the hills along the narrow winding road. Headlights came toward them around a bend and when the bright lights dimmed and the car pulled past them she saw that it was a police cruiser and thought she might have glimpsed Ralph Duggan behind the wheel. She couldn't be sure.

There was a stop sign about a hundred yards from the Danse house. That was where the dirt road began, just past a bridge over a stream rushing along below, flowing into a beaver pond a ways beyond. She told Cindy to pull over and stop there.

"This is where we'll meet," she said.

"I gotta tell you. Now that we got here I'm kind of worried about this."

"I'll be fine," Lydia said.

She didn't feel fine. She felt nervous as a cat lost and alone in the big city streets knowing of nowhere to go where it would ever be safe and warm again. She hoped it didn't low.

"You should have brought something."

"Like what?"

"Like a gun for chrissake! *They've* got guns, right?"

"They've got enough guns to start a war but I don't think me showing up with one is going to help any. I'm supposed to be Miss Emotional Stability, remember? Besides, I'm not going in there. And I don't intend to get seen. I'm looking. They're in the light and I'm in the dark, that's the whole idea."

"Right, yeah."

"Don't worry. What time have you got?"

"8:25"

"I'm five minutes slow. Okay, say ten o'clock, all right?"

"All right."

She opened the door. Cindy put her hand on her arm and stopped her.

"Hey," she said. "Good luck. I hope to hell they just had visitors before. I hope you come up empty."

"Me too. See you in a while."

"Be careful."

The penlight was enough to get her up the hill through the sparse woods headed toward the house. When she reached the field spread out in front of it she turned the light off and proceeded by the dim gray light of the waning moon.

There was still no sign of Arthur's Lincoln. Only Ruth's car and now Harry's pickup parked out front. The bedrooms on the second floor were dark. She could see lights on in the living room and in the hall leading in from the porch. The porch light was off. That was good. It would take a lot of seriously bad luck for them to notice her out here.

She peered through the corner window of the living room. Arthur's portrait, an oil done by a local painter, hung prominently over the fireplace. *Not Harry's portrait. Arthur's.* She'd always thought that pretty odd.

There was no one in the room.

She moved beyond the untrimmed hedges to the side of the house. The dining room was dark but she could see light spilling in under the door leading to the kitchen.

She went around back and moved softly up the three wooden steps and heard them before she saw them, looking in through the screen and the glass panel on the door. Harry, Ruth, and Robert seated at the table.

Arthur pacing.

Back and forth from the sink to the refrigerator.

He had a day or more growth of beard and his white cotton shirt was stained with something in front and had gone yellow under the armpits. He was waving his arms at them, shouting.

Ruth watched him undisturbed.

Harry looked troubled. Two bottles of beer sat in front of him on the table and there was another one in his hand. Robert looked scared.

Even with his back to her she could tell by the inward hunch of his shoulders and when he turned in profile as his father moved past him she was sure.

". . . if the son of a bitch comes back again then I'll just go right on *upstairs* again. We can keep playing that damn game forever. I mean, what are you saying? That you don't want me here? Is that what you're saying? My own *mother and father* for chrissakes?"

Harry said something. She couldn't hear.

"Screw it!" Arthur said. "I'm staying with my son. I have a right to. I have a goddamn *right* to!"

Then she heard Harry say something about a warrant.

"For what? A warrant for what? He can't get a warrant unless he has probable cause, for god's sake. So what have I done? What have I done he can get a warrant for? You tell me. No, dammit, I'll tell *you*. Nothing!"

He walked over and put his hands on each of Robert's shoulders.

She could *feel* him cringe under his father's touch. Arthur murmured something.

". . . love my son," he said. "*Love* this fucking kid!" She pulled open the screen and then the door and suddenly she was inside in the overheated room that smelled of his sweat. It wasn't part of the plan god knows but there was no way she could stand and watch and listen to this bastard say what he had said and see him touching Robert and then just go away again.

"You son of a bitch," she said.

He smiled. "Oho! *Now* look who's here! *My ex-cunt!*" He released Robert and took two steps toward her. "It's *Mama!*"

"Come on, Robert," she said. "We're leaving."

She wasn't even aware that Ruth had gotten out of her chair, but then suddenly the woman was standing between them. One hand raised to her son and the other to her.

"We'll work this out between us," she said. "It's a matter between us and our boy. There's no reason for you to be here."

"No reason? Are you aware that your precious son is breaking the law just by being in this house? That you're breaking the law by having him here? Robert is not staying in this house with him. Do you understand? If you think I'm letting him you're crazy. Come on, Robert!"

"*Mom . . .*"

He seemed rooted in his chair, afraid to move.

"You're trespassing," Ruth said.

She'd had enough of it.

"*Oh, fuck you,* Ruth," she said.

And it was the same as Arthur had done to her so many nights and weeks ago. The fist came out of nowhere. She saw stars and suddenly she was on the floor with her back to the door and Robert was yelling *Mom!* and trying to get away from Arthur, and Ruth was standing right over her.

"Harry, go get the shotgun," she said.

She saw Harry glance at her once on the floor and the glance was empty, empty of all meaning, impossible to read, and then he left the room.

Arthur was laughing. Howling.

"*You better get out of here, Liddy!*" he said. "He'll do it! Mama says do it, he'll do it. He'll shoot your fucking guts out!" Robert was squirming in his grasp. "Trespassers get their asses shot, Liddy!"

Ruth gazed at her calmly.

"What he's saying? You hear what he's saying? That's right," she said.

"Mom! Please! Run!"

And suddenly she knew she'd damn well better run, that these people had all gone mad, that they'd do it and then say they'd mistaken her for a prowler and they'd get away with it too, she was out here on her own in the middle of the night with no car and no apparent justification for even being there and it could happen, they could get away with it, they could kill her right this minute and be done with her.

She hauled herself up. She looked at Robert.

"I'm coming back . . ."

"You better not be coming back, missy," Ruth hissed. She ignored her.

"Robert, I'll . . ."

But Robert was staring down the hallway now, panicked at what he was seeing, struggling with Arthur and screaming for her to *run, run*, and she threw open the doors and plunged down the stairs. She heard the door slam shut behind her and then fly open again against the side of the house and knew that he was coming after her, quiet, sad old Harry with the shotgun.

She ran across the field and didn't look back until she reached the woods. He was halfway across the field, following her, the shotgun resting on his shoulder pointed toward the stars. She fumbled for the penlight in her pocket, then realized it would give her position away. Arms out in front of her she pushed her way blindly through the scrub and trees and branches.

She heard the stream down over the hill below and made for that. She could work her way downstream and find some place to hide from him and wait for Cindy. She felt something wet on the palm of her left hand and saw black blood gleaming in the moonlight. She thought she could hear him behind her and tried to hurry forward but the woods had thickened and she stumbled and fell, heart pounding, breath thick in her throat. She pulled herself up and felt another stab of pain as a broken branch slashed across her wrist.

The water was close now, she could hear it.

And then she could see it just below.

She stumbled sliding down off the bank to the pebble bed of the stream where the water had receded during the cold dry winter— and then stood a moment. Staring at but not able to understand at first what in god's name she was looking at.

A hulk, a shape.

Dark in the middle of the water.

The stream flowing gleaming all around it.

She saw the high rounded head of the thing and the long sleek body half submerged like a stranded sea monster. She moved closer, understanding finally.

It was Arthur's Lincoln.

He'd driven it here. He'd dumped it in the middle of the stream, his precious Lincoln, the water running fast around it.

Above her on the bank to her right she could see where the brush and saplings had fallen beneath its bulk, crushed as it made its way down to the waterline and into the water. She didn't even wonder why.

She didn't need to.

He was crazy.

She had to get Robert.

She crouched listening a moment but she couldn't hear Harry behind her anymore. Maybe he'd given up. Maybe he really had no taste for this after all.

And maybe not.

Staying close to the dark high bank she made her way through the shadows downstream.

She heard the car on the bridge above her and pulled herself up over the embankment.

"Jesus, Lyd! What . . .?"

"*Drive!*" she said.

She hadn't heard or seen anything more of him but she wasn't taking chances, and one thing had become thoroughly clear to her in the long slow minutes she'd been hiding beneath the bridge. That time was everything now. Something could be happening to Robert this very minute, something she didn't even want to think of. And what was to stop him from throwing Robert into Ruth's car or Harry's pickup and driving away? It could be days, weeks, before they found him.

He could disappear forever.

She didn't think he'd go that far—give up absolutely everything—but she'd never seen him as bad as this. He might.

She used a scarf from the backseat to bind the seeping puncture wound in the palm of her hand.

"I've got to get to a phone, Cyn. Fast."

"Your place is closest. And fast is my middle name." She told her what had happened.

The pavement roared by beneath them.

"Jesus, Liddy, you could have got yourself killed," she said. "What are you going to do?"

"Phone the police, phone Owen Sansom. Arthur's living there and that violates the judge's order. I'm going to phone everybody. Get help. And then get back there as fast as I can."

They pulled into the driveway and she was out of the car and at her door before Cindy even got the keys out of the ignition.

"You want to clean that hand up," she said.

"To hell with it."

She was already at the phone dialing 911. Her hands were trembling so that she punched the 1 button three times instead of twice but that didn't seem to matter.

She told the voice on the other end that it was an emergency, that her ex-husband was abusing her son and could very possibly be doing it even as they spoke and that Arthur was living with the Danses in defiance of a court order. It all came out in a rush but she was amazed at how lucid she sounded, how clear and firm she was.

"So you'd like us to go on out there, is that right?"

"Yes," she said. She gave him the address.

"Okay, ma'am," he said. "But I've got to be honest with you, technically speaking we've got the power to go and get your son and take him out of the home—if he's in immediate danger. If he's not in immediate danger you've got to go to a judge and get an order. *Is* your boy in immediate danger?"

"As far as I'm concerned he is, yes."

"As far as you're concerned. See, that's where maybe we've got a problem, like it might be some kind of gray area. That's what I was getting at. Like it's maybe a matter of opinion."

"There's a child molester living in the house with him for God's sake! How could it be a matter of opinion?"

"Ma'am, has Mr. Danse ever been convicted of a crime? Any crime?"

"Convicted? No. But the judge definitely believed that he . . ."

"I know ma'am but, y'see, if he was convicted it would just be a whole lot easier. Tell you what, though—I'm going to speak to my supervisor about this, tell him I think we ought to go on up there and at least talk to these people. And I'll ask him to phone you back as soon as possible. That okay?"

"Can't you . . .?"

"Ma'am, that's really all I can do right now. And I got to tell you it might take a little while. I'd like to give you priority on this but I can't. We've got a five-car pile-up out on highway 93 with one car I know of still burning. I mean, they're all over the road out there. So we're kind of shorthanded right at the moment. I'm sorry."

"How long?"

"A couple of hours, maybe."

Jesus!

And he wasn't promising her any action even then.

Duggan, she thought.

"Listen, is Ralph Duggan there by any chance?"

"Left for home about half an hour ago. Why? You know Ralph?"

"Yes, I do."

"He know your situation?"

"I think he does. Part of it, anyway."

"Well that's a good idea, then. I'll still speak to my supervisor but Ralph might be able to get on it a whole lot quicker than we could. You got his home number?"

"No."

"Let me give it to you."

She wrote it down. She got the officer's name and thanked him and hung up and dialed again.

A woman answered.

"Hello, my name is Lydia Danse. Is Officer Duggan there?"

"No, I'm afraid not. Can I help you?"

"Do you expect him soon?"

She laughed. "Honestly? I never know."

"Please, could you ask him to call me? No, wait. Could you give him a message for me? Could you tell him that Lydia Danse phoned and that Arthur is at his parents' home despite Judge Burke's order and that I'm worried about my son Robert? And then could you ask him to call me?"

She gave the woman her number.

"And could you tell him it's an emergency?"

"Your son's name is . . .?"

"Robert."

"Robert. Yes, certainly. I'll have him call."

She hung up and dialed Owen Sansom, then realized she'd dialed the office number instead of his home so she hung up and dialed again. Cindy appeared from the kitchen carrying two mugs of coffee and handed her one. She tasted it. It was liberally dosed with cognac.

"And don't tell me you don't need that," Cindy said.

"Hello?"

"Owen? Listen, Owen, he's up there."

"Up where?"

"Arthur. He's at his parents' house. He's been living there and god knows what he's been doing. They ordered me off it gunpoint. *Harry* did, of all people. Robert looks awful, Owen. He's terrified. We've got to get him out of there."

"I'll move on it right away. Get a judge to act *ex parte* to remove Robert from their care. Dammit all! It's Saturday night! We're not going to get anything on this until Monday morning."

"It can't wait, Owen! Jesus Christ, you didn't see him. He's crazy. He could do anything!"

"Look, maybe I can find a judge who's home tonight, or maybe Andrea Stone could, somebody who'll . . ."

"*It won't wait!* You're not hearing me! Listen, do either of you have any clout with the police?"

"Andrea might. I . . ."

"Can you call her for me? I talked to an Officer Morton who was going to speak to his supervisor about getting somebody up there as soon as possible. But he said it could be hours yet before they even get back to me. Maybe you or Andrea could light some kind of fire under them. I left a message for Ralph Duggan. I'm going to wait for him to call and then I'm going back there."

"Lydia, don't. You just said they ordered you off at gunpoint. "

"They won't order Ralph Duggan off at gunpoint."

"You don't know that either. Let him handle it. Let me try to get a judge . . ."

"He's my son, Owen. And the courts have already failed him *twice*. Call me back if you get anything, okay?"

"Lydia . . ."

"Call me."

And then there was nothing to do but wait. Somehow the coffee cup had emptied.

Magic.

"You think another cup would get me loaded?"

Cindy shook her head. "With the adrenaline you're pumping, I think it would take a good quart or two to get you loaded. You practically give off sparks."

She took the cup and went to the kitchen.

"I think I'll fix this hand up now," Lydia said.

"Good idea."

The puncture wasn't deep. In the bathroom she washed her hands. The soap and water made the scraped wrist sting and the puncture wound throb. She poured hydrogen peroxide over each of them and wiped the white foam off with cotton balls, poured and wiped again and then sprayed them both with bacitracin. She used a Band-Aid on the wrist and wrapped the hand with gauze and tied it off.

Her image in the mirror startled her. Cindy was right. She did nearly give off sparks. The eyes were wild. There were twigs and leaves in her hair and her face was smeared with mud. She wiped her face with a facecloth and brushed her hair.

She was almost finished when the phone rang.

"I've got it!" she called. She dropped the brush into the sink and ran down the hall to the phone. Cindy was already standing there with two more cups of doctored coffee.

"Hello?"

The silence on the other end was like a weight dropping onto her chest and told her exactly who it was.

"I don't need to talk to you now, Arthur," she said.

"Yes you do."

She glanced at Cindy. She'd set the coffee down on the table by the phone and was watching her intently.

"Don't hang up, Lydia. You know my parents' house, right?"

"Of course I do."

"So you know where the phones are, right?"

"Arthur, what do you want?"

"Do you know where the phones are, Lydia?"

"Yes. One is in the kitchen and the other's upstairs in Ruth's bedroom. So what?"

"So Mom took the guest room for a while. Her room is my room now. Mine and Robert's. So guess where I'm calling you from, Lyd. I mean, guess which room. And guess who's sitting right here with me. Right next to me. Right here on the bed."

"Goddamn it, Arthur, *if you touch him . . .*"

His whisper in her ear was the voice of all her fears—and she knew that somehow it was also the voice of her fate and of her doom. She heard the rest of her life hiss away through the phone line like a nest of snakes surrounding her.

"*Lydia, I can do any fucking thing I want and you can't do shit. You got that? You useless fuck.* I'll be out of here tomorrow, and maybe I'll take him with me and maybe I won't. You want to make trouble about my being here? Who's to say I was here? Your word against mine. Robert's not going to say. The kid's not going to say. He told on me once and he knows where that got him. Don't you, Robert? Don't you, you miserable little *cocksucker!*"

She heard a muffled moan.

She slammed the phone down on the receiver. Coffee spilled across the rim of her mug.

"Stay here," she said. "Wait for Duggan's call. Or no—try calling him back. Tell him I'm on my way up there. If you can't reach him try the police again."

"What . . .?"

"He's going to do something. Maybe he already has. I don't know. I'm going to stop him."

She ran up the stairs to her bedroom and flung open the closet door. She pushed away boots and shoes along the upper shelf until she found the cardboard shoe box with the Smith & Wesson Ladysmith .38 inside and the box of shells. She opened the cylinder and saw it was loaded. She put the shells in her pocket and ran back downstairs again and she was at the door and had it open before Cindy stopped her.

"Liddy, let me try the police again before you . . ."

"No! Goddamn it, *I've gone by the book all the way on this!* I've tried everything. *The courts aren't protecting him, Cindy!* The police aren't protecting him. If the law won't help me get Robert away from that goddamn son of a bitch once and for all then I'll damn well do it myself!"

"At least let me . . ."

"What would you do if you were me, Cyn? Let him spend another night getting raped? Let him go off and disappear with him for a couple of weeks so he can go on getting raped maybe *every* night? Stay by the phone, Cyn. See if you can reach Duggan. Goddamn it, I'm going for my son."

THIRTY-SIX

VISITATION, PART SIX

Robert crouched tight to the bed board and watched his father move back and forth from one side of the bed to the other. Four pillows were spread out in front of him like sandbags—soft ammunition, but all he had if his father should try to come at him again.

His father had a gun, a pistol so shiny it looked almost white. It glinted in the lamplight. He was waving it and walking back and forth across the room.

He felt like he had to go to the bathroom but he wasn't going to ask or say anything to his father, nothing at all. He held it in.

He kept waiting for them to say it was okay to go to sleep. For the night to end.

He heard someone coming up the stairs outside the locked door. His father heard it too. He stopped and turned to the door and waited for the knock.

Instead of a knock Robert heard his grampa's voice. "Arthur?"

He heard the doorknob turn against the lock.

"Come on, son. Let me in. Your mother and I have been talking, thinking. We think y'ought to give it up, son. Take yourself on out of here—just for tonight, you see? Spend the night at your place. Live to fight another day, so to speak. You know? Like you say, as it is right now, nobody can even say you were here at all except her. And we all say she's a liar."

His father just stared at the door.

"Arthur?"

His father'd been acting crazy all day now. Real crazy—worse than yesterday. Talking to himself when there was nobody to listen.

Drinking beer and whiskey. Not eating. Hiding out on Officer Duggan. Robert could tell that even his grandparents were kind of scared of him now.

His father had called him a cocksucker. His father had pointed at him with the gun.

Think I'll shoot? his father had said. Bang. Bang.

"This isn't gettin' us anywhere, son. Duggan comes back, finds you here, it's just going to be More trouble in the courts for you. You got to see that, Arthur. Your mother and I are behind you one hundred percent, but you know Duggan's practically the most persistent man in the damn county. You know that."

More footsteps on the stairs.

"Arthur? *Open up.*"

His grandma.

His father took a step toward the door and then moved sideways to the night table and took the bottle on the table and drank. Robert could smell the stink of it all the way across the room over here.

"Open up the door, dammit."

He drank again.

"Go to hell," he told her.

"*What?* What'd you say to me?"

"I told you to go to hell, Ma. Hey, you can both go to hell. I'll come out when I'm good and ready."

Robert stared at his father in shocked silence. His grandma was always bossy but he had never once heard his father say no to her. Not on anything.

It would be like Robert saying something like that to *him*. The same kind of thing. He'd *never* do it. He'd never dare. And now here was his dad telling his grandmother to go to hell—and something about it scared him almost worse than anything.

There was nothing but silence behind the door.

He guessed they were surprised too.

His father stared at the door awhile longer and then turned to him and Robert saw that he was smiling.

"Just you and me, kid," he said quietly. And started to walk over.

When Duggan pulled up at the house, his wife was standing in the doorway with a coat over her shoulders and she wouldn't even let him get out of the car. He rolled down the window and Alice leaned in. She was holding a piece of paper, reading off it when she needed to.

"Ralph," she said, "you've been getting these emergency calls. Three in the past half hour. First from a Lydia Danse, who says her husband Arthur's at his parents' house, staying there, and she's afraid for her little boy. Then I got two more from somebody named Cindy Fortunato, who's a friend of hers and says Mrs. Danse has gone to get her son now and that she's carrying a weapon, a gun, and she wants you to call her right away. But I thought that maybe you should just go on out there and I should make the call. To save time."

"Thanks, Allie. Call her up. Tell her I'm on my way."

He leaned over and kissed her and started the car.

"You be careful," she said. "Domestic disputes, right?"

"Domestic disputes." He nodded. She knew as well as he did that they could be pure hell. "I will," he said.

As he started back down the drive he radioed in for backup.

"We're already on the way," the dispatcher told him. "The Fortunato woman called a few minutes ago. We got a car out as soon as she did. I got to tell you, this one really got screwed up, Ralph. Morton thought it was nothing all that urgent on the first call. But there wasn't any mention of weapons then, you know?"

"I know. Don't worry about it. I think everybody screwed up somewhere on this one."

He signed off. And Morton probably the least of them, he thought. Everybody'd fucked up. Fucked up bad. The judge, lawyers. Everybody.

Even him. Though he didn't really know how. There must have been something he'd missed, something he hadn't done that needed doing and that now saw him out here in the middle of the night trying to outdrive a lady with a gun.

To hell with it, he thought, now's what's important. Now you've got a chance to do something. And he drove toward the mountain.

The wooden beams jolted her in the car seat and then she was over the bridge. She slowed to thirty on the old dirt road and drove a little ways and then cut the headlights and stopped the car and got out. There was no point announcing herself.

All the way here she'd been praying to a god she rarely even considered that Arthur hadn't hurt him, that the man raving in the kitchen and taunting her on the phone had burned himself out, exhausted with sheer craziness, and gone to bed. *Alone*, she thought, saying it like a mantra. Please god.

Alone.

This had to be the end of it. She could take no more from Arthur Danse and neither could Robert. The terror had to stop now one way or another. She'd take Robert and run. Where didn't matter. It didn't matter either anymore that they'd probably be poor, that the work she was trained for was going to be forever out of the question. Poor was still alive and poor was still unabused.

The house was brightly lit. Upstairs and down.

So they hadn't gone to bed.

No matter.

She cut across the field and felt the tall wet grass brush her right hand holding the gun. She brought it up to waist-level, the weight of it comforting in a way no gun's feel or heft had ever seemed remotely comforting to her. It was as though the gun were the ally she had needed all along but had never thought of. Not Sansom, not Andrea Stone, not the courts and not the police. Just this cold weight of metal.

Her final advocate.

She stepped up toward the porch. She knew the front door would be open. She knew that all the doors would be open. It was inevitable.

It was all of it inevitable and always had been.

He saw the headlights sweep the bedroom curtains as the car came up the hill and then immediately go dim. Robert didn't see them but he did.

She was coming.

She or Duggan.

It was starting. Something.

Trespassers, he thought. Thou shalt not trespass.

No way thou shalt, you fucking pieces of shit.

He unlocked the door and saw his mother and father standing

there looking at him and the 9mm semiautomatic in his hand. His mother looked mad at him. The old man looked nervous and worried.

So what else was new.

"Daddy, grab the shotgun," he said. "We've got company."

It felt good to say that to his father. To command him.

He knew that when this was over he'd be in a position to command both of them. Because they both would be just as guilty as he was for what was about to happen here—as guilty as he'd ever been for anything in his life. They'd carry that.

He could use that against them the rest of their lives. It was about time.

It was whatever he wanted now.

He pushed past them down the stairs.

"Get the shotgun, daddy," he said. "And I mean move."

She'd been right, the door wasn't locked. She turned the doorknob and it opened with barely a sound and she saw Arthur in the doorway by the stairs, a black shape pointing at her, backlit by the light from the kitchen and she felt something slam into her chest and throw her back against the door and then she heard the explosion.

She raised the gun and fired, she didn't know how many times, and the figure fell away. She looked down at her body and saw there was blood all over her. She saw movement in the kitchen and then Arthur's father was coming toward her out of there shouting something that she was far too deaf to hear and she saw the double-barrel shotgun in his hands pointed in her direction so she fired again. Plaster showered down over her head and shoulders as the shotgun flashed and roared. Harry fell and lay slumped against the kitchen door.

She saw Ruth behind him and she tried to raise the gun again but the strength was gone from her arm and she felt herself sliding down the front door to the rough nappy doormat that lay askew between her knees. Ruth was shouting too, her face twisted and red and awful and angry but she couldn't hear.

Lydia saw her move quickly from Harry's body to Arthur's and when she got to Arthur she stopped and fell to her knees and put her hands to her cheeks and rocked there. She reached down and touched his face and then stared a moment at her bloody hand then she was screaming again, looking up at Robert in his pyjamas standing there frozen halfway down the stairs and screaming, not at him she thought or even at her or at anybody at all but in some mad incredible rage that Lydia could almost understand, could almost feel and know.

The room was swimming.

She saw Robert gaze in her direction, saw him register all the blood across her breasts and belly, saw the terror in his eyes and heard herself dimly and far away saying, "It's okay, baby. Everything's all right now. Nobody's going to hurt you anymore. It's all right, baby."

She felt hands at her shoulders, big hands, calloused hands, and looked up into Ralph Duggan's ashen face and heard what must have been sirens and then he was fading away into light and darkness and she couldn't see him, couldn't feel him, she could only hear the ringing in her ears until even that was gone. She imagined she felt her heartbeat And then there was only silence and darkness and an end to what she had come here for, to where time and maybe all her life had brought her.

EPILOGUE, PART ONE

IDENTIFICATION

There was a subtle reek to human death that not even cold and disinfectant could subvert—the dark wet mold on a decaying flower, bland meat only just beginning to turn. They stood and looked down at the corpse of Arthur Danse and Duggan felt the young woman tremble beside him and thought, hell, you still scare people, Arthur. I guess you've just got a knack for it.

He'd read the coroner's report by now and noted the clean black wound that had ended him, Lydia's first shot and a classic—straight through the heart. He imagined her luck and the shattered organ sewn up inside him. Her two other shots would not have done the trick. One had chipped the left side of his pelvic girdle before careening off into the wall a foot above his head. The other had sheared a flap of skin off his cheek and cracked his lower jaw. Knowing Arthur, he would have kept on coming.

Not luck, he thought. Providence. Finally in all of this, the hand of mercy.

It was the broken jaw that was his problem though. Marge Bernhardt had not been able to identify Danse through the morgue photos. It was not surprising. The dead, he thought, simply did not look like the living. And the smiling amiable snapshots they'd taken from his home seemed not to correspond to the memory of that dark figure attempting to nail her to a tree in the frozen woods. His only hope now was that despite the facial wound and the pale softening of his features there would be something about the mass of him, the man in his totality, that would jar her into a moment of recognition.

But it wasn't going to happen.

"No," she said. "Or maybe. Oh, God! I can't tell!"

She hardly knew Duggan. Yet she leaned into his arms as though urged by a gust of wind.

He held her gently until the shaking subsided though her body and even her hands were cold and then he asked her to look again.

She shook her head.

"I keep thinking," she said. "What if it's not him? What if he's still *out there*? I know you want to—what do you call it?—close the books on this. But what if it's not him? And then I say it is."

He understood. This was a brave intelligent woman and she needed to be sure. So did he. If he was pretty certain that Arthur Danse had lived his double life so completely and successfully that not his wife nor even his parents had ever fully known what he was capable of, if he had escaped even in death, Duggan would just have to live with that.

The woman was right. What if he was out there—trolling the streets in a dark car, some splintered soul mate to Arthur Danse who was of him yet not him, searching out the vulnerable under the winter moon.

He pulled up the sheet.

She was right. In the long run Danse didn't matter. Danse was legion. It was what they had inherited even in this quiet town, and it would never pay to close the books on that, not for a moment.

He led her quietly from the room and closed the door and listened to the tired weight of their footsteps on the concrete floor and imagined all the bodies settling cold into their frozen beds behind him and thought of how many would follow.

EPILOGUE

SAFETY

The reporter studied the face of the woman in front of her and contrasted that with the photos she'd seen and the news footage covering the woman's arrest and trial. She knew that Lydia Danse was just two years older than she was but she looked older by nearly a decade. She had put on weight. She was still quite an attractive woman in the reporter's estimation, but the eyes looked puffy from lack of sleep, the mouth more pinched than in the photos.

The reporter, who had no children of her own but who had talked on the telephone with Andrea Stone at DCYS and the woman's own lawyer and who had listened to her firsthand story for almost an hour now, could fully understand the change.

Over a year later it was still clearly difficult for her to talk about the killings and what had happened to her son. Knowing most of the details of the case beforehand the reporter thought she had guts even to agree to the interview. When he heard what Lydia had to say, she amended the word guts to courage.

Her article was on the subject of why women kill. She was now some three months into researching it. She'd seen good deal of courage. Some madness.

And a lot of desperation.

"So his bullet grazed your lung," she said. "Then passed through your back."

"That's right. They found it in the door behind me. I was lucky because the bullet was the kind with a metal jacket and that meant the exit wound was clean, not as bad as it might have been. I was in the hospital a couple of weeks. Then they transferred me."

"So your lawyer said they were asking for two hundred thousand dollars in bail?"

She nodded.

"And you didn't pay it."

"I was already incredibly in debt on legal fees as it was."

"In court you used Robert's videotaped confessions to contend that you had reason to believe that he was in danger at the time, at that very moment maybe, that you were afraid he'd be molested again, and that you went to the house to protect him."

"Yes."

"And the state asked for first-degree murder. The death penalty. I find that . . . just incredible."

Her smile seemed to say, *Believe me, you don't know the half of it.* The reporter had yet to see the slightest sign that Lydia Danse was sitting here feeling sorry for herself. *Even though it was death by hanging in this state.* Even her occasional bout with tears had only spoken of sadness and waste and her son's emotional pain.

She thought that was incredible too.

"They didn't get it, though," she said.

"No, thank god. They gave me aggravated life."

The reporter took a breath. It was hard not to be furious—she was furious, what was hard was not to show her fury—at the whole damn justice system.

"I don't get it. Why not self-defense? He shot you first. Forensics proved it. He couldn't have fired *after* you did because he was dead the moment your bullet hit him."

"We couldn't get self-defense because I went to the house with the gun. Because I thought about it long enough to take the gun out of my closet and put it in the car and bring it there. That made me the aggressor. That's the way they saw it. There was even a big deal about my not having a carry permit."

"And the videotape?"

She shrugged. "Either they didn't believe the videotape or they chose to discount it. The jury, not the judge. The judge took it into consideration and that's what got me life. My lawyers and I never could figure it out, to tell the truth. One of the jurors came forward later and said that he believed the tape right from the beginning and another came forward and said he never did. I don't know why the ones who did believe Robert voted the way they did. Straight law and order, I guess. I suppose it was the gun."

"You're aware that Ralph Duggan and the State Police had been investigating a number of serial killings at the time. And that these murders apparently have stopped since?"

She nodded again. "I'm glad they've stopped. But it doesn't really matter in my case, does it? They never proved it was Arthur. Maybe it was and maybe it wasn't. But I don't know that it would have mattered to me in court or would even have been admissible even if they did."

The reporter glanced at the uniformed matron in the corner of the conference room to their left. The matron was making an elaborate show of not overhearing them. Gazing off into space, arms folded in her lap. It was like every prison she'd ever seen. Every sound echoed in there. Every scrape of a chair. The matron was hearing all of it.

The reporter felt strangely vulnerable knowing that. "And you haven't been out of prison since, have you?" she said.

"No."

"And you haven't seen Robert?"

"They won't let him visit. The court won't. Not until he's fourteen. If your article can do anything for me maybe it can at least do that. Get them to allow us to at least see each other now and then."

Secretly the reporter doubted that it would. She felt that Lydia Danse was still fighting a losing battle with the system. But she wasn't going to say so. This was a woman who had already failed in one appeal for clemency. She couldn't imagine how trapped she must feel. The reporter wasn't going to add to that.

"How many years before you're eligible for parole, Lydia?"

For the first time during the interview her eyes flashed bright with anger.

"Fifteen years," she said.

"Before parole is even possible?"

"Yes. Robert will be twenty-four. A man. I'll have lost the rest of his childhood. All of it."

Her eyes said she'd been cheated in a nasty game that was never of her making and that she knew it. What Lydia Danse had been through and was still going through seemed to press in on the reporter like an invisible heavy weight. A kind of push. It was personal.

What would I have done in the same situation? she thought. What would any woman have done?

The reporter had seen Robert's tape and knew he was telling the truth about his father. She believed the tape completely.

She thought that Lydia Danse had walked through fire and that the fire was still burning.

She felt suddenly ashamed at simply being able to leave this place. At being able to walk free on the outside while this woman whom she suspected was far stronger and braver than she was wasn't free and probably would not be free—not for a very long time. And for being part of a world that had put her here.

Fifteen years.

She didn't know what to say.

Unless something happened to change things Lydia Danse would be a woman approaching old age.

My god.

"How do you . . . I don't know how to say this but . . . God! How do you live with that? How do you possibly *bear* it?"

She watched Lydia draw herself up in the hard metal chair.

"Robert's with Ruth now," she said, "he's with his grandmother. The very same woman who raised his father. Who broke the law allowing Arthur to stay there in the first place. For some insane reason the courts decided Arthur forced that on her and would rather give custody to her than to my sister Barbara, basically because Barbara's single.

We're fighting that and I don't like it one damn bit but that's not the point. The important thing is that the men in that family are all dead. That nobody's pointing guns at anybody anymore. The important thing is that I know Robert isn't being abused by his father anymore, that he's safe. That's the one good thing I can see coming out of . . . all of this. If it weren't for that I'd probably go crazy. But I have that much, anyway. He's safe."

Even the matron was looking at her openly now in what

appeared to be a kind of stony empathy.

"I have that much," she said.

The reporter found that she could think of nothing more to say.

She's just fallen through the cracks, she thought. Another one the system's failed to protect. This one had fallen deeper and harder than any she'd met—yet look at her, she thought. She's refusing to be buried by it all. She wants out, yes. Badly. Of course she does. Yet something in her clearly remained uncircumscribed by dull gray walls and bars and empty looks and all the monotony of her days. Something which stood outside these walls, in the mind and body of her son—and grew there, with her and without her.

It was a waste. It was a goddamn crime.

The reporter could despair for her and feel for her and knew that she would do exactly that in anger and in cold print for the audience of a major national magazine just a couple of weeks from now. But Lydia Danse was not despairing.

She's done the right thing, the reporter thought. And she knows it. No matter what anybody thinks.

There's a nobility in that.

There's grace.

The reporter realized that Lydia Danse was gazing deeply into the reporter's own troubled eyes and knew that the interview was over.

Ruth watched him from her armchair in front of the television. He was working on his homework at the dining room table. Erasing with a pencil.

Persevere, she thought. That's right. *Persevere.*

He'd grown taller in the year since it happened—taller and skinnier. She thought the skinniness suited him as it had suited Arthur at that age and didn't fuss when he left a bit of the food on his plate at dinnertime. Just so long as he ate a little something, she was happy.

In fact she was having no trouble at all with him these days. Oh, he was still too quiet, he still stumbled into furniture not looking where he was going sometimes, but the stuttering had stopped and she was thankful for that because the stuttering, to be honest, had always embarrassed her. His work was going well at school. He was diligent and respectful.

He was a good boy.

The same way Arthur was a good boy.

Most of the time he was.

The only problem she had with Robert was—and it didn't happen nearly so often now, but god knows at her age once a month was still quite enough to frazzle her—the only problem she had was this messing the bed at night. She'd wake up in the morning or even in the middle of the night sometimes to a smell like something had crawled up into her house and died. And there would be the boy, sleeping in his own shit or else stripping the sheets off the bed or else just sitting there looking sad and guilty.

She made him wash his sheets when it happened and kept plastic on to protect the mattress underneath at all times. But she wasn't buying any diapers for him. She wasn't spending money on diapers for a nine-year-old.

She'd have to find some way to break him of the habit. And soon.

She couldn't stand the god-awful stink when it happened. It wasn't correct.

It wasn't sanitary.

And it wasn't necessary.

He was far too old for dunking.

She'd have to find some other way.

Of course there was always what had worked with Arthur what helped to put him back in line when he was out of line—on those rare occasions. But the world was different now than it was when Arthur was a boy and people were a lot more nosy. Teachers were nosy and they had counselors at school who were nosy and even other parents got nosy a whole lot of the time. She'd heard stories. People who had their kids taken away from them by the goddamn county. She'd have to be careful.

She'd have to use it where it wouldn't show.

A thin peeled stick. Birch.

It had always worked for Arthur.

And then afterwards in the darkness of his bedroom she'd go to him and hold him close to her breast and feel his sweet warm tears soak through her housedress and she'd rock him and tell him that it was all right now, it was over, that he was her boy, her good boy, her one and only child and the love of her life, forever, never mind old Harry, never mind anybody because nobody else in the world mattered the way he mattered—they belonged to one another forever there in the sight of God and she would stroke him, stroke him, stroke him.

AUTHOR'S NOTE:

In 1831, about the time that Edgar Allan Poe was being court-martialed from West Point, President Andrew Jackson felt threatened by supports of the Second Bank of the United States, led by the bank's president Nicholas Biddle. Jackson confided to Martin Van Buren, "The bank is trying to kill me, but I will kill it." That statement is the heart of the fictive conspiracy against Jackson, but no such conspiracy has ever been verified.

ABOUT THE AUTHOR

JACK KETCHUM's first novel, *Off Season*, prompted the *Village Voice* to publicly scold its publisher in print for publishing violent pornography. He personally disagrees but is perfectly happy to let you decide for yourself. His short story "The Box" won a 1994 Bram Stoker Award from the HWA, his story "Gone" won again in 2000—and in 2003 he won Stokers for both Best Collection for *Peaceable Kingdom* and best long fiction for *Closing Time*. He has written twelve novels, arguably thirteen, five of which have been filmed: *The Girl Next Door*, *Red*, *The Lost*, *Offspring*, and *The Woman*, written with Lucky McKee. His stories are collected in *The Exit at Toledo Blade Boulevard*, *Peaceable Kingdom*, *Closing Time and Other Stories*, and *Sleep Disorder*, with Edward Lee. His horror-western novella *The Crossings* was cited by Stephen King in his speech at the 2003 National Book Awards. He was elected Grand Master for the 2011 World Horror Convention.

Curious about other Crossroad Press books?
Stop by our site:
http://store.crossroadpress.com
We offer quality writing
in digital, audio, and print formats.

Enter the code FIRSTBOOK
to get 20% off your first order from our store!
Stop by today!

Made in the USA
Columbia, SC
11 February 2021

32808785R00137